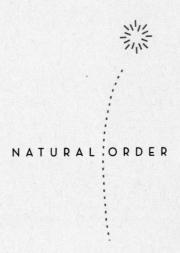

NATURAL ORDER

BRIAN FRANCIS

NATURAL ORDER

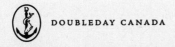

DOUBLEDAY CANADA

Doubleday Canada and colophon are registered trademarks

LIBRARY AND ARCHIVES OF CANADA CATALOGUING
IN PUBLICATION
Francis, Brian, 1971–
     Natural order / Brian Francis.
ISBN: 978-0-385-67153-8
     I. Title.
PS8611.R35N38 2011   C813'.6   C2011-902500-0

This book is a work of fiction. Names, characters, places
and incidents are products of the author's imagination or
are used fictitiously. Any resemblance to actual events or
locales or persons, living or dead, is entirely coincidental.

Text and cover design: CS Richardson
Cover image: © John Kuss/Corbis
Printed and bound in the USA

Published in Canada by Doubleday Canada,
a division of Random House of Canada Limited

Visit Random House of Canada Limited's website:
www.randomhouse.ca

10 9 8 7 6 5 4 3 2 1

For Mom,
my best publicist

NATURAL ORDER

The Balsden Examiner
July 27, 1984

Sparks, John Charles May 5, 1953–July 25, 1984. After a sudden illness, John passed away peacefully in Toronto in his 31st year. Survived by his loving parents Charles and Joyce Sparks of Balsden, his Aunt Helen and Uncle Richard, Aunt Irene and Uncle Dwight, cousins Marianne, Mark, Rebecca and Patricia. Friends and family will be received at the Floyd Brothers Funeral Home, 927 George Ave., on Sunday, July 29, from 7–9 p.m. The funeral service will be held at St. Paul's United Church, 70 Ormand St., on Monday, July 30, at 12 p.m. Reception to follow. Interment to follow reception at Lakeside Cemetery. In lieu of flowers, the family requests donations to the Canadian Cancer Society.

I lived in hope. I prayed in vain
That God would make you well again.
But God decided we must part,
I watched you die with a broken heart.

CHAPTER ONE

THE BUZZERS keep me awake at night. That's one thing that hasn't gone—my hearing. Most everything else has faded. My taste. Vision. Even my voice, which comes out sounding like a scratch in the air.

The buzzers bleat in the hallway like robot sheep. We keep our strings close to us so they're easy to reach and pull. Mine is attached to my purse. Before I go to bed, I always set my purse on my night table. During the day, when I'm in my room, I keep it on my bed. I always have it near. Sometimes, at night, when the sounds wake me, I'll stare at my purse until I fall asleep again. It's not a particularly nice purse. I don't even think it's real leather.

Most of the buzzers you hear aren't for what you'd call real emergencies. Usually, someone needs an extra blanket. Or someone had a bad dream. More often than not, I think people pull the buzzer just to see how long it takes for someone to come to their room. I did that, the first few months after I came here. I'd pull the string and count the seconds, panic building.

17, 18, 19

What if I'd fallen out of bed? What if I was having a heart attack?

34, 35

What if I'd broken my hip?

42

What if I was dead?

Joyce Sparks.

My name is on the wall outside my room next to a straw hat with a yellow ribbon and a couple of glued-on daisies. The hat reminds me of my sister, Helen, although it isn't hers. The social coordinator had us make our own hats for a tea party last spring. I don't know why someone decided to hang my hat outside the door. I didn't do a nice job of it. I've never been good at crafts. I don't have the patience.

Ruth Schueller is the name on the other side of the door. She's my roommate. She doesn't have a hat next to her name because she wasn't at the home in the spring. Instead, there's a black-and-white photograph beside Ruth's name, taken during her younger years. I hardly recognize her. Frightening how much damage time does to a face. Ruth is eighty-two. I turned eighty-six in July.

Ruth snores something awful. Not at night, usually. But during her daytime naps, she makes the most horrific sounds.

She'll fall asleep in her wheelchair and her head will flop down like a dead weight. That's when the snoring starts. Some days, it's so loud I can't concentrate on the television, even when the volume is turned up all the way—which it usually is. I'll have to throw the Yellow Pages at her. (Never at her head, although I've been tempted. Only at her feet.) Then I'll watch her out of the corner of my eye as she tries to sort things out. What was that noise? Where did this Yellow Pages come from?

Last week, I wheeled into the bathroom and found my hairbrush on the back of the toilet tank. This bothered me because I always keep my brush next to the faucet. I wheeled out of the bathroom, carrying my brush like a miniature sword.

"RUTH, DID YOU TOUCH THIS?"

She blinked back at me like I was talking another language.

"IT'S NOT RIGHT!" I said. "YOU CAN'T DO THINGS LIKE THAT!"

I don't know why they can't give me a roommate who can talk. Ruth is the second mute person I've had in the past year. She replaced Margaret, who was also soft in the head. She'd sit in her chair, knuckle deep inside a nostril for most of the day.

"If you find an escape route up there, let me know," I'd say to her. Then Margaret's liver shut down and she turned bronze. She lay in her bed, day after day, while a string of family members I'd never seen before came in and out of our room. They stood at her bedside, joisted fingers over their bellies, looking down at Margaret and shaking their heads as though this was one of the greatest tragedies they'd ever witnessed.

It's not nice having someone die in your room. I'll say that much. I woke up in the middle of the night, the sheep bleating in the distance, and even though I couldn't see her, I knew Margaret was gone. There was a stillness in the air, a cold pocket. I thought about reaching for my purse, but then wondered if it mattered. I didn't want to deal with the commotion that would follow: the lights turning on, whispers, white sheets. So I lay there with my hands at my sides and said a short prayer for Margaret. Although she couldn't talk, I could tell by her eyes that she'd been a good person. Kind. Gentle. She hadn't deserved her fate. After a while, I fell back asleep.

One week later, Ruth moved in. She'd been living on the second floor where the other soft-headed people are, but her family wanted her on my floor, the fourth. Did they think she'd be more stimulated up here?

I suppose it could be worse. There's Mae MacKenzie down the hall, trapped with that horrible Dorothy Dawson. Dorothy keeps the divider curtains shut so the room is cut in half. She even safety-pinned the flaps together. She means business.

"She trapped herself in once," Mae told me. "Kept pawing her way around, trying to find the opening. It was the best entertainment I've had here yet."

Dorothy doesn't talk to anyone. Mae says she's a bitter woman. There's been some talk of a husband who had wandering hands. A daughter into drugs.

"Some people get a rough ride in life," Mae said with a slow shake of her head.

I held my tongue.

The room that Ruth and I share is small, but big enough for two beds, two dressers and two wheelchairs, which I suppose is all the space that a couple of old ladies need. We're on the south side of the building, so we don't have the nice view of the lake. Instead, we face the street. I guess I can't afford the lakeside setting. I'm guessing because I don't know for certain. My niece, Marianne, handles my finances. She lives in Brampton. I call her once a month or so, but we don't talk for more than five minutes. It always seems like someone is pulling on her arm. The last time I saw her was January. She showed up in my doorway wearing a dark brown blouse. She'd put on weight.

"Happy belated New Year, Aunt Joyce," she said and sat down on the edge of my bed.

She looked like a bonbon left out on a hot day.

I shouldn't be critical. That was Helen's problem—always after Marianne and her son, Mark, to live up to some idea of perfection. Now look at them. Marianne is fat and divorced and Mark had a heart bypass two years ago. But I was grateful for Marianne's company that day. I don't have visitors, and living here makes you feel removed from the simplest things. I don't remember the last time I went grocery shopping. Or to Sears. Or ate in a restaurant. Or visited the cemetery.

Sometimes, when I look around my room, I think, "This is the last place I'll live." When I go, they'll be able to pack all my belongings in a cardboard box. I like to think I'm simplifying my life. Maybe it's the other way around.

I've been here at Chestnut Park for six years. Marianne pressured me into it. I'd fallen in the bedroom in my senior's apartment. I couldn't be trusted on my own anymore.

"You've always taken care of others, Aunt Joyce," she said to me. "Now it's time to let people take care of you."

I hadn't taken care of anyone in my life. If anything, the opposite was true. But I was too tired and frightened to argue. My arm was stained with bruises and my ankle was swollen like a cantaloupe. I'd lain there, sprawled out between the bed and my dresser, for what seemed a lifetime. (They figured it was close to a day before the superintendent let himself in. Imagine my relief—and my shame when he found me on the floor, my legs wide open.)

I don't remember much of the time in between. What I mean is, the time between my fall and the superintendent coming in. I was in and out of consciousness. I know I tried to reach for the telephone on the night table. And I remember seeing how dusty the floor was under my bed. Cobwebs everywhere. I was mortified. I wondered if these were the kinds of thoughts people had while they waited to die: the embarrassment of filth and the fear of discovery.

Mostly, I thought of my son.

There aren't many bright spots in our days, but Hilda, the social coordinator, tries to keep us entertained. Every now and then, she brings in a children's choir. Other times, there's a tea social that only leaves us nostalgic for the lives we used to live. Once, Hilda brought in a dog. A black and brown beagle with a tail like a flagpole. I didn't like the way it looked at me with its rheumy eyes and twitching snout. I refused to pet it.

"I didn't know you were afraid of dogs," Hilda said.

"I'm not," I said. Then, because I knew that answer would likely lead to more questions, I said, "I'm not good with animals."

I sit with three other people during meals: Irene, Henry and Jim. We don't talk much. Mainly nudge and point to the things we need. Irene chews with her mouth open. Half the food tumbles out and down her bib and onto the table. It's nauseating, and if I don't keep my eyes down at all times, I lose my appetite. I told one of the nurses that I wanted to move to another table and she said she'd look into it, but I know that nothing will come of it. Nothing comes of anything in this place. The staff don't listen to you. They bully you into taking your pills or making your poops or eating your food so that they can leave for home. I watch them tear across the parking lot towards their cars, a blur of uniform.

I do my best to finish my fish sticks, but they're horrible. Soggy. The cooks bake them, which I know is healthier. But I'm eighty-six now. I'll take my chances with trans fats. All around me, I hear the clatter of cutlery against plates and the occasional wet plop of something hitting the floor. Someone starts hacking (likely that woman from 405—she's a smoker) and I think how sad that these are my final meals.

After lunch, I'm wheeled back to my room and positioned between the bed and the wall. I'll usually try to nap in the afternoon as it helps to quicken the wait until dinner, but Ruth is already passed out in her chair. I press my eyes shut, willing myself to fall asleep before the snoring starts, but it's a lost cause.

"Hello, Joyce."

I look up to see Hilda coming into the room. She's a tall woman, although everyone seems tall when you're in a wheelchair. There's a strand of chunky turquoise beads around her neck.

"How was lunch?" She sits down at the foot of my bed.

"Fine," I say. "We had fish. Is it Friday?"

She nods. "Are you Catholic?"

"United," I say.

"They have a service every Sunday downstairs."

"I know."

"Are you a religious woman?"

"Not particularly. But we'll see what happens on my deathbed."

"I have a new volunteer starting tonight. A young man. Do you mind if I send him to you?"

"What does he want?" Most of the volunteers are women.

"Nothing. He's coming for conversation or errands or whatever you like." She leans in and lowers her voice. "He goes by Timothy. Not Tim. He was quite firm about that."

She waits for me to respond. I say nothing.

"A friend once told me that when a man goes by the long version of his name, chances are . . ." She laughs. "It's nice, though, having a male volunteer for once."

There are a handful of puffy women volunteers, running around before the bake sales or planting impatiens in the front garden, their eyeglass strings swaying this way and that. Well intentioned, I suppose, but intrusive. They make me uncomfortable when they come into my room, asking if my plants need watering or my pillows need fluffing or my water jug needs filling. No, no and no, I say, anxious for them to leave. I don't need their short-breathed fussing. This is my room. I didn't ask for their help, did I?

"Timothy will be coming in after dinner," Hilda says, standing up from the bed. "Around seven." She glances over at Ruth, who is now sucking back air like it's food at a buffet.

"I think you'll like him, Joyce."

"The only thing I'd like . . ." I begin. Hilda leans towards me, waiting. She wants something from me. A surrender. This will make her dogs and choirs worthwhile.

"The only thing I'd like is a nap," I say.

For some reason, I never thought I'd spend my final years in Balsden, even though it's the only place I've ever lived. I grew up on Shaw Street, and then spent my married life on Marian Street. After I sold the house, I moved into a seniors' apartment building on Finch Avenue. Now I'm here. And while Balsden is a small city of forty thousand, it's only now that I realize how tiny my world has been. The four cornerstones of my life have been within a ten-minute drive of one another.

"There isn't anything on earth you can't find in your own backyard," my mother used to say.

I remember as a girl standing on our back porch, contemplating the pine trees and the wire fence that circled the yard, the laundry poles and the ants whose grey-sugar castles sprang from the cracks in the concrete. I believed in these things and my mother's words. Perhaps, in some ways, I still do. In other ways, I think they're lies.

I was certain I'd end up in Andover, a much larger city, only forty minutes from Balsden via the double-lane highway or the old one with its winding single lane winding through towns and farmers' fields. Life seemed better in Andover. People were cut from a different cloth. There was a university and a downtown park with a bandshell and a rink where people went skating in the winter. When we were young, my best friend, Fern, my older sister, Helen, and I would take the train to go shopping for back-to-school clothes. That seems so far back in the past, I question it. That's the problem with getting old. Time bends and shifts. Memories spring up, uprooted. Sometimes, I'm not sure if my life happened the way I remember it, and there's no one left to verify the facts.

Fern moved to Andover after she sold her house. She had a cousin there and asked me to go with her.

"We'll get an apartment," she said. "Raise some hell."

But I was grounded by fear, afraid that my money would run out in a larger, more expensive city. And I had to consider

Helen. She'd been in and out of the hospital on account of her heart. When she died a year later, I reconsidered. There was nothing left for me in Balsden. I was alone. But then Fern was found dead one morning. And when her cousin called to tell me, I became aware of something I never thought possible: that solitude had another floor down.

No matter. Maybe I deserved it. No freedom for someone like me. No respite from guilt. Everything I ever did in life, I did wrong. Everything I touched, I destroyed.

I spend the rest of the afternoon trying to watch my soap opera. I wish I had a pair of earphones. Stupid Ruth. Oh, it doesn't matter. My mind is fluttering around like a distracted bird anyway. Timothy. Not Tim. I rub my hands, trying to loosen muscles that feel more like strips of jerky.

A while later, an attendant comes in with our afternoon snack. Today, I get two digestive cookies and a blood pressure pill.

"You're looking well today, Mrs. Sparks," I'm told. It's the Filipina woman. I forget her name and I can't read her badge. She's just a wisp of a thing, a pink peppermint stick in her uniform. "How are you feeling?"

"My neck hurts," I say, even though it's no better or worse than usual. "My hands, too."

"Mmm-hmm," Filipina woman says, tipping the contents of the tiny white cup into my palm. She hands me a glass of apple juice with a straw bent like an elbow. I could've told her I was pregnant and she would've asked me if I wanted ice in my glass.

I'm nervous after dinner. The meatballs I ate roll up the sides of my stomach, threatening escape. I don't want to see anyone. I can't be bothered to make small talk with a stranger. I'll wheel out of the room and sit at the end of the hall. He won't know where to find me.

I have to go to the bathroom, but there isn't time. That's the problem with being in this chair. Everything is such a production. They have to wheel in this monstrosity of a machine, hook me under my arms, manoeuvre me to the bathroom and lower me over the toilet. The entire process pulverizes whatever shards of dignity I have left. Once they get me on the toilet, they leave me there. I was once in the bathroom for a good thirty minutes before someone decided to come back. It frightened the daylights out of me.

No. I can't risk the bathroom. I'll have to hold it in. I wheel around to grab my purse when there's a soft knock at the door.

"Mrs. Sparks?"

I freeze. Should I fake deafness? Or sleep? I won't talk to him. I don't want to meet any—

"Ma'am?"

The voice is closer now. He's stepped into the room. I make out his reflection in the window. I won't have it. Hilda had no right to do this.

"Yes, I'm Mrs. Sparks."

"I'm Timothy. The new volunteer."

"I don't need anything right now," I say. "The nurse already came by and filled up my water jug."

"Oh." There's a pause. "I didn't know I was supposed to do that."

I turn and am shocked by his youth. He could be my son. No, I remind myself. John would've been in his sixties by now. Impossible to believe. This young man looks around thirty (although most people look thirty to me). His hair is dark and short. He's wearing a white polo shirt and his arms are hairy. I smell nutmeg. Cologne? He smiles awkwardly and half waves at me, as though we've just spotted one another from across a field. I look down at his shoes. Sneakers with white laces. Stylish, I suppose. I suddenly feel self-conscious. Why has Hilda sent him to me? She knows nothing about me.

"You have a lovely room," he says, stepping towards the window.

"The view isn't much." I rub my hands. "At least we don't get the late-day sun. Those rooms on the west side heat up like ovens. You'd think we deserve air conditioning at this stage of our lives."

"Have you been living here long?"

"Yes."

"And you?" He turns to Ruth.

"She can't hear you. She's not of sound mind." I tap my temple to make sure the message is clear.

He nods and blushes.

"I'm afraid Hilda misinformed you, Timothy. I don't need a volunteer. I get by on my own just fine."

"Oh."

13

"It's her job, you see. To try and make us feel better. About being old. About being in this place. There are other people who could use your company more than me."

"I shouldn't have waltzed in like that."

"You didn't know."

"Better to be up front with one another than to sit suffering through polite formalities." He glances over at the photo of John on my night table. "Who's that?"

My back stiffens. "My son."

"Does he visit?"

"He had cancer. He died a long time ago." My finger pokes the air. "Did Hilda tell you that already?"

"Of course not."

"Then why are you asking about him?"

He crosses his arms. "I didn't *ask* you about your son. I only asked about the picture. I was simply trying to make conversation."

"That's the problem with this place. Everyone sticking their noses into everyone else's business."

"On that note." He turns around. "Have a nice evening, Mrs. Sparks."

My fingers grip the arms of my chair. It doesn't have to be this way, I remind myself. *I* don't have to be this way. I clear my throat.

"I suppose Hilda gives you a list of people to visit."

He eyes me cautiously as he pulls a piece of paper from his pocket and hands it over. I hold the paper close to my face and scan the names. "Maureen will talk your ear off. Francie complains all the time. Who is this? Doris? No. Doreen. She's hard of hearing. Ronald tends to cry. He had a stroke a few months back. Looks like you've got your work cut out for you." I pass the list back to him.

He takes the paper and folds it into a small square. I notice his hands. They're nice. Strong. John's hands. I feel my heart fold up like the piece of paper.

"Take care, Mrs. Sparks," he says, and gives a quick nod in Ruth's direction.

I watch him walk out of the room.

CHAPTER TWO

I FOLD UP Helen's engagement notice from the newspaper and tuck it in my vanity drawer. I don't think she
and Dickie are in love. Not the kind of love you should be
in if you're going to stand in front of God and everyone
else and declare your devotion for all eternity. If you ask
me (which no one does, because all anyone ever talks about
is Helen now that the wedding is two weeks away), my sister hasn't even been thinking about love or Dickie or what
will happen the day after the wedding. All she cares about
is the ceremony and her dress and the flowers and what
will be served at the luncheon afterwards. But this is my
sister's specialty—controlling the things she can touch and
see and smell.

"There's nothing wrong with those shoes, Joyce," she said
to me the other night. "They're a perfectly good height."

"I got a nosebleed the last time I put them on."

"Don't be ridiculous."

You'd think a maid of honour would have more influence, but she sees me only as her younger, inexperienced sister. Any suggestions I've made or concerns I've had have been batted away like fruit flies over a ripe banana. Of course the heels aren't too high, Joyce. No, your dress isn't too tight in the bust. The colour is perfect for your complexion. And I'm sorry that you have to be paired up with Dickie's cousin, but he's not *that* overweight and everyone will be on high alert to ensure he doesn't drink too much.

Last night, at the dinner table, I listened to my mother and sister go on about the hat for Helen's honeymoon dress (she and Dickie are boarding a train to Montreal after the reception), and as I passed the plate of Saltines to Dickie, I noticed he looked shell-shocked. Not that Dickie ever looks anything *but* shell-shocked (Helen says he has bad nerves, nothing serious), but he seems even more so lately. His eyes searched for something to land on.

"Cracker?"

He nodded and took the plate from me before passing it along to my father. My eyes lingered on him. I watched as he carefully spread a thick wedge of butter across one of his crackers. Then he took a bite and I could tell he didn't have the slightest clue what was in his mouth. If I had a different sort of relationship with Dickie—and my sister for that matter—I would've put my hand on his arm and told him to hang in there. But I don't have that relationship with him. So my hands stayed on either side of my plate and my eyes contemplated the pink circle of ham that was waiting on my plate to be sliced.

I know Helen suspects me of jealousy, but I honestly have no desire to get married. Not yet. I'm only seventeen. Even twenty, the age Helen is now, is too young. I don't see what the rush is about.

"You'll find someone soon enough," my mother keeps telling me, even though I haven't expressed one doubt or desire. "When you least expect it, love will come knocking."

I've been on a few dates, but none of the boys have left much of an impression on me. Maybe I'm not cut out for love. That's true for some people.

"My aunt never married," Fern says. "Of course, she's a teacher."

"What has that got to do with it?" I ask.

We're sitting at the lunch counter in Woolworth's. Fern works the afternoon shift on Saturdays. Sometimes I come by in time for her break. She looks down and scratches a piece of dried food from her name tag.

"Men don't want a woman with a job. My aunt didn't start teaching until her mid-twenties. She must've given up on marrying someone by that point. Once that window of opportunity passes you by, well . . ." She takes a long sip of her Coke. "You have to take control of life before life takes control of you. I'm getting married by twenty."

Fern is one to talk. She's completely controlled by her mother. Mrs. Dover's first child was stillborn, the umbilical cord wrapped around the baby's neck.

"It was a girl," Fern once whispered to me. "She was blue by the time she came out."

When Fern arrived a few years later, Mrs. Dover was so terrified of something happening that she clamped on to Fern and never let go. Fern is bound by a lot of rules. She can't date, she can't stay out past nine (which is ridiculous, considering we're practically adults), she has to call her mother whenever she arrives at and before she leaves a destination.

I don't think things would be as bad for Fern if the Dovers had had another child, but once Fern was born alive and pink, Mrs. Dover had an operation. She wasn't going to take any more chances. When Fern talks about taking control of her life, it's all I can do not to arch an eyebrow. I'm not sure that her mother will ever let Fern out of her sight long enough for her to find a husband.

In any case, I don't want to discuss marriage anymore. Not weddings or dresses or spinster aunts. And I have to leave for work, which makes Fern's comment about men not wanting women with jobs sting all the more.

When I get to the Dairy Maid, Freddy Pender is on the phone with his mother. I don't know how they find as much to talk about as they do, although I suppose the same could be said about Freddy and me.

"Well, how much does she want to pay?" he's saying as I pass by. The small of my back brushes up against his stomach and I immediately feel my face turn crimson. About a month ago, I came to the realization that I have a crush on

Freddy, but I'd die if he—or anyone else—ever found out.

You could say that Freddy and I are friends, but I've never really been friends with a boy before, so it's strange thinking that way. Most boys I know are clumsy and either too shy or too bold and usually only after one thing. And once they get it, they're on to the next girl. (I've never given it. Never given anything, for that matter. Sometimes I'm proud of that. Other times, embarrassed.) But Freddy isn't like most boys. He's fun and loves to talk and I've never once caught him looking at my chest instead of my eyes. He calls me his Cinema Princess (he's the Theatre Prince) because every Friday night for the past two months, we've been going downtown to the Odeon Theatre. Freddy's crazy for movies. I like movies and looking at people on screen who are better looking and lead more important lives and always say the perfect thing at the perfect time. Sometimes it's easy to convince myself that that's how real life could be, if only I lost a few pounds and had more confidence and knew how to dress. But for Freddy, the movies mean much more. Something happens to him. I can see it in his eyes when the screen goes bright. Like he's under a spell. It seems so personal for him. Private. I asked him once if he would prefer going on his own and he got very serious.

"You're part of the magic," he said, and those words rolled and rolled inside by head. I wanted to tell Freddy that he was part of the magic, too. That while I was sitting in the movie theatre next to him, the darkness around us, I felt like the first tear of a wrapped present.

Last week, we went to see *A Place in the Sun*, and when Montgomery Clift told Elizabeth Taylor that he loved her even before he saw her, I was certain that Freddy was going to reach for me.

"Wasn't Montgomery sensational?" he said as we left the theatre. I nodded, still thinking about the scene where Elizabeth says to Montgomery, "Tell Mama . . . Tell Mama all," and then they kiss passionately. What would that be like? To give yourself over to something so completely? I hoped Freddy might take my hand as we walked home, but instead, he was preoccupied with the remains of his popcorn and his talk about Hollywood.

Being around Freddy is frustrating, because I can't seem to get him to "see" me. I don't know if that makes sense, because it's not as though he doesn't notice me. We go to the movies. We've gone for bike rides along the river and lain in the grass at Donlan Park all afternoon and sometimes we share a cigarette behind the Dairy Maid when it's not busy. In other words, all the things that a boyfriend and girlfriend would do. Only we're not that. But I want more. And I think Freddy does, too. It's so complicated it makes my brain hurt sometimes.

I go to the backroom that Mr. Devlin, the owner, refers to as the "Gussy-Up Room." There's a sink and a mirror and a shelf stocked with cologne, aftershave, a razor, shaving cream, hair spray, a tube of lipstick (the most unnatural shade of red I've ever seen), a tortoiseshell compact that a customer left behind and a tin of black shoe polish. Mr. Devlin insists that all staff arrive at least ten minutes before their shift so that everyone has a chance to primp before stepping behind the counter to serve up banana splits and Tiger Tail ice cream.

I've been working at Dairy Maid for just over three months. I took the job when school finished to bide my time until I figured out what I wanted to do. Now it's Labour Day weekend, and I still haven't taken any definitive steps. Leaving Balsden is top of the list. I hate this town with its belching smokestacks and zombie citizens and the prevailing attitude that you might as well give in and give up before even trying. That's what bothers me most about Helen. She's only marrying Dickie because he asked.

"There are other guys in the world," I said to her. "It's not like God created Dickie and then shut down the factory."

"People get trapped into thinking that anything worth having must involve some big journey," she said. "Sailing on icebergs and thrashing through jungles with machetes. But what if it's already here, Joyce? What if what you have now is as good as you'll ever have?"

She slipped on her veil and examined herself in the mirror, her face blurred through a wall of netting.

"I'm the practical sort," she said. "Like Mom. She told me that when she and Dad got married, she had her doubts. It's expected. But over time, you can learn to love anyone. You, on the other hand." She turned around. "You still think you're in store for magic. Stars and firecrackers. But that's because you're young. You'll see in another few years."

"See what?"

"That your life is already mapped out whether you realize it or not. There's a natural order to things, Joyce. You might as well make the best of it."

I gather up my hair, fasten it into a ponytail and bobby-pin my paper Dairy Maid hat into place. Then I check the temperature of the hot fudge because Freddy always has it too hot and it slides off the ice cream.

"I suppose, Mother," Freddy sighs. "But I'm not crazy about the idea of private lessons. She's got about as much poise as a greased pig. What is it she wants to learn? The rumba? And by the end of summer? Kill me now. All right. You call me back after you've spoken to her. But this is the last time, Mother. I mean it."

He hangs up and adjusts the paper hat on his head. He's always been very particular about this. The hat has to sit just slightly off to the side. "I never sacrifice personal flair for uniformity," he said once.

"Oh. Joyce," he says when he sees me. He always says my name like I'm some kind of surprise.

"Hi, Freddy," I say, trying to sound as nonchalant as possible. I'm having trouble looking at him lately because I can't stop noticing his blue eyes. There are other things, too—his blond wavy hair, the straw splat of freckles across his nose and cheeks. The cleft in his chin, just like Kirk Douglas's. "Has it been busy?"

"Moderately," he says. "We're out of rum-and-raisin if anyone asks. I told Mr. Devlin last week to get some in, but he didn't listen. Nothing new there." He squints at me. "Did you colour your hair?"

"No," I say, feeling my face stain red again.

"You should. It would soften your complexion. I got my mother to take the plunge, but it wasn't easy. She said school-teachers don't bleach their hair. I told her that was a pile of garbage. Now she can't stop looking at herself. Someone told her she looks like Lana Turner in *The Postman Always Rings Twice*. I wouldn't go *that* far, but I think she looks younger. Now if only she'd lose twenty pounds."

I can't imagine Mrs. Pender blond. Both Fern and I had her as our teacher in grade six. I never liked her. She was stern and wore too much blush and would whack the desks with her yardstick if anyone got out of line. Fern thought Mrs. Pender was romantically frustrated.

"No man wants a woman with a child," she said. "Damaged goods."

A number of years ago, maybe eight or nine, Mrs. Pender's husband died in an accident. He was on the roof during a storm, got hit by a bolt of lightning and then fell to his death. No one could say for sure whether it was the lightning or the fall that killed him, although my father thought it was likely a combination of three things.

"The lightning, the fall and a spectacular lack of common sense," he said.

I've never heard Freddy mention his father. All he ever seems to talk about is his budding career. He's convinced he's going to be a movie star. When he's not serving ice cream, he's teaching tap dancing to women in a studio above the mechanic's shop on Bowden Street. I overheard my mother's friend talking about him once.

"He certainly isn't the most masculine thing on the planet. But he does have ambition and they say that's half the battle."

"He's as fruity as they come," Helen said once. "Baton and all."

"That's not true!" I shot back, even though I wasn't entirely sure what "fruity" meant. But I knew it wasn't a compliment. "You don't know the first thing about him."

Freddy was in my sister's grade and was, among other things, the baton twirler for the high school marching band.

"I didn't think there were boy baton twirlers," Fern said to Helen.

"There aren't," Helen answered out of the corner of her mouth.

"Of course there are," I said. "Lots of them."

Two years ago, before I even knew Freddy, there was a championship game between our high school football team and the Catholic high school team. I'd never seen so much hoopla in my entire life, which was largely the result of our school not having made it to the finals in years. You'd have thought the new Queen Elizabeth was coming. Still, it was hard not to get caught up in the excitement. For once, it felt as though I was part of something magical and important. Fern and I planned to go even though we couldn't have cared less about football.

The day of the finals, a parade was planned to run along Parker Street and eventually lead straight onto the football field. Fern and I stood bundled and huddled under the grey November sky, waiting for the parade to wind its way to us.

The sidewalks were thick with people wearing hats and ear-muffs, and breath hung in the air like small clouds. Eventually, we heard the distant notes of trumpets and drums. Everyone began to clap and whoop and little kids jumped up and down and tried to break free from their parents' arms to run into the middle of the road.

"I hope they're not expecting Santa," Fern said.

I stood on my tiptoes and leaned over just far enough to catch sight of the band turning onto Parker Street. I caught a flash of something white and it wasn't until the band got closer that I realized it was Freddy Pender, leading the parade with his baton. For some reason, he'd chosen to dress not in the band uniform, but in a white suit. He was wearing a hat like my father puts on for his Elks Lodge meetings, only it was white to match his suit. An oversized pompom dangled from it, bouncing to the beat as Freddy's knees slapped the sky. His blue eyes were frozen on some distant point on the horizon, his smile hard and wide, like the grille of a car. He stopped in front of us, threw his baton up in the air, spun twice and caught it in his white-gloved hand on the descent. I'd never seen a boy so . . . I wasn't sure what the word was. I'm still not sure. *Feminine* didn't seem right. It wasn't like he was wearing a skirt. But he was garish. Outrageous.

Un-Balsden.

Based on the laughter and half-hearted claps Freddy gener-ated as he passed, I could tell the crowd felt the same way. But I didn't see anything wrong. In fact, I think he had more cour-age than any of those pea-brained football players. Everyone spends so much time trying to be like everyone else. At least Freddy knew who he was. And maybe, even before our paths had crossed, that moment in the parade was when I *really* fell for Freddy.

I thought a lot about him after that. It was as though there was a rebellious and glorious version of myself in that white suit and hat, sending that baton up like a missile into the November sky. I imagined myself beside him, my skin clear and glowing, teeth perfectly straight, my posture full of conviction. I'd wear a skirt shorter than I'd ever dare to dream and send white pompoms flying through the air like soft explosions. I wouldn't care about what anyone thought of me. I'd know no boundaries. No maps. No predetermined destinations. But the reality is I *do* know the boundaries. So I stood there that day, anonymous in the crowd, watching Freddy as he passed by. I wondered which one of us was in the better place.

"You said Freddy Pender was as fruity as they come," I said to my sister a few weeks after the parade. "What did you mean?"

"Weren't you there? Didn't you *see* him?"

"I saw him. But do you mean fruity because he's a baton twirler?" I suddenly felt nervous.

Her eyebrows bumped together and she looked at me hard for a couple of seconds. Then she got up off the bed, shut the door and came back.

"Fruity men do things with other men," she said in a low voice.

"What things?"

"Sex things," she hissed. "Like women and men. Only it's two men."

"How is that even possible?" I asked.

"One squeezes his legs together and the other one sticks his thing between and goes in and out. You remember Barbara Carter? Her father is a police officer and she overheard him tell her mother that he found two men in a car on a country road one night."

"What were they doing?"

"What do you think? Officer Carter took them both in for questioning but let them go. Disgusting."

Later that night, when Helen was asleep, I pressed my legs together and worked the handle of my hairbrush between my thighs. How was something like this pleasurable? Why would men want to be with other men in the first place? And what gave Helen the right to think that about Freddy? If anything, I knew him better than she did, even though I'd never said a single word to him. I wanted to protect him. I wanted to keep him safe from the crowds.

A couple of years later, I got hired at Dairy Maid. On my first day, I was stopped dead in my tracks when I saw Freddy standing behind the counter.

"This place will suck your soul dry," he said with a roll of his eyes.

Helen is furious with Dickie. She keeps pacing back and forth on the plank of floor between our beds, whispering,

"Unbelievable," over and over again. They were on their way home from a Sunday afternoon visiting Dickie's grandmother in the country when Dickie announced that he had to go to the bathroom. Helen told him to pull over and be discreet. So Dickie got out of the car and walked into a thicket of woods. Helen said she started to get a little nervous when Dickie didn't come back in what she thought was a reasonable amount of time to pee, so she got out of the car to look for him.

"Couples are found murdered in similar situations," she says. "The girlfriend is left alone, the boyfriend gets beheaded, et cetera."

It didn't take long for her to find him, though. He was squatting between a pair of maple trees with his pants around his ankles.

"Like it was the most natural thing in the world. I watched him use a leaf to clean himself, Joyce. A leaf!"

"Maybe he couldn't help it."

"Oh, he could help it, all right. He just couldn't be bothered to wait until he got home. His country bumpkin roots are showing." She drops her head into her palm and sighs. "I don't know if I can marry someone like that."

"What are you talking about?"

"I'm just . . . oh, I don't know. We're still getting married, of course. There's no stopping this train now. But I was so . . . *disappointed* when I saw him, Joyce. Never in a million years did I ever think I'd be witness to something like that. And my fiancé, of all people. All I kept thinking about was a gorilla.

I'm marrying a gorilla. There are other things, too. Dickie gets down in the dumps sometimes and I have no idea why. It's like a raincloud suddenly appears over his head. He won't ever talk to me about it. All he wants is to be left alone. His mother calls them 'spells.' Dickie's father gets them, too. She told me they last anywhere from a day or two to a week. Usually the wintertime is worst. She said I'd get used to it and not to take it personally."

"But are you happy with him?"

She flexes her fingers to examine her nails. She's been trying to grow them for the wedding. "I don't think about happiness. I mean, I never sit down and ask myself if I'm happy or not. But when I close my eyes and picture happiness, I see a whirlwind. People. Voices. Telephones ringing. A to-do list a mile long and a day that never has enough hours. So in that context, I'm the happiest I've ever been."

"What happens after the wedding?"

"A house," Helen says. "Babies. Building a life."

"And after that?"

She shrugs and the corners of her smile disappear. "We grow old together."

I never thought I'd say this, but I'm grateful for my Dairy Maid job. It gives me a convenient excuse to get out of the house. And, of course, to see Freddy. It's Friday and Freddy is dying to see *Show Boat*.

"Ava Gardner is a goddess," he said the other day, and I wished Helen were there to hear him say those words. It would've put her fruity theories to bed once and for all. Not that Helen has much time to pay attention to anyone but herself and her wedding. This morning, she was crying because Dickie had forgotten to tell her that some of his relatives from up north were coming.

"How many is 'some'?" she asked.

Dickie wasn't sure. Maybe ten or so.

"That's a whole table!" Helen complained to me. "We don't have room. You've seen the size of that church basement."

I told her to relax. "Set up a table in one of the nursery school rooms."

"It's not the way I envisioned things at all," Helen said, more to herself than to me.

I'm more than happy to put on my uniform and pedal away from the latest debacle in my sister's perfect-wedding world. It's a beautiful mid-September day. Warm with lots of sunshine. There's a hint of fall in the air, like a dab of perfume behind an ear. I love those days when the weather tricks you. For example, I can be standing outside on an April day and swear it's November. Or I'm walking along the sidewalk and for the tiniest fraction of a second, October will feel like May. Just when you think things are going steadily along, there's always another force working in the opposite direction, like an undercurrent. Something unknown and unpredictable and completely out of your control.

I've been thinking about asking Freddy to be my date for Helen's wedding. It's true that I'll have to contend with Dickie's cousin for a while, but it's not like we're glued to one another.

After the ceremony, I'll shake him off. Then Freddy and I can enjoy each other's company for the rest of the afternoon. I haven't breathed a word of this to anyone. I have a feeling that Helen wouldn't approve, but I don't care. In some ways, I'd love to see the expression on her face. My little piece of revenge.

Still, the thought of asking Freddy makes me nervous. What if he says no? And on the other hand, what if he says yes? I think about him showing up in that white suit from the parade and my stomach feels queasy. Surely he must have another one. Preferably black. I'll try to bring it up in an inconspicuous way.

In any case, what I keep asking my bedroom mirror is this: "Joyce Conrad. What's more terrifying? The thought of asking him or the thought of *not* asking him?"

This always puts things in perspective.

Freddy is on the phone again when I get to work, but something's different. His back is turned to me and his usually boisterous voice is low. I try to listen in as I make my way past.

"Well, of course it's not true, Mother. I don't know why she'd say something like that."

I go back to the Gussy-Up Room and scrutinize my face. Maybe Freddy is right. I should colour my hair. I'll do it just before the wedding. I bite down on my lip, imagining Helen's reaction. She'd have an absolute fit. Freddy's voice gets louder.

"She's delusional. And jealous. Plain and simple!"

I take a step back to get within better earshot.

An older man came to pick up Freddy from work last week. Someone I'd never seen before. He stood in the far corner, looking nervous and pushing his glasses up his nose.

Freddy came out of the Gussy-Up Room doused in cologne. He introduced the man to me as "a family friend" and winked. The man coughed. I felt sick inside as I watched the car pull out of the parking lot, trying to keep my dark thoughts at bay.

"*You* were the one who arranged this in the first place. Don't sit there and try to wash your hands clean. It's always about what you want, isn't it? Never about what I want! You're selfish and cruel and I won't be your puppet anymore. Do you understand?"

The phone slams down, followed by a cloud of silence. I hold my breath, not wanting to go out there. I've never heard Freddy yell like that before. I don't think today will be the day I ask him to Helen's wedding. I stare into the mirror, still trying to imagine myself as a blonde, but I can't. I'm trapped inside myself. I put my hat on top of my boring chestnut curls, count to ten, spread a nonchalant smile across my face and walk out. Freddy is still standing next to the telephone, one hand pressed down on the freezer lid, as though he's trying to prevent something from getting out.

"Hi, Freddy," I say as I squeeze past. "Has it been busy today?"

He looks up at me. "What? Oh . . . No, not busy."

After I turn down the temperature of the hot fudge, I top up the sundae canisters, keeping one eye on Freddy as he wipes down a table. I'm ten minutes into a shift and he has yet to say my name like it's a surprise or mention Hollywood or offer any tips to help my complexion. A couple of customers come into the shop, and when I hand over their strawberry sundae and chocolate-dipped cone, Freddy is still wiping the same table. Eventually, he steps back behind the counter and both of us manage our way through a small swarm of customers. When the last of them leaves, Freddy leans up against the counter and sighs so dramatically, my bangs ruffle.

"I hate this place."

"It's not so bad," I say. "We get free ice cream."

"I'm not talking about *this* place, Joyce. I'm talking about this *place*." He swings his arms in a wide semicircle. "This shit hole. I can't wait to get away."

"I'm moving to Andover," I say, surprised by my confession. Truthfully, it's been on my mind. I was planning to move after Helen's wedding. I could get a job typing. My own apartment. I'd make new friends and have them over for dinner. I'd smoke too much and stare out of my kitchen window onto the street below.

"Well la-di-da," Freddy says and twirls his paper hat on his finger. "No one ever said you weren't living on the edge."

I cross my arms. "What exciting place have *you* got in mind? Toronto?"

"Someplace bigger, toots."

"I can't wait to get away, either," I say, more to myself than him. "I'm sick of all this stupid wedding business. Helen always has to have centre stage. It's so typical of her."

He narrows his eyes. "Joyce Conrad, do you know how to cha-cha?"

I can't help but laugh. "How to *what*?"

"What time does the movie start tonight?"

"Nine," I say.

"Then we've got time."

"For what?"

"You'll see."

Later, after we close up the shop, Freddy pushes the chairs and tables against the wall to clear a space. I watch him from behind the counter, paralyzed. He takes the transistor radio from Mr. Devlin's office and sets it on one of the tables. After some static and high-pitched whining, he finds a station and turns up the volume. He starts to snap his fingers.

"Take off that dirty apron and get on this dance floor," he says.

"I don't think I can do this, Freddy." My mouth feels full of dried glue.

"If I can teach the fat, middle-aged women of Balsden the soft-shoe shuffle, I can teach you how to cha-cha."

I untie my apron and hurry into the Gussy-Up Room to check my hair. I can't put on lipstick without looking too obvious, so I tap and pinch my cheeks to give them some colour. Then I breathe into my cupped palm and sniff.

"Joyce!" Freddy calls. "The orchestra is waiting!"

"Good lord," I whisper to my reflection. Things are about to change for me. I can feel it.

The steps, he assures me, are very simple.

"Just take one step forward and then two half-steps back. Like this." He demonstrates. "Can you do that?"

I try, but mix up the order. It's hard to concentrate. "I'm horrible at these types of things."

He tells me to wiggle my hips more.

"I don't think I can," I say. I'm light-headed. His hand presses around mine. I can smell everything about him: his cologne, his skin, a hint of vanilla ice cream.

"You're only as bad as you allow yourself to believe," Freddy says.

We keep practising, and eventually I get it right. My hips unlock. I didn't know I could move this way. I feel free. Ungrounded.

"Forget Cinema Princess. I'm going to call you Ginger Rogers from now on," Freddy says as we spin around the room. We crash into one of the tables and start to laugh.

"If Mr. Devlin saw us, he'd have a heart attack," I say.

"He'd spew whipped cream out his ears."

"His hot fudge would boil over."

Then Freddy tells me he's going to dip me. "Hang on."

My body stiffens instinctively as I fall back towards the floor. The heels of my sneakers slide against the tiles.

"Don't worry," he says. "I've got you."

And he does. I see that now. Freddy has always had me.

He pulls me back up and then I kiss him. It's the first time my lips have ever touched anyone else's. My breath catches inside my mouth and my skin becomes a blanket of pin pricks. I feel Freddy press his lips against mine and if freedom ever felt like anything, it's this moment. Then he pulls away and drops his face between my neck and shoulder. I hear him inhale, as though sucking me in.

He lifts his head and I notice his eyes are glistening. "That wasn't so bad," he says in a peculiar voice.

I can't believe I've done something so bold. He lets go of me and walks over to the radio, which is now broadcasting the news. He's going to find another station playing music. Something slow and romantic. Then he's going to walk back to me and take me into his arms again and—

"I'm not sure about the movie tonight," he says quietly. He switches off the radio. "I have some things to take care of."

"Oh?" I manage.

"But why don't you come for dinner on Sunday night?" His voice is back to its usual pitch. "Mother will positively squeal with excitement. Do you like roast? She makes one every Sunday. Tough as shoe leather, but I don't have the heart to tell her. Just sharpen your teeth before you come."

Helen and Fern want me to go over the details again. We're sitting in Helen's bedroom with the door closed.

"Was his mouth open?" Fern asks.

"Of course not." I told them that Freddy was the one who kissed me.

Helen's nose scrunches up. "I don't know about this. It's *Freddy Pender*, after all."

"What do you mean by that?"

"You know what I mean." She rubs half a lemon against her elbow. I watch a sprinkle of juice land on the carpet.

"I'd kill for someone to kiss me," Fern says. "Anyone at all."

"Be careful what you wish for," Helen says.

"Do you like him?" Fern asks.

"I'm not sure," I say, feeling myself blush at the lie. Ever since our kiss, I can't stop thinking about Freddy. He's so much more interesting than anyone else I know. He's passionate and funny and he's got talent in spades. But there are things about him that make me feel uncomfortable, too. Shouldn't I want a quarterback instead of a baton twirler? Could I have someone like that as a boyfriend? I glance at Helen. She said Freddy was a fruit. But she was wrong. I know what I felt the other night. I know that Freddy felt it, too. That's what those tears meant, wasn't it?

"He obviously likes you," Fern says. "Otherwise, why would he invite you to dinner?"

"Something's fishy," Helen says and begins to work on her other elbow.

"The only thing fishy around here is your attitude," I say, hearing my voice get louder. "It's not always about you, Helen. It's not always about your dumb wedding."

Mrs. Pender and Freddy live on Bleeker Street, on the west side of Balsden. It's not far from the refineries, so most people avoid that area if they can help it. The streets are wide and the bungalows are set back from the sidewalks in a way that makes them seem shy. I'm carrying a banana loaf wrapped tightly in waxed paper. My mother made me take it.

"It's good manners," she said. She seemed nervous. "Don't be late."

"Stay off the roof," my father said.

Mrs. Pender's house isn't hard to find. It's the only one on the street painted burgundy and buttercream. Freddy picked the colours.

"It came to me in a dream," he'd told me. "Mother said it seemed more like a nightmare to her, but she came around. She always does."

A crooked path leads me to the front steps. On the porch, there's a large wicker rocker with an overstuffed floral-print pillow and a Hollywood gossip magazine draped over the arm. From inside, I hear piano music. I stop and gather my nerves. When I get Freddy alone, I'm going to ask him to Helen's wedding. Then I'll kiss him again. I don't care if it makes me seem bold. There's too much at stake.

The piano stops abruptly when I ring the doorbell. Freddy appears behind the screen.

"Hello, stranger." He holds the door open for me. He's wearing a crisp white shirt. I can see a snippet of chest hair poking out and my knees turn to gelatin. "It's nice not seeing you knee-deep in maple walnut."

I wait for him to touch me, to put his hand on my arm. Or even peck my cheek. But all he does is hold the door.

"I brought this," I say, passing him the loaf. "My mom . . . made . . . banana . . ." Where did my words go?

It's hard for my eyes to adjust to the darkness once I'm inside, but I begin to make out the shape of a sofa. An armchair. A radio in the corner. And then Mrs. Pender, coming out of the kitchen wearing a blue apron with white daisies.

"Look who's here!" she says. Her hair looks like white candy floss and her mouth is a circle of red lipstick. "It's been years since you were in my class. Now here you are. All grown up. I'm glad Freddy has someone besides me to take to the movies now. I was so excited when he told me you were coming for dinner."

I feel Freddy pinch the back of my arm. She offers me iced tea in a jam jar. I notice dried orange pulp around the rim. The tea isn't sweetened, she says, and hopes that's not a problem for me.

"I'm trying to cut back on my sugar intake. Freddy was just practising some songs." She reaches for Freddy's shoulder. "Why don't you play a few songs for Joyce while I finish up in the kitchen? Joyce, have a seat on the couch."

Freddy rolls his eyes and whispers, "Sorry." Then he goes over to the piano and plays a song I think I've heard before, but can't place. My eyes wander the cluttered living room. Everywhere I look, there's a chair or a lamp or a footstool. It's as though one day the room shrunk in half and all the furniture got pushed towards the centre. On the mantel, a large picture of Freddy with his baton smiles back at me. He's wearing that same white suit.

A silence interrupts my thoughts and I realize the song is over. Freddy has swung around on the piano bench, facing me.

"That was very good," I say.

"You weren't even listening." The name of the song, he tells me, is "Bewitched, Bothered and Bewildered." "From *Pal Joey*."

"Of course," I say. I have no idea who Pal Joey is.

He comes over and sits next to me on the sofa.

"Can I be frank with you for a moment?"

"Sure," I say. I try not to stare at his lips. In my mind, I say, "Tell Mama . . . Tell Mama all."

"I'm glad you came, especially after the other night. It took me by surprise."

"Me, too. But I'm glad it happened."

"I like you, Joyce. You're smarter than most girls. If things were different, I think we could have hit it off."

"Could've? What do you mean?"

"There's something you don't know." His mouth stretches between a grin and a frown. "Can you keep a secret?"

"Sure."

"I'm taking off for New York City in two days," he whispers, and waits for me to respond. I hear a sound, a low rumble like the approach of a tornado, inside my head. I press my eyes shut to try to block it.

"This woman took a tap class with me and one day, her husband came to pick her up. We got talking and I told him about how I wanted to get going on my film career. Turns out he's originally from New York. He offered to take me there and help get me started. Says he knows a bunch of people who'd be *very* interested in me."

The sound grows louder. I jab my pinkie fingernail into the pad of my thumb.

"He's going to drive me there and set me up with one of his friends. Then he has to come back. He wants to stay, but it's complicated. He's married, after all."

"And your mother doesn't know this?"

"She'd blow a gasket."

42

"But she wouldn't want you to go to New York alone."

"I'm not going alone. I told you. Besides, I have to get away from her. You have no idea what it's like for me. I can't breathe."

Then Mrs. Pender's voice comes floating from the kitchen. "Freddy, I'm not hearing any music."

"Please don't tell anyone, Joyce. I'm counting on you."

Over dinner, Mrs. Pender makes a point of telling me things about Freddy. He sang in the church choir when he was a boy. He used to put on plays for her and Mr. Pender. He once broke his wrist doing a cartwheel. He started dancing at eleven. He has such a natural flair. An innate showman. She has no idea where it comes from, although can't remove herself entirely from taking credit.

I feel like I'm going to vomit all over Mrs. Pender's plates and cutlery. I can't concentrate. Inside, I'm stone. Set in place.

"I used to write poetry," Mrs. Pender confesses as she heaps another mound of mashed potatoes onto my plate. "Sonnets and that sort of thing. I guess that's why I loved teaching English so much. You were a good student from what I remember, Joyce."

Throughout dinner, Freddy remains silent. The colour of his face varies from light pink to crimson. Occasionally, he looks horrified. Other times, apologetic. But most of the time, he seems constrained, as though he's been strapped to his chair. At one point, I drop my napkin. When I reach down to pick it up, I see his leg bouncing like a jackhammer under the table.

She wants me to stay after the chocolate pie has been finished, but I tell her I have to go.

"My sister is getting married next week. There's so much to do."

"Did you hear that, Freddy?" Mrs. Pender says. "Joyce's sister is getting married."

There's a flick of a blade in her tone.

"I know," Freddy says, his eyes on me.

Mrs. Pender insists I stay for one more song. Her voice has gotten higher, her mannerisms more exaggerated. It's like she's doing an impersonation of someone, but she doesn't know who that person is. We go into the living room and Freddy takes his place on the piano bench while Mrs. Pender and I sit side by side on the sofa.

"What would you like to hear?" he asks.

"Why do you even need to ask?" Mrs. Pender says.

Freddy rolls his shoulders and begins to play. When the song ends, I look over at Mrs. Pender and see that her eyes are sparkling with tears.

"That's called 'You'll Never Walk Alone,'" Freddy says, and his voice is both gentle and robotic. "From the musical *Carousel*."

"Look at me," Mrs. Pender says with a wet laugh. "I turn into a complete mess every time. Freddy, pass me your handkerchief, will you?"

I say I have to leave then and hurry out the door before I'm forced to endure any more. When I reach the end of the crooked path, I turn around briefly and see the two of them standing side by side, watching me from behind the gauze of the screen door. They look like they're trapped inside a box, but I know it's really the other way around.

I manage to hold my tears until I reach the end of the street.

CHAPTER THREE

THERE ARE TREES behind our house: evergreens and maples and birches with thick curls of white bark that flap like flags. On the other side of the trees is an open field filled with clover at this time of year, dense constellations in a green galaxy. I like June. The days are warm with thick clouds and the nights are cool for sleeping. Daylight breaks early, as well. It's comforting to open my bedroom curtains and see sunlight spilling across the backyard.

The trees won't be around for much longer. A second phase of housing is planned to start soon. That's what the Sparrows told me. Hal and Eileen live across the street. Eileen seems to know most things that go on in the neighbourhood. Charlie claims to have caught her looking at him with a pair of binoculars once, but Hal told me she bird-watches, so I don't know. She seems to pay Charlie a lot of attention, but I could be reading into things. I have a habit of doing that.

The new development is scheduled to start in a few days. I'm not looking forward to the commotion. John is six, an exploratory age. I keep imagining him sneaking off and falling into a mud pit or getting pinned underneath some dinosaur-ish piece of machinery. I play these scenarios over and over in my head until I feel nauseated.

"Everything around here is about to change," Charlie likes to say. He'll stand out on the back porch, his hands in his pockets, rocking back and forth, the swirl of his growing bald spot like the eye of a hurricane. "We made a good decision with this house."

"When do you think the basement will be ready?" I've been anxious for him to finish the rec room. No one else we know has one, not even Helen, who seems to have every-thing under the sun, even though Dickie can't make *that* much as an electrician. I'm desperate to have a party. I think of laughter and music, a passed plate of hors d'oeuvres, tin-kling ice. I imagine myself in a dress that I'll never be able to afford, pearl-drop earrings that I don't own, a trail of per-fume on my neck. Who is this woman? I sometimes wonder. Where did she come from? How could she possibly fit into this landscape of shift-working husbands and exhausting six-year-old boys?

"Soon," Charlie will say. "We'll have everything soon enough. Maybe another baby, too."

"Don't talk like that. You know what the doctor said."

"Doctors don't know everything. You just need a little faith."

I'll be sad to see the trees go. There's something peaceful

and hypnotic about the dark pockets between their trunks. I once saw a deer step out from the trees so matter-of-factly that I couldn't believe what I was seeing. I watched it walk towards the edge of the backyard. I would've called for John, but he was at school, and Charlie was working days. The deer cocked its head and paused. I held my breath. Then, as quickly as it appeared, it slipped back into the trees.

I think about that deer often. I wonder what will happen to it once the dump trucks and bulldozers and chainsaws move in. Who will protect it? Where will it go?

We moved here five years ago, when John was just a toddler. Before that, we lived in the apartment on Cecil Street. It was small and dark and I hated smelling what strangers were having for supper. Charlie was working overtime shifts whenever he could and I did some sewing on the side until I got pregnant. We used to drive by the areas we wanted to live in, wondering what it would be like to have a backyard. A porch. Our own driveway. Charlie wanted a workroom more than anything else. He can build or repair just about anything. He's quite the handyman, Charlie Sparks. Born and raised in the Prairies. When the work out there dried up, he bought a car and drove east.

"You didn't know *anyone?*" I asked him once.

He shook his head.

"But how could you leave like that, without knowing what might happen?"

"You take your chances in life," he said. "Things usually work out for the best."

I wanted him to talk about me in that moment; about how fate drew us together. I wanted him to use the word *love*. But he has trouble talking about those sorts of things.

"Most men aren't good with emotions," Helen said once with an authoritative nod. She's always making pronouncements like this. Grand overviews. Hard-and-fast rules about life and men and marriage. I think she feels it's her responsibility to set me straight. She wants to teach me.

I met Charlie at the dance pavilion one summer night. He was shy and I was lonely. By that point, I believed what Helen had told me—that my expectations were too high; that love wasn't some kind of explosion. And even if it were, it wouldn't endure. Life was moving steadily along, so what was the point in chasing after the idea of something that didn't even exist?

Charlie and I were married six months later. Helen was my maid of honour. Dickie was the best man. I remember walking down the aisle on my father's arm and seeing Charlie waiting at the altar in the suit he'd borrowed from a friend at work. I was thinking about the luncheon menu, my parents, my dress. I wasn't thinking about him. It was only in the months after, once all the commotion died down and a silence settled in between us, that I began to wonder what we had in common.

Not that he's a bad man. He comes from a good family, although I'm not sure how they feel about me. His mother and sister came for the wedding. It was the first time I'd met them. His father left Mrs. Sparks and the children at some early stage in the marriage. Charlie didn't offer many details.

Only that the last he'd heard, his father was somewhere in Manitoba.

His sister, Irene, was tall with a twisted front tooth.

"You can practically smell the wheat coming off her," my mother whispered.

His mother was older than I expected. She walked with a limp and her white hair was tightly curled against her head, revealing a grid of pink scalp. She treated her son cordially, as though he was someone she'd just met. Everything was "please" and "thank you" and she seemed to feign interest in his stories of life "out East" as he referred to it and how Balsden was an up-and-coming city on account of its refineries.

"It's a city of the future," he said as we drove past the massive oil drums and tall smokestacks like smouldering cigars. "People are calling it the Yukon of the south."

I noticed a desperate edge in his voice, and the look Mrs. Sparks and Irene shared told me they had detected it as well. I realized for the first time what it had meant for him to come here, to leave behind the only world he knew.

"It's so hilly," Irene commented later.

"Really?" I asked. I couldn't think of a single hill in Balsden.

I was anxious to make a good impression on Charlie's family. I didn't want them to think that he'd made a mistake in moving east. And even though he assured me that they liked me, their stone Prairie faces did little to convince me.

"Do you ever think about your father?" I asked once. I wanted to tell him that although I'd never been abandoned in that way, I knew about loss. In the eight years since I last saw

Freddy, I'd never so much as breathed his name. I'm afraid that if I ever tell Charlie about him, he'll ask me if I still have feelings for him and I won't know how to answer. I'm not in *love* with Freddy. I never was. But he offered me something different, exciting. The crack of an open door.

Charlie considered my question about his father. I knew it was the first time he'd been asked.

"You don't miss the things you never had."

"Let me get this straight," Helen says. The three of us are sitting in my backyard, keeping one eye on the children over the horizons of our coffee cups. Helen's eight-year-old daughter, Marianne, is playing with John in the sandbox. Mark, her five-year-old, is asleep on the lawn. "What did the teacher say again?"

"She said that John had been a good student but that he exhibited behaviour throughout the year that concerned her."

"The kitchen set?" Helen's eyes widen. She recently had her brown curls cut short and dyed red. It makes her complexion too washed out, but she says that's the point. It's all about alabaster skin.

"Among other things." I shouldn't have said anything to her. It will come back to haunt me. I glance over at John, who is scooping sand into a bucket. He's the spitting image of me. Brown hair, stern face, long arms. He catches me staring and waves.

"Are you and your cousin making sandcastles?" I call out.

"Sand *houses*, Mommy," he says with irritation.

"Don't get too dirty."

"I personally don't see what the fuss is about," Fern says, shifting in her lawn chair. "Most of the world's greatest chefs are men." With her index finger and thumb, she pinches out her top. She does this all the time so that her clothing doesn't catch in the folds of her stomach. She's put on weight this past year and blames it on her mother's cooking.

"Were there other things?" Helen inquires, leaning towards me.

"Not really. I think she's blowing it out of proportion. She was very snooty to me." I don't mention Miss Robinson's other comment.

"Teachers can be like that," Helen says. "No offence, Fern."

"None taken," Fern says, but her tone says otherwise. She's about to finish her first year of teaching.

"I almost went crazy," she confessed to me. "They're horrible little creatures. All snot and smelly feet and pestering questions."

"Then why did you go into teaching?"

"It was either that or sit at home with Mother all day. I picked the lesser of two evils."

I look over at John. Miss Robinson was younger than me, with pouty red lips like glue bottle dabbers. Her nylons made whispering *whish-whish* sounds each time she crossed and uncrossed her legs. How much happiness can be found in a pair of perfectly shaped calves? Everywhere I looked in the classroom, there were rectangles: the green chalkboards, the beige desks, the melamine backs of chairs.

"About John," Miss Robinson began.

"John," I repeated, tucking my legs under the seat.

She assured me he was a good student. "Just the other day, he held the classroom door open for me." She laughs lightly. "The perfect gentleman."

"He's very considerate."

"But I have concerns." She twisted around, her legs jutting towards me. She gestured behind her back with an index finger. I saw a miniature oven, a sink. Shapes that looked like plastic fruit. "John likes spending play time in the kitchen area."

"He helps me at home," I explained.

"I'm sure he does." Miss Robinson cleared her throat. "There are other things, Mrs. Sparks. John also enjoys playing with dolls."

Did this woman think she was revealing things I didn't already know? "He likes taking care of people. He's . . . he's a very caring soul."

Miss Robinson nodded. I was hot under my jacket. The warm June morning was building to a hot afternoon. I was glad Charlie wasn't there.

"I'm not questioning John's intentions," she said, pressing the pads of her fingertips together. Her fingernails matched her lips. "I'm concerned about the end result of those intentions. Most boys in this class couldn't care less about the kitchen set and they certainly aren't playing with dolls."

Dolls and kitchens. Kitchens and dolls. Was that all she could focus on? What about his spelling?

"I'm sorry, Miss Robinson. But I'm not sure what it is you're trying to tell me."

She looked up. "If I see a child exhibiting abnormal behaviour, I have a responsibility to address it, Mrs. Sparks. My conscience won't allow me to turn a blind eye." She leaned in. "Is everything all right at home?"

"Of course."

"No upheavals or change in the environment that might cause John to act out in peculiar ways?"

"Nothing that I can think of."

I watched her tongue poke the inside of her cheek. A large clock above the chalkboard ticked the seconds away.

"When the children play tag at recess," Miss Robinson finally said, "John lines up with the girls. He wants to be chased by the boys. You'll need to keep a close eye on him, Mrs. Sparks."

I say nothing to Charlie. There's no reason to get him involved. I try to keep certain things about John a secret; things I know Charlie wouldn't be good with. Besides, he'll only blame me.

"You coddle him too much," he tells me. "He can't keep running to you whenever he's got a problem."

"What do you expect me to do? Turn my back?"

"I see the way he is around you."

"You never give him the time of day."

"You won't let me near him."

"You're too critical."

"You make excuses."

You. You. You. I don't know when this blame game started. It's a jagged piece of glass between us.

I buy celebrity magazines when I go grocery shopping, glancing over my shoulder before tucking a rolled-up copy between the items on the conveyor belt. It's not as though I'm doing something shameful or unusual. These magazines are created for women like me, looking for escape, for straight-toothed glamour and perfumed necks, for comfort when fantasy gets run over by reality. The cashiers see right through me.

You want to find Freddy, their eyes say.

I keep the magazines hidden under my mattress. When John is at school and Charlie is working, I'll take them out and pore over every inch of every photograph, reading all the articles, even the advertisements in the back, searching for him.

Rising star Freddy Pender has just signed on with 20th Century Fox to headline in the studio's next major motion picture.

This is what I'm expecting to read, even though I've never come across the actual words. I've even dug out the magnifying glass to scrutinize the party pictures. He may be in the background, smiling or laughing or tapping someone on the shoulder. Is his hair still blond? Has he outgrown his freckles? Does he even go by his own name?

He's in Hollywood now. Mrs. Pender told me. A few years back, I ran into her in the grocery store, in the canned goods aisle. She wore a pleated skirt and black shoes with fat soles. As soon as I saw her, I came to an abrupt stop. My heart froze.

"Joyce Conrad," she said. Her eyes travelled to the stroller where John was sleeping. "I see you've been busy."

I managed a sound resembling a laugh. "This is John."

She bent over to peer into the stroller, and I resisted the impulse to pull it away. Her once bleach-blond curls had gone back to their natural shade of brown. Her black shoes were scuffed at the toes. She had a run in her panty-hose, a thin trickle down her right shin. Her earlobes dangled like pale berries.

"He's a fine-looking boy," she said.

"Thank you. I got married a couple of years ago."

"Oh? And who is the lucky fellow?"

"Charlie Sparks."

Her mouth curved downwards. "Name doesn't ring a bell."

"He's not from here. He grew up in the West and moved here a few years ago. We met at the dance pavilion and hit it off right away." Why was I telling her this?

"And what does he do?"

"He works at one of the refineries."

"I don't know what this town would do without that industry. Say what you like about pollution, but it's giving people the means to earn a living and there's no crime in that."

"We just bought a house on Marian."

"I'm not familiar with that street."

"It's on the east side."

"I see."

I didn't want to ask the question, but couldn't help myself. I cleared my throat and hoped I sounded casual. "How's Freddy?"

She looked over her shoulder before leaning closer. A pink-peach line of foundation ran along her jaw, a morning horizon. "He's in Hollywood, if you can believe it."

"Hollywood? I thought he was going to New York."

"Broadway wasn't for him. He got tired of the repetitiveness. He was on stage for eight performances a week. It was too much and not the best use of his talents. So he packed up and headed for 'La-La Land,' as he refers to it. He's getting into movies."

"Movies," I repeated, as though it was the first time I was hearing the word.

Her chin tilted up. "My boy is on the road to stardom. He even has an agent. Freddy said that when he lands his first starring role, he'll send a white limousine to whisk me away. Needless to say, I keep my curtains open and a packed bag by the front door."

A shadow slipped across her face.

"I worry about him being on his own, though. Especially in a place like that. I write him every day to keep him in line. I need to keep an eye on him."

John began to stir.

"It must be difficult for you," I say. "Being on your own."

"I have friends, Joyce."

"I didn't mean—"

"And my church."

"Of course. Are you still teaching?"

She nodded. "Grade four this year. It's a good age. Right before they turn all saucy."

I heard John yawn. "I should be going. He's not usually in a good mood when he wakes up. Please send my regards to Freddy."

"Keep an eye out for the limousine," she said and turned her shopping cart to leave.

Since then, I haven't come across a single picture of Freddy or a mention of his name in any of the magazines. But that doesn't stop me from buying and hiding them.

Sometimes, when the weather is nice, I'll sit out on the front porch and watch for the flash of white tearing down the street. Ridiculous, I know. Mrs. Pender doesn't live anywhere near us.

From where I sit, I can see John's school. The sight of those yellow bricks reassures me.

He's in there right now, I think. Safe. Contained.

When I pick John up from school today, he passes me an envelope. There's a clown on it. Balloons. Another birthday party invitation.

"Who's Benjamin?" I ask.

"He's in my class," John says.

"Are you friends with him?" I think parents spread the net too wide with these invitations. It's all for show. They're setting their children up for disappointment later in life. Still, I shouldn't complain. Better too many invitations than none at all.

John shrugs and grips my hand tighter. I hope, when he's older, he remembers our walks home. I hope he remembers the feeling of my hand and the pebbled sidewalks and the smell of early summer. The party is Saturday afternoon. Today is Thursday. Is it too much trouble to ask for *some* advance notice?

"We'll have to get Benjamin a present tonight," I say. "Remember we're going to Aunt Helen's for dinner tomorrow."

"I don't want to go there," John says. "I don't like Mark."

"Now John . . ."

"Marianne is bossy. And Uncle Dickie looks funny."

What am I going to do with this boy? He's going to give me such a run in this life.

"It's not nice to talk about your relatives that way," I remind him. He looks up, scrutinizing my face, gauging my sincerity.

Charlie gets home from work shortly after six. He's on days this week. Twelve hours, from six to six, then he's off for three days and back for three nights. He sits down at the table in his beige work shirt with matching beige pants. Sometimes, when he's coming home from a night shift, I'll meet him in the kitchen wearing my short purple nightie. We'll sneak down to the laundry room or the unfinished basement, the smell of crude oil and night air still on his skin. I love him desperately in those moments, this abandoned young boy with a dream. I can almost believe what he says. That every-thing *does* work out for the best.

I take his dinner plate from the oven and set it on the table in front of him. Charlie won't eat a vegetable to save his life. Everything he puts in his mouth is either white or brown. John and I have already eaten. It's better when it's just the two of us. John loves vegetables. His favourite is carrot medallions. I let him peel them.

"I have to go to Woolworth's," I say to Charlie. "John's been invited to a birthday party on Saturday. You can come if you want. To the store, I mean." I know he won't, so I feel safe putting it out there.

"You go ahead," Charlie says around a mouthful of meat loaf. "Don't spend too much. I need to get the car fixed."

"What's wrong with it?"

"I don't know. That's why I'm taking it in."

"Is it safe to drive?"

"So long as you don't use the brakes."

I swat him with my tea towel. "Don't joke about things like that. You know I'm a nervous driver."

"I need some socks. Wool ones."

"I'll pick some up."

The store isn't busy. We pass through the empty aisles and when we come to the perfume section, I almost stop. I'm desperate for some kind of indulgence these days. I saw a dress in the window of Purdy's on the weekend and just about cried. It was dark blue with a lace collar. I used to have a dress just like that, although I have no idea what happened to it. I have a hard time connecting with my younger self. My teenage years seem like memories belonging to someone else.

"What do you think Benjamin would like?" I ask John as we make our way towards the toy section.

"He plays cowboys and Indians a lot."

"Do you ever play with him? You'd make a good cowboy."

He shakes his head. "I don't like playing that."

Charlie wanted to sign John up for baseball this past spring. He was excited about being a father, about making up for all the things he never experienced as a kid. The first time we took John out West to visit Charlie's family, Charlie was so proud of his son. I'd never seen him so happy.

"He's got my ears," he said to his mother. "Unfortunately."

"It's a sign of intelligence," Mrs. Sparks said.

"It's a sign of big ears," Charlie laughed and lifted John high into the air.

"Treat him right," Mrs. Sparks said. "You be everything to him." I heard the slightest quiver in her voice. It was the closest I'd seen her come to revealing the damage Charlie's father had caused the family. When Charlie broached the idea of baseball with John, we both thought it was a good idea. Our boy needed more physical activity. But John crossed his arms against his chest and howled as though we'd just told him Santa Claus had died. I pleaded with him to give it a chance. Charlie even made him a wooden platform with a pipe to practise hitting the ball, but John would have none of it. I remember the hurt expression on Charlie's face when he took the platform out to the curb for garbage collection. Later that afternoon, my son and I made a zucchini loaf. I told John to wrap a slice up and set it into his father's lunch box.

"It'll be a nice surprise for Daddy when he's at work."

John was so careful with the waxed paper that it broke my heart. My husband and son seemed frozen on parallel lines.

The toy section is a whirl of reds and blues and yellows. "Now remember what I said, John. We're here for Benjamin. Not you."

We go to the boys' section and he surveys the shelves of trucks and war figurines. I take a bag of small plastic soldiers from the shelf. The price is reasonable.

"Do you think Benjamin would like this?" I ask. He shrugs. There's also a toy gun with a holster. "Or this?"

Another shrug.

"Bag of soldiers it is. Now we need to get a card. And wrapping paper. Did we pass that section on the way here?"

I walk towards the end of the aisle to get my bearings. I'm still thinking about the perfume we passed. Why does Benjamin get to have all the fun? I'll give myself a squirt or two of something. Just to test it out before we have our rec room party. Maybe I'll stop by the dress department before we leave.

When I turn around, my son is gone. I'd be more panicked if I didn't know where to find him. He's moved to the next aisle—the one filled with pink boxes, with plastic faces and eyes half-hidden behind black bangs.

This is the real reason I didn't invite Charlie.

"John," I whisper, standing at the threshold of the aisle. "Come away from there."

"But there she is!" he says. Without even explaining, I know the doll he's referring to. Curly Q Sue. A girl brought one to school a couple of months ago. Ever since, John has pleaded for one non-stop.

"What did I tell you?" I glance over my shoulder. "Let's go." My voice is an urgent hiss.

"Please, Mommy," he says. His arm stretches out towards the doll.

"I don't have time to fool around, John."

"Please."

"Come here."

He turns to me and I see his wide eyes. "*Please.*" He sounds like a wounded animal.

"John."

"*Mommy.*"

I sigh and look at the fluorescent lights overhead. I don't know what's worse—to deny him the things he wants or to allow him to have them. I march over and grab the doll box from the shelf and put it into the cart.

"Come," I say, louder than intended.

"But I want to carry her."

"Oh no you won't." I grab his wrist and pull him along. I pick the first birthday card I find and a package of the cheapest paper. I'm in such a rush to get out of the store I don't even pause at the perfume and I don't bother with Charlie's socks. I'll have to make up an explanation for the extra expense. Plastic soldiers have gone up in price.

Once we're safely inside the car, I establish the rules.

"Daddy will be very angry if he finds out," I say. "We have to keep the doll a secret. The only time you can play with her is while Daddy is at work. When I say it's time to put the doll away, the doll goes away. No arguments. You cannot bring the doll to school or mention the doll to any of your friends. If you do, I will take the doll back to the store. Do you understand?"

"Yes. Can I hold her now?"

I can't help but smile when I pass him the box and watch his face light up. How could I deny my child such joy?

"I won't tell anyone, Mommy. Promise."

I'm hanging out the laundry on the back line. John is playing in the sandbox. Charlie is driving posts into the ground. He's working on a fence that will circle our backyard. He plans to paint it white.

"We'll have to invite the Queen back to see it," he says to me.

"I'm sure it will be first on her list," I reply.

The royal tour is coming to Balsden next week. This is the biggest thing to happen in our city in years. There's a motorcade that will run along Parker Street and stop at city hall while the mayor makes a speech and a high school band plays "God Save the Queen." Then the motorcade will start up again and wind past the river before ending in Century Park. There, Queen Elizabeth and Prince Philip will watch performances by a children's choir and Ukrainian dancers and the Queen will be presented with a gift on behalf of the city. (Fern says it's an oil painting of the refineries by a local artist, which sounds just awful to me, but she insists it's nice and if anyone would know, it would be Fern.) Afterwards, the Queen and Prince Philip will visit one of the refineries. I screamed out loud when I read that, as Charlie is working that day, but he says it's not his refinery they'll be visiting.

"Likely Nordoc," he said. "It's the newest one."

John and I will go downtown to watch the motorcade. He's convinced he's going to meet the Queen in person. I've tried to quash those expectations but with little success.

"Well hello, neighbours!"

I turn from the towel I'm hanging to see Hal Sparrow standing at the edge of the yard, wearing a bucket hat.

"Hi, Mr. Sparrow. I haven't seen you or Eileen around for a while."

"Eileen's under the weather lately."

"Oh? Nothing serious, I hope."

"She'll bounce back." He waves to Charlie. "I could use a fence around my yard, too."

"That so?" The back of his shirt is patterned with dark shapes of sweat.

"Good you're getting that done before the construction starts," Hal says to me. "I just hate to think of those trees going."

We stand in silence for a few moments, watching Charlie hammer a post into the ground. A cicada's trill stretches through the air.

"It's a shame about the Pender boy."

It takes a moment for the name to register with me. "Pender?"

"Yeah. Anne Pender's boy. Freddy. That was his name, wasn't it? He's dead."

"*Dead!* That can't be true. Who told you that?"

"Eileen heard it. Apparently he was on a ship. Some Alaskan cruise. I think he was a singer or something. Anyway, he went overboard."

"He *what?*"

John's head turns towards us.

"The official word was that it was an accident."

I look over at Charlie as he rears back the sledgehammer. He hasn't heard any of this. John is emptying a bucket of sand on the ledge of his sandbox. Clothes flap on the line. I smell detergent. On the other side of us, the trees.

"Freddy was in Hollywood. He was getting into movies," I hear myself say. I think of the magazines pressed flat under my mattress. "When did this happen?"

"A week or so ago. There's no body, of course, which makes it harder. They say when a child dies before the parent, it's the worst possible thing. Especially in *those* circumstances, if you catch my drift. Did you know him?"

Charlie's sledgehammer rises and falls. Rises and falls. "Yes," I say.

"I'm sorry. I didn't realize."

"No, no. It's all right. I didn't—we weren't—"

A scream. "A bee stung me, Mommy! A bee!"

I rush over to the sandbox. My son is wailing, tears running into his mouth, a finger pointing to his knee. Charlie calls over, asking what's wrong.

I can't let Charlie know, I think, and then wonder, Why can't he know about a bee?

Charlie drops the sledgehammer and begins to hurry over, his face set with concern. I hold my hand up. "It's fine. I've got him," I say, but my voice cracks. "Nothing to worry about."

"Poor little guy," I hear Mr. Sparrow say.

I scoop my screaming son up and carry him into the house.

The date squares turn out as perfectly as I'll ever get them. I ask Charlie to taste one. He chews for a minute.

"Not dry, are they?"

"Why didn't you make that carrot cake?"

"Older women like date squares," I say, annoyed. I remind him that John is in his room. "I won't be long."

"Who died again?"

I brush some crumbs from the tablecloth. "An old friend. Anne Pender's son."

"What was his name?"

I feel my face go warm. "Freddy."

He meets my eyes. There's a playful look on his face. "And did you date this Freddy fellow?"

"No. It wasn't like that." I can't let him know anything about Freddy. I can't let *anyone* know about Freddy.

"You seem a little preoccupied."

"Someone I knew died, Charlie. What do you expect me to do? Tap dance down the street?"

"Sorry, shouldn't have said anything."

"It's fine."

I should've just sent a card, I tell myself as I gather up my purse and the tin of squares. Or flowers. I'm not good with these face-to-face things.

"Do you want me to go with you?" Charlie asks.

"It's fine," I say. "You stay home with John."

"I can't say I'm surprised," Helen had said when I called her with the news. "Freddy wasn't right."

"He was a nice person, Helen."

"He was troubled. Anyone could see that. I don't know what you saw in him."

I turn down Mrs. Pender's street. The elm trees lining the boulevard are in full leaf, branches reaching over the road. She could be away. Or she might not be open to receiving visitors. I should've called first. I pull over and step out of the car. Is she watching me from inside? I don't know why I feel so afraid. She's just been through a horrible tragedy. Still, the tin wobbles in my hand.

The front walkway is cracked. Burgundy paint peels away from the eavestrough in curls. The second porch step feels soft under my shoe. I press the doorbell and hear the echo of the chime bouncing off the walls inside. There's movement on the other side of the window and for a second, I imagine it's Freddy.

The door opens. A figure stands behind the screen.

"Mrs. Pender?" My eyes try to adjust. "It's me, Joyce Sparks. I don't mean to disturb you. I can't even begin to imagine what you're going through. I just thought—" I look down at the tin in my hands. The door opens with a metallic scream. Dark eyes, long nose, lips that would melt away if it weren't for lipstick.

"It's you, Joyce Conrad." She sounds bothered, as if I promised to come earlier.

"I made these," I say, holding out the tin. "Date squares."

"You didn't have to." She takes the tin from me. I wait for her to invite me inside. Somewhere, a wind chime tinkles on a nearby porch.

"I just can't believe it," I say. "I can't believe Freddy's gone." A lump catches in my throat.

"Freddy was many things, but predictable wasn't one of them."

"Do you know how it happened?"

"He got himself mixed up with a bad crowd in Hollywood. Showbiz types. Old men. They influenced him. They used him, Joyce. A bunch of filthy men took my son and squeezed his soul dry. He called me one night, crying. Said he couldn't live with himself. He was ashamed. I remember his words to me. He said, 'Mother, I feel diseased.' That was his word. *Diseased.* Do you know what it does to a mother to hear her own child say that? I told him to come home right away. He could get a job in Balsden. There was no shame in it. But he refused. He said he couldn't come back here a failure. The next time I heard from him, he'd taken a job on a cruise ship. He was looking forward to seeing the Atlantic."

She clears her throat and stares at a point just over my shoulder. "So he went out to sea. One night, he was on the deck and went overboard."

"No one went in after him?"

"I'm not sure anyone noticed. Until it was too late, of course.

The current would have pulled him under very quickly. He wasn't a strong swimmer, my boy."

"You don't think he . . ." The words slip out before I consider what I'm saying.

Mrs. Pender looks at me. She says, "You knew about Freddy, didn't you?"

"Knew what?"

"His . . . predilection."

"I'm sorry?"

"His *way*, Joyce. Those men saw it. They used my sweet boy and then tossed him aside. They might as well have pushed him over the rails themselves."

A drop of sweat rolls down my back. I'm not sure what to say, so I keep my lips pressed together. I think of white suits and hard smiles. Pompoms and the cha-cha.

"A mother always knows when something isn't right with her son," Mrs. Pender says. "It's her job to protect him, especially when he doesn't have the wherewithal to protect himself." She looks down at the tin. I hear her inhale deeply. When she speaks again, her voice is thicker. I think it's the first time I've heard her real voice. "I failed my boy. And, in the way these sorts of things tend to go, he failed me. I'm just not sure which of us failed the other first. But I have the rest of my life to figure that out."

"I'm not sure I understand," I say.

But I do.

That night, I take John into the living room.

"Listen to me," I say, holding him by the shoulders. "I'm signing you up for baseball. We'll go to the store tomorrow and get you a baseball glove and a hat."

"I don't want to play ball!"

"Your father can practise with you in the backyard. You should be spending more time with him and not with me."

"No!"

"I'm not arguing with you, John. You're playing ball this summer whether you want to or not."

He squirms under my grip. *Please don't start to cry*, I think. *Please.*

"You'll make lots of friends. You'll make your father happy. You'll make me happy, too. Don't you want to make us happy?"

"No!" he screams.

My hands are vises on his tiny shoulders.

"I bought you that doll," I say.

He stops. I see the hurt in his eyes. Then the anger. Then resolution. My son and I have reached a new level of understanding.

A few days later, the construction crews move into the neighbourhood. By noon on the first day, half the trees behind our house are gone. Hal drops by and we sit out back, drinking coffee, listening to the chainsaws. And although I know I won't see it again, I can't stop myself from looking for the deer.

- - - -

My roommate Ruth is dead. I'm certain of it.

She came down with a dry cough a week ago that turned into a gurgling hacking. I wasn't able to sleep with the racket, especially when they brought in that hissing oxygen machine with its see-through green plastic mask and coiling hose. I felt like I was sleeping across the room from an alien. My nerves were raw. I resented having to put up with this commotion. How did I know she wasn't contagious? I'd had a tickle in my throat for two days but no one paid me any attention.

"Try sucking on a peppermint," the Filipina nurse suggested.

"You should've been a brain surgeon," I said.

I sat in my wheelchair and watched Ruth trying to pull air down into her lungs. She'd open her eyes from time to time and I could tell she was disoriented. I'd wheel over and wrap my hand around the cool metal bedrail.

"YOUR NAME IS RUTH SCHUELLER," I'd yell over the hissing machine. "YOU LIVE AT CHESTNUT PARK IN BALSDEN. YOU ARE SICK."

She'd blink back at me, her mouth opening and closing under her mask. Was she trying to tell me something? Sometimes she'd try to take the mask off, but I'd clamp my hand over it, holding it firmly in place.

"IF YOU TAKE THE MASK OFF, YOU WILL DIE."

I wasn't sure how true that was, but figured the strong-arm approach was the best one to take.

Other times, her eyes would meet mine and I'd see her fear, pure as the white in her hair. My hand would move from the bedrail to her forearm. Her skin was loose sand beneath my palm.

"YOU'RE IN GOOD HANDS."

I don't think either one of us believed that one.

After dinner the other night, two orderlies marched into the room with a stretcher.

"You are being taken to the hospital," one of them told Ruth in a robotic voice. "Your doctor has been notified."

I watched as they lifted her from her bed, her tiny purple-spotted feet dangling.

"Which hospital?" I asked.

"We're not allowed to say, ma'am," one of the orderlies said as he draped a blanket over Ruth. "Patient confidentiality."

"What if her family calls?" I knew this wouldn't happen. Ruth's phone had yet to ring once in the year we'd been sharing a room. But still. It was a matter of principle. I was her roommate, after all.

"The family can call the nurses' station, ma'am."

I watched them wheel Ruth out. I didn't even get a chance to say goodbye. They took the oxygen machine with them. The room was suddenly silent. I stared at the wrinkled sheets of her empty bed, the indent on her pillow. The walls around me seemed to nudge closer. I wheeled myself into the tight space between the wall and my bed and traced the crooked veins of my hands.

"I-23! I-23!"

I massage my temples.

"G-49! G-49!"

Bingo Friday. The recreation room is next door to mine. The racket wouldn't be so bad if Hilda didn't use that damn microphone to call the numbers. There's no escaping it. I turn up the volume on my TV, but it's no use. I can't concentrate. The only thing I can do is hope someone gets lucky soon. These games can go on for hours.

I'm supposed to go for my shower this morning and I'm not looking forward to it. They hose you down like a farm animal and the chemicals in the cheap soap turn my skin to crackled mud. They don't even take the time to blow-dry my hair. No wonder Ruth came down with pneumonia. That's what one of the nurses told me yesterday. I think her name is Mary. Or Marjorie.

"Apparently, she's had it for some time," she said under her breath. "It's lucky they caught it in time."

"She'll pull through?" I asked, incredulous. I almost felt myself rise out of my wheelchair.

"I suspect so," Mary/Marjorie said. "If all goes well, she'll be back in a week."

"N-35! N-35!"

"For god's sake," I mutter as I press the volume button on my remote control. "Somebody win already."

There isn't much television worth watching at this time of the day, but I settle for my soap opera, even though I don't have a clue what's going on most of the time. The dialogue is so fast and I can't remember who did what to whom or which twin sister ran off with the other one's husband or who robbed the bank to pay for the kidney transplant. So much life packed into a single hour. I wheel myself closer to the set, squinting at the screen. Two young men are talking in an office. One of them is wearing a tie and seems agitated.

Now who are they? I wonder.

The other man is wearing one of those hats. What do they call them again? Visors. He looks like he's just come in from the tennis court. He grabs the arm of the man in the suit.

"B-5! B-5!"

I reach for the ginger ale sitting beside the TV. It'll be warm and flat by now, just the way I like it. Just as my fingers touch the plastic ridges of the glass, the two men step towards one another and kiss.

"O-73! O-73!"

My fingers stop. Have I got my channels mixed up? Is this one of those hidden camera shows? I wait for studio-audience laughter, but nothing comes other than the sweeping strains of an orchestra. This doesn't appear to be a joke. But surely it must be. It's the middle of the afternoon.

"Ready for your shower, Mrs. Sparks?"

A hand touches my shoulder, startling me. I turn my head and see it's one of the nurses, the fat one with the bright red hair and orange streaks. When did women decide it was attractive to have fire on their heads?

"Now what is going on here?" she asks, bending towards the TV.

Shame sweeps over me. I fumble for the remote control. "I don't know what this is. I turned on the TV and this came on."

"The one in the suit is a real looker," the nurse says. "Just look at those two go at it. There's nothing they won't put on TV these days."

"Take me to the showers," I say, louder than necessary. We're halfway down the hall when I hear a "Bingo!" but the victory comes too late.

"Let me know if the water's too cold."

A cool shower on my calf. Lilac soap. A drain in the floor like an armoured mouth.

I keep my head down while the water spills over me. I won't come clean. Firewoman can ram the shower head down my throat, but this guilt will never wash away. It's impenetrable. A stain under a crust of ice.

"Can you lift your arm for me, Mrs. Sparks?"

My tears, at least, go undetected.

"Mrs. Sparks?"

My eyes open. I lift my head. The back of my neck throbs.

It's him. Standing in the doorway, a cautious expression on his face. He's wearing a yellow sweater this time. It looks soft and I imagine how nice it would be to have his arms around me, taking me in. I don't remember the last time I was hugged.

"I'm sorry to bother you," Timothy says. "But Maureen in 407 is worried about Ruth. She asked if I'd check with you."

"Pneumonia," I say. "They say she had it for quite some time. God knows who has what around this place. How is

Maureen doing herself? I haven't seen her in the dining room for the past couple of days."

"She's been having dizzy spells," he says. "She fell out of bed a few days ago. Her arm is all bruised." He takes a step back. "Thanks for the information about Ruth. I'll pass it along. Sorry to have bothered you." He turns to go.

"I've always been a private person, you see."

He pauses. Turns back. Takes one step into the room. My eyes dart down.

"I gathered that."

"That photo you commented on," I say. "It was taken the day my son graduated from chef school."

He walks over to it, picks it up. My heart quickens. "I can see the resemblance," he says.

"We had the same nose."

I watch him sit down in the chair opposite me and stare at John's picture.

"He was a good cook. I couldn't boil an egg to save my life. My husband wasn't much good in the kitchen, either. I don't know where John got his talent. Strange, isn't it? How people can be so different, even in families."

I never knew my son. Not in the way I should have known him.

"He made a big birthday cake for me once. An apple cake, sprinkled with cinnamon and sugar. And writing on the top. 'Happy Birthday, Mom' in white icing. I'd never seen anything so—"

I press my eyes shut to block the tears. I won't cry.

"That's all in the past now. No point bringing it up."

Timothy looks from the picture back at me. I feel as though my clothes are suddenly made of Saran Wrap.

"He was thirty-one," I say. "If that's what you're wondering."

CHAPTER FOUR

ANOTHER DAY, another funeral. This one for Louise Arnold. According to Fern, she'd been dead a few days before she was found face down in her laundry room, the spilled contents of her laundry basket around her.

"Can you imagine?" Fern said, looking like she'd just sucked a lemon wedge.

"Who found her?"

"Her neighbour. Apparently, Louise's son was trying to get in touch with her. He lives in Andover, you know. Anyway, he called and called and never got an answer. The neighbour had a key and went in. I can't imagine. If I ever don't answer the phone, Joyce, call the police. For god's sake, don't come into my house."

I made date squares yesterday for the after-service lunch-eon. I'm nervous about them, even though they look more or less like I remember them. I tasted a few oats off the top. The possibility of food poisoning worries me. I hear about these things on the news sometimes. Bake sales that lead to man-slaughter charges. One bad egg and your entire life is over.

I'm also nervous because I haven't made date squares in I don't know how many years. I can't remember the last time I did *any* baking, for that matter. I've got a whole Tupperware container full of index cards and torn magazine pages and spiral-bound church cookbooks, but I never look at them. The box is an artifact from a previous life, when I had people to bake for.

Besides, most things you can buy. They taste just as good and look so much better. Icing smooth as glass. Nuts chopped finely as sand. Loaves with splits running down the centre like healed scars. That's the convenience of modern life for you. I remember my mother baking up a storm. It was work to her in a way it isn't to me. She'd be appalled at my laziness. She'd tell me to take pride in my efforts. She'd say something about tasting the love in homemade goods. Mother died when she was only fifty-eight. Heart attack. My father died of leukemia at sixty the following year. I don't think he knew how to live without her. For reasons completely unknown to me, I've somehow outlived them. Last month, I turned seventy-two.

In spite of my reservations, I decided to make something from scratch for Louise. It was the least I could do, given the unfortunate circumstances around her death, although I don't think she'd care one way or another. She wasn't much of a baker herself. We used to bowl on the same team. That was back in the late '80s, when I decided to make an effort again. I'd spent too long inside the house, roaming from room to room, my grief a worn carpet trail. I needed something to take my mind off things, even if it was only for a few hours on a Tuesday afternoon. The league was called the Silver Balls. Charlie had a comment or two about that. I bought a pair of ugly shoes, a carrying bag and a ball that looked like Jupiter. I'd make small talk with the other women, concentrate on the crimson arrows and dots painted on the alley's floorboards and bring my arm down in finger-snapping frustration every time I missed a spare—which was most of the time. Sometimes, after the game, we would all go to the bowling alley's restaurant for coffee and club sandwiches. They'd talk about their children and grandchildren and I'd listen, jabbing my thumb under the table with a cellophane-tipped toothpick.

Louise had big hair back then. It was burgundy—much too dark for someone her age. Some women think they can keep up the same styles as their younger days. She had silver rims around some of her teeth, and her fingertips were always slick with nail polish. She was a good bowler. And a nice person. The last time I saw her was a few years back in the watch department at Sears. Her battery had run out.

"No replacing it this time," I say out loud. I sit up and swing my legs to the side of the bed. It's necessary that I sit still like this every morning for a few minutes. If I stand up too quickly, I get dizzy. My blood is thinner these days and takes longer to get circulating. Salmon swimming upstream.

The end of August. Summer is about to take its final bow for another year. Thank god. The humidity has been terrible this year. I felt claustrophobic every time I went outside. I asked Fern one sticky afternoon if she thought the weather was getting worse. She said no. "It's *us* who are getting worse."

She has a point. In any case, the fall weather can't come soon enough, as far as I'm concerned. I need a change. I'm looking forward to wearing jackets and going on a bus trip or two before the snow settles in and traps me. Helen says she wants to go to Turkeyville. It's in Michigan, although I've never heard of it. I'd rather go see a musical. Something robust with good-looking young people and smiles so wide their ears disappear.

"What's in Turkeyville?" I asked her.

She frowned. "Turkeys, I suppose. Although that doesn't seem like much of an attraction, does it? Let me check with Joan Franklin. She went a few years back and raved about it."

"I'll think about it."

"Don't think too long. These trips fill up fast, you know."

Yes. I'm sure turkeys are as popular as the pyramids.

There's a throbbing in my left leg. My varicose vein. It bubbles under my skin, a river of jelly. The heat makes it worse. I go to the window and open the blinds. Mr. Sparrow's bedroom blinds are up. Good. It's our way of checking in on one another. If the other person's blinds aren't up by seven-thirty, something is wrong. One day last fall, I forgot to open my blinds. At eight o'clock there was pounding on my door. It was Mr. Sparrow. He stood on my front porch with a baseball hat perched on his bald head, small chest heaving, his eyes darting like goldfish behind the thick frames of his glasses.

"Your blinds," he gasped.

I apologized profusely.

"Just glad to know you're okay," he said. "You can't be too sure anymore. Too many crooked people are running amok these days. I told you about my bird bath, didn't I?"

I've heard the story a dozen times. It happened last summer. "And you're sure someone stole it?"

"It was either a burglar or a very powerful chickadee, Joyce."

Mr. Sparrow's blinds are usually up before mine. The man is an eighty-seven-year-old firecracker. I don't know where his energy comes from. Eileen died over forty years ago and there were never any children, so I think he fights off his loneliness by keeping busy. He tends to a massive garden in his backyard. I'll open my front door to find a basket of green peppers or beets or carrots on my porch at least once a week. It's sweet of him, but I end up throwing most of it away. What am I going to do with eight peppers? Still, those baskets are a comforting sight. Someone, it seems, is taking care of me. But I live in fear that Mr. Sparrow will one day discover his vegetables rotting in my garbage.

I make my way to the bathroom with Louise's demise still on my mind. I should have bars installed next to the toilet and the bathtub. I've gotten in the habit of using the towel bar for support, but it's not sturdy and certainly not meant to withstand the precarious balancing of a senior woman stepping out of the shower. Outfitting the bathroom would mean having someone—a stranger and likely a man—come into my house. I don't like that idea. There are lots of ideas I've grown to dislike, now that I'm older. Driving is one of them. I was never the most confident driver, it's true. Charlie was the one who made me get lessons after John was born. And I got by. I even remember driving to Andover a few times with Helen. But since Charlie's death, I'm afraid of driving. I'm fine on my routes: to the bank, to Sears, to church, to the grocery store. But anywhere beyond that is treacherous territory, the highway especially. I close my eyes and imagine speeding trucks, teenage boys tempting fate, darting wildlife. Sometimes, death is only a rabbit away.

I hoist my nightgown around my waist and ease onto the toilet. My sparse pubic hair creeps like a half-hearted weed down my inner thighs. I never shave my legs higher than mid-calf anymore.

My stool is loose this morning, which alarms me. This is the second day in a row. I think back to what I ate yesterday, but there was nothing out of the ordinary. Shreddies and juice for breakfast. A salmon salad sandwich for lunch. A chicken breast cooked in cream of mushroom soup with broccoli for dinner. Had that been everything? I try to remember. My short-term memory is getting worse. Details slip down a steep hill and land in a pile too large and tangled to sort through. But I have to remember. Sometimes, the smallest detail can have the most significance.

Two loose stools mean nothing, I assure myself, and promise I'll throw open the worry floodgates if tomorrow's stool is similar. I don't remember when I starting worrying about such foolish things. I reach behind and flush, imagining my anxiety spiralling away. Helen calls this "visualization." She read a book about it and it's all she can talk about. She gets that way. Fixated on things. She wouldn't eat bread for the longest time. Then she joined that mall-walking group. There was the choir last winter, the one where they forced children to sing old songs alongside old people. She took a six-week Chinese cooking course that culminated in a single dinner of pebble-sized chicken balls and rice dripping in soy sauce. She hops from one thing to the next, informing me each time she lands on something new, passing on her insight. I don't know what kind of response she hopes to get from me. Sometimes I think she wants me to jump up and down in gratitude. Other times I think she wants me to tell her she's the stupidest person on earth. I give her neither response, which perhaps frustrates her more.

Her latest is visualizing things into existence.

"*See* what you want, Joyce," she said to me. "Picture it in your mind and concentrate very hard. Feel as though you've already received it. The other day, I lost my keys. You know I'm bad that way. I searched high and low but I couldn't find them anywhere. Dickie was no help, of course. I worked myself into an absolute frenzy. Then I stopped, sat down on the sofa, closed my eyes and visualized those keys. In less than a minute, I found them."

"Where were they?"

"In the front door."

"Haven't you left them there before?"

"Yes. But I've never found them so quickly. Tell me something you'd like to happen, Joyce."

I'd like this to end.

That's what I wanted to say. But Helen would've thought I meant the conversation. Then she would've taken offence and cut the conversation short. A few days later, after she had sufficient time to turn my words over in her head, she'd call.

"The other day," she'd say slowly. "What exactly did you mean? Are you feeling down? I don't want to see you get like that again."

My sister isn't good with things she can't fix. She needs solutions, even if they're fleeting.

"I'd like to go on a cruise," I told her instead. "Eat my way through a buffet and then stretch out on a deck chair and count the stars."

Helen asked me to find a picture of a ship. "Tape it to your medicine cabinet mirror. Every morning, close your eyes and *smell* the sea air."

"Or I could call a travel agency," I said.

I turn on the kitchen radio to catch the tail end of the morning news. I've missed the big stories. Not that there are many in Balsden—sometimes a fire or a burglary. Every once in a while, a murder. Drugs seem to be at the root of most problems. Or love gone wrong. Good intentions can turn down such dark paths. Mostly, the news has been about the refineries shutting down. Unemployment has skyrocketed. People wonder what's going to happen to this place.

I used to love my kitchen. It was my favourite room in the house. I redecorated it after Charlie's death eight years ago. I needed a distraction. I went with a butterfly theme and it worked out nicely. There are butterfly patterned curtains that match the butterfly chair pads that match the butterfly wallpaper border that match the butterfly tablecloth. The butterflies used to comfort me.

Now, they look old and faded. Wallpaper borders aren't in style anymore and my chair pads are too thick and bulky. Most of the strings that tie to the spindles have ripped off. I can't be bothered to fix them. I haven't sewn anything in years.

Helen had her kitchen redone last winter. She took an interior decorating course at the college.

"It made me think about space in an entirely different way," she said.

Now, everything in her kitchen is so clean and sparse. Her countertop is granite. Her cupboards are cream coloured. Her floor is ceramic tile, hard and smooth and cold. Dropped plates explode like land mines. But that's how "everyone" is doing things these days. Laboratory kitchens.

Swap Shop comes on while I'm eating my cereal. It's a radio show where people call in to sell their items. One woman is offering a hardly worn purple velour pantsuit, size 16. "I got it in Vegas," she says, as though this will motivate the fence-sitters.

Another caller, a man, sounding like he's chewing a mouthful of crackers, wants to sell a birdcage. It's in good condition, he assures the host. He's asking twenty dollars and offers to throw in two boxes of birdseed to sweeten the deal.

"Do you mean *tweeten* the deal?" the host asks with a chuckle.

"Pardon?" cracker man asks.

I should call *Swap Shop*, but I'd be on the air for an hour, going through all the things I need to get rid of. Last fall, Helen and I went through the shelves and closets in the basement. There were winter boots and flannel sheet sets and a brown-speckled toaster oven and a set of 1984 Olympic commemorative glasses that Charlie bought at a gas station.

"Why do you still have all of this junk?" Helen asked. She was wearing a strand of old Christmas lights like a boa.

"I don't know." *She* was the one who had suggested a purge. I was fine to leave everything as it was. It was all stowed away, at least. "Charlie couldn't throw anything out. He always thought something might come in handy again."

"I'm all for frugalities, Joyce. But three dozen margarine containers?"

"We used them for . . ." What did we use them for? "I suppose your house is just spotless. Helen. Clean as a whistle."

"Well, it's certainly better than this." Her face softened then. A hand went to my arm. "Have you called that real estate agent I mentioned? He sold Pat Kipling's place. She said he was very patient with her."

"I have his card somewhere," I said, rearranging a box of newspaper-wrapped mugs.

"Well, don't delay things too long. The market is very good right now. Especially for Balsden. You don't want to lose out."

Lose out.

Helen thinks I'm going to sell my house and move into her basement. She and Dickie had it finished while Mark was living at home. There's a bathroom and a bedroom and a kitchenette.

"It's got everything you need," Helen told me. "Even your own entrance. You can come and go and I'll be none the wiser."

I resisted the idea at first. Rejected it completely, in fact. The possibility of living under Helen was unimaginable, especially after all these years. But this past winter weakened me. The snow piled up to my back door. The neighbour boy I pay to shovel my driveway was sick for two weeks. I couldn't get out for food. I sat crying in the living room with a bag of stale oatmeal cookies. Where would I be in another five years?

But to sell my house. The thought of it turns my heart to charcoal. I have lived here for fifty years. I know every crack and corner, every carpet ripple, every smell (Charlie's work-room, the linen closet, the root cellar). How can I walk away from everything I've ever known?

I stop by St. Paul's United to drop off my date squares, feeling guilty that I haven't attended service for most of the summer. But it's more spiritually depressing than uplifting to sit there among the half-empty pews.

"The United Church is dying," Helen said with a slow shake of her head. "Every other religion is going strong as ever. Do you know why? The United religion is too liberal. You have to put the fear of God into people. That's the only way to get them out of the house on a Sunday morning."

Neither Charlie nor I were what you'd call religious people, but when John was old enough, we started taking him to St. Paul's.

"He might as well learn one side of the coin," Charlie said. "He'll make up his own mind when he's old enough."

I thought the structure of church would be good for my son. I wanted him to understand that Christmas was more than presents, that Easter was more than bunnies and chocolate. I wanted to expose him to things that didn't have price tags. Maybe I was being a hypocrite, because I never went to church before John was born. I believed in God but I didn't think about him very much. That's especially true these days. It's funny because I always assumed that as you got older, you naturally became more religious. I attributed it to fear; a sort of spiritual insurance. But it doesn't happen that way. At least, it hasn't for me. The closer death gets, the less sense God makes.

John enjoyed church. He'd get up early on Sunday mornings to shine his shoes and pick out a tie. He had quite the collection at a young age, from what I remember. He'd sit between Charlie and me, fidgeting while the hymns were sung and the Scriptures read out loud. Then the minister would call the children to the front of the church and John would be the first one running down the aisle, even though I told him to always walk. After speaking with them about the importance of sharing or forgiveness or respect, the minister would send the children down to Sunday school in the basement. Even to this day, I can still see the happiness on John's face when he passed by our pew. Sometimes he'd stop and pat my arm, as if reminding me not to worry. He'd only be a few steps away.

If only I had that same reassurance now.

When he turned seven, John joined the junior choir. I was so proud, watching him sing at the front of the church. Charlie was, too. I remember the soft smile on his face. There were only three boys amidst the rows of curly-headed girls, but John had one of the best voices. I could always hear its clarity through the cloud of the other children.

"That boy of yours is quite the charmer," I remember a woman telling me once. "He's going to be a heartbreaker one day."

I had my fingers crossed that John might become a minister. It seemed like a natural fit for him. He was good with people, especially older women. They doted on him terribly.

Precious. That's the word I heard the most. "He's just the most precious thing."

I never left him alone with any of the older women and always made a point to pull him away if the conversation lingered too long or if the compliments became too many. *It's not good to have his ego stroked like that,* I thought at the time. *Or to be around women so much.*

I've been remembering things lately. Small, random memories. I don't know why. The other day, I thought about the time we hit that dog.

The three of us were on our way to a winter play day at the United Church Centre. John was in the back. I remember his boots pressing into my seat. I used to scold him about this.

"Your soles are filthy," I'd say, and he'd drop his feet down, but it wouldn't be long before I'd feel them again, like a burn on my back. Even then, we were always testing one another's limits, seeing how far one of us could go before the other broke.

Charlie was driving. I remember feeling anxious about trees. A boy had been killed earlier that winter when his toboggan ran into the trunk of an evergreen. He was eight years old, the same age as John was at the time. I was saying something to Charlie about black ice when a dog appeared out of nowhere and darted onto the road. Charlie slammed on the brakes, but it was too late. I can still see the flash of brown. I can hear the tight squeal of the tires. Then the soft thud. I turned around to see a dog spinning in the centre of the road, as though it was performing a trick. Charlie pulled over and got out of the car. John was asking what had happened.

"Nothing," I told him. "Stay seated."

He didn't listen, of course. He never did. He clambered up to look out the rear window. Charlie was slowly approaching the dog, which was now lying still. Its ears were brown and its belly as white as the snow that covered the front yards on either side of us. John started to cry.

"What's wrong with the dog?"

"It's sleeping." The stupid things parents say.

"Daddy hit it."

"He didn't mean to. It was an accident."

"Daddy is a murderer."

"John, don't say that."

Charlie crouched down beside the dog. His hand hovered a few inches over its side. There was a look of hopeless loss on his face that I'd see again years later, but that loss would be one that neither of us would recover from. He came back towards the car and opened the trunk. I rolled down the window.

"You're not putting it in there, are you?" There was a casserole. The toboggan. A Thermos of hot chocolate.

"I'm getting a blanket."

The open trunk blocked the scene momentarily. John turned back to me, his face as red as the scarf around his neck.

"Daddy killed a dog!"

"Please, John."

We should've turned around and gone home, but Charlie insisted we continue on.

"We're halfway there," he said.

I could see that he was shaken, so I didn't argue. Instead, I passed John a box of tissues. He didn't say another word until we were sitting in the dining hall, eating dinner.

"You hit the dog on purpose," John said, and Charlie got up from the table and walked over to the windows. He stood there for some time, staring out at the white hills and the children sliding down, before returning to us. His eyes were pink. He quietly announced it was time for us to leave and started gathering our dishes.

Charlie brought this up a few years after John had died. The two of us were sitting in the living room, watching television. He asked if I remembered the day he had hit the dog.

"Yes," I said.

"Why didn't he believe it was an accident?" Charlie asked, his gaze never leaving the TV. "He thought I hit it on purpose."

"He was young. And upset."

I watched the reflection of the TV in Charlie's eyeglasses, twin mirrors of a flipped world, frightened by the realization of how haunted he was, and would continue to be, during all those empty years in our post-John world. I'd done my best to protect my husband from his son. And my son from his father. That was how I saw my role. That was how I believed things worked.

Funny.

Turns out I was the only one they needed protection from.

When I step into the St. Paul's kitchen, I see Arlene Disdale and a few others from the social committee, prepping sandwiches for the luncheon.

"Joyce Sparks," she announces, tossing a tea towel over her shoulder. "I've been meaning to call you."

"Oh?"

"My bridge club is looking for a new person." She lowers her voice. "You know. Louise."

There's a fine line of hair above her top lip. Wasp legs.

"The club gets together on Wednesday nights. You already know Shirley and Bev. We all take turns hosting. The next meeting is at Shirley's. You know where she lives, right? In the north end? I don't mind picking you up. How about six-thirty?"

"I'm not much of a card person," I say. She's bullying me

into it. I don't like Arlene, let alone bridge. "I don't even know how to play."

"It's very easy. I'll teach you." She takes another step closer. "We're not competitive. Well, Shirley can be a sore loser, but she gets over it quickly. I'll call you later this week."

I exit through the kitchen door, a dark cloud over my head. All I had to say was, "Thank you, Arlene. I'm not interested." Now I've somehow managed to trap myself. Again. Between my loose stool and Arlene, this day hasn't gotten off to a good start. I head to the Clip N' Curl for my appointment.

My hairdresser, Connie, informs me she has a mole on her back. "I'm convinced it's cancerous. My brother tells me I'm a . . . what's the word?" She stares at the mirror with a twisted expression. "Not hippopotamus."

"Hypochondriac," I say, surprising myself.

"That's the one." She snaps her fingers and I wonder how anyone can keep her nails that long. Connie's are at least two inches. I once bought fake nails for a wedding on Charlie's side. Everything was fine until I went to the bathroom. Three of them landed in the toilet when I pulled my pantyhose up.

"Did you see the moon last night?" I ask.

Connie presses a hand against her cheek. "Wasn't that something? Nothing like a full moon to get me feeling all romantic again. Isn't it a shame, Joyce? Here we are, two vital, passionate women and not a man in sight. They're all married or dead."

I'd never get married again. A second chance isn't in the cards for someone like me. I don't deserve happiness. Besides, those last years with Charlie—when the cancer bit down and wouldn't let go—still haunt me. I'll never get over the horror of watching him fall apart, piece by piece; how he clung to me and sobbed when the results of his biopsy came in. I was all he had left in the world. I pressed his head against my breast, terrified of what was to come. He would die. I could do nothing but watch. And then, I would be alone. I wanted to die with Charlie. I wanted his cancer to seep into my body. I didn't want to face life without my son and husband. I didn't think I'd be able to cope, to even get out of bed every morning. I've since come to understand that getting out of bed every morning is punishment for what I've done; for what I destroyed between Charlie and John.

Charlie wasn't sure how to react to John's interest in the junior choir. He could hardly criticize his son for doing something as noble as praising God every Sunday morning. And yet, while he sat beside me, he wouldn't stop fidgeting when John and the rest of the choir performed their songs. I'd press my hand on his thigh in an effort to keep him still, but he wouldn't settle out. He'd cough and glance at the other faces in the pews around us. What was he looking for? I wondered. Their approval? Couldn't he find happiness in his son's happiness? I became annoyed with what I sensed was his discomfort—and disapproval—of his son.

"You're not pushing him, are you?" Charlie asked me once. "He shouldn't be made to sing if he doesn't want to."

"He wanted to do it," I said. "And I don't push John into anything."

"I'm not so sure about that."

"At least I'm encouraging him. You hardly ever compliment him."

"That's not true."

"There's nothing wrong with being outgoing, Charlie. There's nothing wrong with singing."

"I never said there was. Stop putting words in my mouth."

Charlie was still smarting from his Little League loss. We'd tried for two years to keep John interested, but he hated playing baseball. Charlie bought him a new glove and a Louisville Slugger bat with an orange handle.

"I'm afraid of the ball," John had confessed to me once. "What if it hits me in the face and then I have to go to the hospital and have an operation?"

"The ball won't hit you if you practise catching it," I pointed out, but my words were useless. I knew my son. The more we encouraged, the more he resisted. I'd sit on the bleachers and look at the misery on his eight-year-old face in right field, his glove hanging grotesquely at his side like a monster's hand, and wonder how much it was worth in the end. I'd have to clamp my arms around my legs and fight the urge to run out onto the field and rescue him.

But I couldn't do that. I'd made a promise to myself to always protect my son. To help him. To keep him on a path towards happiness. Charlie wouldn't have understood this if I'd spoken to him. He didn't know what I knew. He couldn't see the darker side of things that I did. He didn't know what was at stake.

It was Charlie who finally pulled the plug on baseball. I don't think he could bear to watch John suffer through it anymore, although that wasn't the reason he gave me.

"It's too expensive," he said one night while we lay in bed. "There's no point spending the money if he's not willing to put up the effort."

"He's tried, Charlie," I said, hoping to hide the relief in my voice. John would be over the moon when I told him. "It's just not his thing. We'll get him involved in something else. Soccer, maybe. Or swimming."

"He hates the water."

"He likes drawing. We could sign him up for art classes."

Charlie was silent. I looked over at him. His jaw was peppered with stubble. I noted the tiny beginnings of lines around his eyes. We'd been married for almost ten years. I knew his favourite foods and the faint brown ring around his penis and that he was often constipated on account of shift work. I knew that he could spend hours listening to country music in the den and that he kept a childhood photograph of himself and his sister in his wallet and that he wrote his mother a letter every Saturday night, slipping a lined sheet beneath a blank one so that his words appeared as neatly as possible. But I didn't know *him*. At least, not the way I thought husbands and wives were supposed to know each other.

"I'm not sure what I've done wrong," he said after a while. "John always seems uncomfortable around me."

"That's not true," I said, even though I noticed it as well. I didn't understand. Charlie wasn't an intimidating figure by any stretch, but it seemed that was how John saw him. There was an air of caution about John when he was around his father, as though he was taking the tentative first steps on an ice-covered pond.

"He's all peaches and cream with you," Charlie said. "I just don't know how to be around him. Maybe it's my own fault. What kind of experience can I draw on? I barely even remember my own dad."

"You're a good father," I said. "I can see that. *John* can see that. He's just at an awkward age."

"Then why does his world revolve around you?"

I didn't know how to answer this.

It was true that I couldn't shake John off me. Everything was "Mommy this" and "Mommy that." It was suffocating at times. I remember when we took John to see Santa at the mall. Something spooked him and he bolted off Santa's lap and came barrelling down the red carpet. Charlie was with him at the time. I was across the way at a clothing store, trying to steal a few uninterrupted minutes. John ran straight past Charlie and over to me. He buried his face so forcefully in my jacket that I almost toppled over. I looked up to see Charlie, bewildered, surrounded by a landscape of cotton-batten snow and sparkle-dusted mechanical elves.

"John, you could've run to Daddy," I whispered. "He was right there."

"I wanted you," he said through his tears, his hands clutching my coat. "I wanted my pretty mommy."

He'd started calling me "pretty mommy" a few months prior. He was taking a bath and I was sitting on the toilet, chin in hands, preoccupied by my doubts about my marriage, my choices, my life.

"I don't like it when you're sad," he said.

"I'm not sad. Don't be silly."

"When you're sad, you're not my pretty mommy."

I looked down at my worn-out pants, the toenails that peeked out from the fuzzy border of my slippers. I couldn't remember the last time I'd painted them.

"There's nothing pretty about Mommy," I said.

Then my son carefully placed a small mound of crackling bubbles on my knee. "Now there is," he said, and I almost cried.

I suggested that Charlie needed to make more of an effort with John. "If you're concerned about the way he acts around you, then do things with him."

"But he doesn't want to do anything with me."

"You have to take the lead."

So off they'd go to the movies. Or they'd sit in the work-room together while Charlie repaired or built things. But there was always a forced quality to it, a sense of formality, as though the two of them had been dropped into a scene with-out knowing the dialogue.

John gave up baseball, but excelled at choir, with songs about the birth of Jesus and doves and God's ever-watchful presence. It wasn't such a terrible exchange, I'd reason, pulling myself up higher in the pew to get a better view of my son. It was better that John do something *meaningful*. I didn't see where God could be found in a baseball diamond.

I'm not sure Charlie felt the same way.

I decide to pop into the Golden Sunset on my way home. I haven't been by to see Mrs. Pender in a few weeks. Excuses are easy to come by whenever she's involved, but the library called the other day. The last book I signed out for her is now overdue. She claims to enjoy mysteries, but I know she never reads any of them. It's all about appearances with her.

The Golden Sunset Home for the Aged isn't terrible, all things considered. I've been in places that looked more like asylums than nursing homes. But there isn't much to choose from in Balsden and I've heard about waiting lists a mile long. I don't know how true that is, but it worries me to think that when my time comes, I might not end up where I want.

Two years ago, a group of us from St. Paul's volunteered to serve Christmas dinner to the Sunset residents. It got me out of going to Helen's and listening to my niece and nephew natter on about their dull lives.

While passing a turkey platter, I heard a voice behind me. "That you, Joyce Conrad?"

It took me a second to realize the name was mine. I hadn't heard my maiden name in years and I felt a sudden tug of melancholy, as if someone had mentioned a friend I hadn't missed until that moment. I turned around to see a tiny, elderly woman sitting in a wheelchair, covered in a blue terry-cloth bib. She was no bigger than the ornaments hanging from the Christmas tree in the corner. I searched for a familiar face underneath the wrinkles and almost dropped the platter when I discovered it.

"Mrs. Pender?" I whispered. It wasn't possible. Not after all these years.

"This turkey is terrible."

My doubts disappeared.

Since that holiday dinner, I've made a point of visiting her every now and then. I don't enjoy our time together and more often than not, I'll leave with a blinding headache. But she has no other visitors and deep down—deep, *deep* down—I think she looks forward to seeing me. She'd never admit it, though. She may be ninety-seven, but her edge is still razor sharp. Maybe that's what's kept her alive all these years.

Our visits typically consist of me sitting on the edge of her bed, fiddling with the straps of my purse and trying to look engaged while she runs through the travesties of her life, tapping each one into the centre of her palm with a crooked finger.

The staff at the Sunset is terrible. "You get the bottom of the barrel in places like this. The decent ones go work in hospitals."

The food in unpalatable. "Today they served that fish. For the second day *in a row*."

Mrs. Ogilvy is insane. "She came up behind me the other day holding her spoon like a dagger."

"You can't stab someone with a spoon," I reminded her.

"You can stab with anything if you push hard enough," she said.

This morning, a few of the residents are sitting outside their rooms. A sharp smell hits me as I pass the linen bin and my hand instinctively goes to my nose. I pull it away, conscious of the eyes on me. I wouldn't be able to work with the elderly. Positioning straws into mouths and wiping rear ends and helping people into their backless clothing. I wouldn't be able to clean off the decay at the end of the day.

"Nice morning," I say loudly to a kind-looking woman in a wheelchair. She's wearing a fuchsia jogging suit. I've seen her before.

"I wouldn't know," she replies.

I pass a whiteboard announcing activities in scrawling red marker. Kraft Korner with Kay! 10 a.m. Classical music hour! 1–2 p.m. Chaplain visit! 3 p.m. So many exclamation marks in one day.

Mrs. Pender's room is on the second floor, at the end of the hall. She shares it with Mrs. Ogilvy, who suffered a stroke a few years ago and can communicate only by saying "Whuh-whuh-whuh" in various tones. The door to the room is partly closed. A brown paper acorn is stuck to it with a Scotch tape square. It's too early for acorns, I think with a frown. We've got another month to go before warty gourds start showing up on magazine covers. It strikes me as bad taste, as though the staff is trying to hurry time.

I knock on the door, push it open and see Mrs. Ogilvy napping in her bed. On the other side of her, Mrs. Pender sits hunched over in her wheelchair, white hair hanging down, draping her face. She looks so fragile. Although I'd never openly admit to it, I feel we have something in common.

I don't think she knows about my John. She's never asked me any questions and I'm more comfortable keeping my personal life to myself. But there have been a few quiet moments between us when the words bubbled inside my mouth.

I lost my son, too.

But to bring it up would only open the door to questions. So I say nothing. She doesn't talk about Freddy anyway. Instead, he stares silently at us from the framed black-and-white picture she keeps on top of her dresser. Our sons never get old behind their glass enclosures.

"Mrs. Pender?" I say softly. Her head slowly turns to the side. Eyeglasses and a nose poke through the curtain of hair. "How are you doing?"

"I lost a tooth this morning."

"How did you lose it?" I sit down on the bed.

"The biscuits. Hard as rocks. I'd like to go have a word with that cook, I'll tell you that much. I thought coloured people were good at biscuits."

A barrette dangles from her hair. She's a ghoulish little girl.

"I saw a sign in the hallway. There's a garden party tomorrow. You should go."

"I don't care about a garden party."

Sometimes I mention things to get a reaction. Garden parties. Kay and her kraft sessions. Christmas carol singalongs in the auditorium. All the social delicacies she can't stand. It gives me perverse pleasure to watch her flare up in disgust and anger. Perhaps it's my revenge for the headaches.

"Are you sure? It's supposed to be a beautiful day."

She clamps a hand over her wrist and stares straight ahead. So, she's in fine form today. I glance at the clock next to her bed. Ten minutes tops. Then I'll say something about having to pick up groceries.

"Whuh."

"Hello, Mrs. Ogilvy. Nice to see you again."

"Don't bother with her," Mrs. Pender says. "She's as stupid as they come."

"Whuh-whuh!" Mrs. Ogilvy shouts.

"The library called," I say. "I need to return that book I signed out for you. It's overdue."

"But I'm not finished it."

"I can sign it out again, if you like. But I'll have to pay the fine first."

"How much?"

"Fifty cents or so."

"Hand me my purse."

"I can afford the fifty cents, Mrs. Pender."

"My purse."

I sigh and pass it to her.

"I'm a woman of my word," she says as she begins to dig through it. She pulls out a jar of Noxzema. A whirlwind of tissues. A magnifying glass. "I believe in settling accounts."

She hands me a small black change purse and asks me to open it. "I'm all claws," she says.

"Hello, Mrs. Pender!"

A short woman in yellow enters the room. She smiles absently at me. "It's time for you to get weighed."

"No, it isn't."

"Oh yes, it is." She steps behind Mrs. Pender's wheelchair. "We have to make sure you maintain your girlish figure. The scale is just down the hall." She tells me they'll be back in a bit.

I see this as the perfect opportunity to cut the visit short. "I'll see you next time, Mrs. Pender," I say, setting the change purse on the bed.

"I'll only be a minute," Mrs. Pender says as she's wheeled past.

I pretend not to hear.

It starts to rain again. Large, lazy drops hit the windshield, and I flick on the wipers. My stomach growls. Maybe it wasn't the salmon salad that gave me loose stool. How am I to know? And what difference does it make? It's time to go home.

When I turn the corner, I spot a familiar figure standing in front of the post office. I consider driving past, then think better of it. I pull over, give the horn two quick honks and roll down the passenger window.

It's hard for me to believe my sister is seventy-five now, in spite of her lined face. She's wearing a straw hat with a red ribbon. She's taken to wearing hats lately and informed me she's always had a hat-shaped head. She simply never realized it before.

"Joyce! What a surprise. I was out for my morning walk and needed to get stamps."

"Get in and I'll drive you home."

"You don't have to do that," she says, opening the passenger door. "I was sending out cards and came up one stamp short. Isn't that always the way? You did remember cousin Renée's birthday, didn't you?"

"Of course." I've spent most of my life lying to Helen. It's easier that way. For both of us. I'll have to get a card this afternoon.

Helen's seat belt clicks into place. "I hope it doesn't get muggy after this. You know how it is after a rain. All those worms. That smell. Nauseating." Her eyes narrow. "Your hair is so big. Are you coming back from the hairdresser?"

"I was there earlier. I'm just coming back from the Sunset."

"I honestly don't know why you keep in with that woman."

"I don't keep *in* with her."

"Well, I suppose everyone has their good deeds." She leans over to adjust one of the air vents. "How's the old gal doing?"

"She lost a tooth."

"Is she all right?"

"It's just a tooth."

"I suppose."

We drive for a few minutes in silence, the rubber wipers pulling noisily across the windshield. A metronome, I think, remembering back to when I was young and took piano lessons. I didn't last long. I had no patience and my fingers slipped off the keys as though they were greased. Helen kept up with it, though. She'll still play the odd song, usually at Christmas, although she complains her fingers are too stiff now. She was always the more artistic of the two of us. John had that in him as well. He must've gotten it from

Helen because neither Charlie nor I were artistically inclined in any—

"Damn it!" I say so loudly Helen yelps.

"What's wrong?"

"I forgot the library book. That's why I went to see Mrs. Pender in the first place."

"Well, turn around and go get it. I'm in no rush to get home."

"Of all the stupid things," I say as I flick on my turn signal. I can't seem to concentrate on things like I used to. I need to focus more. Pay attention.

"How's Dickie doing?"

She lifts her hat from her head and places it delicately in her lap. "The same."

"Have you considered getting some help? You can't do it all on your own. It's too much work."

"It's fine. *I'm* fine. I have the kids, too. If I ever need them."

I don't know what help Mark and Marianne would be. Neither of them lives in Balsden, although Mark is in Andover. My nephew works with computers. I've never known exactly what it is he does with them. I asked him once and he started to explain. My eyes must've glazed over because he seemed to get annoyed.

"I fix them," he said and reached for the TV remote.

Helen says he spent too much time with his computers and not enough with his family. He got divorced about fifteen years ago. There are two children, girls in their early twenties by now, but I never see them. Helen says Mark is dating someone new now, another divorcee, but Helen doesn't like her. She thinks the divorcee is after his money. I never knew he had much in the first place. You certainly can't tell by the way he dresses. He's worn the same white polo shirt for the past twenty years.

Marianne lives in Toronto with her husband and massages people for a living. She became a Buddhist last year.

"What does that mean exactly?" I asked Helen.

"Something to do with trees and rocks and grass. Honestly. I don't know when everyone decided they could go out and believe in anything they felt like."

I see Marianne and Mark once a year, at Christmas. Mark looks like Dickie. Marianne looks like Helen. They'll ask me questions but don't seem interested in the answers. Maybe they sense my own lack of interest. I try to mask it, but I'm never sure if I'm doing a good job. Besides, it's not a matter of interest. It's a barricade. John would've turned fifty-three this year. I can't even imagine what his face would look like, and I feel a sharp pull of sadness. All the life he never had.

"Did I tell you how angry Marianne was when she received the invitation for my seventy-fifth birthday?" Helen asks. "She said she was planning a surprise party. I said to her, 'Marianne, you wouldn't expect me to sit around waiting for something to happen.'" Helen sighs and places her hat back on her head. "I know what she's saying, Joyce. But at the same time, what if they'd forgotten about it? Then my milestone would come and go without any fanfare at all. I couldn't take the chance."

"You shouldn't be so controlling," I say to her, as I've said for most of her life, although I don't think she's ever heard. "They wouldn't forget something as important as that."

"I'm not so sure." The hat comes off again. "I was afraid it'd be nothing more than an obligatory phone call after dinner. They get so easily distracted. I can't trust them."

"I'm sure Dickie would've—"

"Dickie wouldn't have done a thing. Dickie *couldn't* have done a thing."

We ride in silence for a few moments. For a brief second, I wonder why I'm taking this route. Then I remember. The book. I turn onto Bleeker Street and pull into the Golden Sunset parking lot for the second time today.

"Well, it isn't much to look at," Helen says. "Is it nice inside?"

"About what you'd expect," I say.

"I sometimes wonder if Dickie would be better off in a place like this."

"It would make things easier for you."

"But the guilt. I couldn't do it." She cocks her head. "Poor Mrs. Pender. No son to visit her."

My hands tighten around the steering wheel.

"Oh, Joyce. I didn't—"

"It's fine," I tell her.

"It's not that I forget. I don't. I'll never forget poor John."

"Do you want to wait here?"

"Sure. Just don't be too long. The car will heat up."

I tie my rain cap over my head and step out, making my way towards the front entrance. My sister knows nothing about guilt.

———

Mrs. Ogilvy is asleep in her bed and Mrs. Pender is nowhere to be found. Would she still be getting weighed? That stupid book. It has to be here somewhere. I tiptoe over to her night table and slowly slide open the drawer. There's a folded newspaper inside and a box of peppermints. I open the drawer farther. If she's lost the book, so help me. Beneath the peppermints, something catches my eye. A greeting card. I glance over my shoulder to make sure Mrs. Ogilvy is still sleeping, then lift it out.

It's a Mother's Day card. There's a faded picture of a monarch butterfly on the cover with impossibly perfect script that reads, "To a Dear Mother." My heart catches in my throat. How long has it been since I received such a card? Inside, there are three verses about a Mother's love. I can't bring myself to read the words. At the bottom of the card, under Freddy's signature, is this line:

Moved to Miami three months ago. Will send new address.

Miami? Freddy never lived in Miami. He went to New York and then to Hollywood. Is there a Miami in California? I shake my head. No, stupid. Hollywood is in California. Miami is in Florida.

There's a date written in the top corner of the card. I fish my glasses from my purse and hold the card out. The writing is faint, but I can just make it out.

May '77.

My breath catches. I put the card back into the drawer and hurry out of the room.

CHAPTER FIVE

HELEN DOESN'T shut up the entire ride home and I'm too preoccupied to listen.

"I just don't know, Joyce. On the one hand, having a computer would mean that I could email the grandkids. And Marianne says it's the easiest thing in the world. You just turn it on and away you go. But I'm not good with technology. Have you ever thought about getting one?"

I feel her eyes on me, but I don't look over. I keep seeing those sevens on the Mother's Day card. How is it possible? He's been dead for years.

"I don't want a computer." I reach over and turn up the radio.

"What happened to the book?" Helen asks, her voice overpowering the radio host without any effort at all. "Did you forget it again?"

I'm so angry, but I don't know why. What a ridiculous morning.

"I found a card in her room," I blurt out. "From Freddy. It was dated 1977."

She looks at me, eyes wide. "That's not possible."

"I know it isn't. He died in '59."

"You're sure it was from him?"

"Yes."

"And you didn't ask Mrs. Pender about it?"

"She wasn't in the room."

We pull up in front of her house with its lush lawn and bright red impatiens. She always had more of a green thumb than me. My flower beds have sat empty the entire summer. My lawn looks like straw. I could water it, but pulling out the sprinkler and hose seems like a Herculean effort. I haven't taken care of anything since Charlie died. My house is an eyesore. Shame seeps through me like ink.

I put the car in park and we sit in silence. Helen's hat is pushed back on her head, giving her a straw halo. I scan the dashboard. Crisp bugs lie on their backs, legs like broken matchsticks. When was the last time I cleaned the car? Everything, it seems, is falling apart.

"Funny," Helen says, "I don't remember what Freddy looked like. Was he a redhead?"

"Blond."

"You dated him."

"No."

"Something happened between the two of you. I remember you talking about it."

"Nothing happened."

"He was a singer, wasn't he?"

"More of a dancer."

"He supposedly killed himself, right? How did it happen again?"

"He jumped off a ship. Mrs. Pender said that he'd fallen in with the wrong crowd."

"What—?" But then her lips clamp down. For once, my sister's thoughts catch up to her words. "I see."

The air inside the car thickens, making it hard to breathe. My lungs stick together. Withered balloons. I open the window partway. Raindrops hit my shoulder.

It's only when I'm stopped at a red light a few blocks away that my lungs begin to open. I sit and wait, gulping for air while the traffic light turns into a fireball.

When I pull into my driveway, Mr. Sparrow is stepping down from my front porch, wearing his baseball hat. He waves and raises it, revealing a shiny dome. I'm in no mood for small talk, but I have no choice. I press a smile onto my face and step out of the car. The rain has stopped, leaving behind a heavy humidity. I look down at my driveway and see a brown-pink worm patiently pulling itself across the asphalt towards some unknown destination. They'll be everywhere shortly. My sister will be mortified.

"How about that rain?" Mr. Sparrow asks.

"Yes. How about it. Seems like we've had more rain than sun this year."

"I was just dropping off some zucchini. They've come in real nice."

"I see that."

There's a basket full of them waiting in front of my door. What am I going to do with all those zucchinis? I don't even like them. Oh, Mr. Sparrow. Bless you and nature's bounty, but I'd be happy with a solitary tomato every now and then.

"Looks to me like someone just got back from the beauty parlour." He leans in closer for an inspection. "That's a good head of hair in my opinion."

"Thank you," I laugh, feeling myself blush. "Connie tends to backcomb a little too much. It takes a day or so to settle out. How have you been?"

"Oh, fine. All things considered. You?"

"The same. I'm looking forward to the fall."

"You're looking forward to what?"

I take a step closer. "The *fall*. Autumn. Cooler weather."

"Speak for yourself," Mr. Sparrow says. "Cooler weather brings cold weather. And cold weather brings snow. You know that neighbour boy is going away to school this year, don't you?"

"Trevor?"

"I ran into him the other day. He's going to the university in Andover. Science or something like that. In any case, he won't be around this winter."

"But who will do the shovelling?" I remember the stale oatmeal cookies and my helplessness.

He shrugs. "We'll find someone. The snow won't come until December."

I may be gone by December, I think. I have to call that real estate agent. I try to nod encouragingly at Mr. Sparrow. I watch him cross the street, his bowed legs working furiously. Once I'm gone, who will make sure his blinds are up every morning?

I have just enough time to change into my navy blue suit and slide some lipstick across my lips before heading out to Louise's service. I'm grateful for the distraction. If I were sitting at home, I'd be thinking about that Mother's Day card. I'll go see Mrs. Pender tomorrow and get that book. I won't say anything to her about the card. I can't admit to snooping through her drawers. Besides, I decide, it's nothing. A mistake. I won't think about it any more.

The attendance for Louise's service is sparse. Her two sons come with their families. There are a handful of relatives. Friends scatter themselves among the pews. I recognize a few former Silver Balls.

"I hope you like ham salad sandwiches," Fern whispers to me. "Because that's all we'll be eating for the next week."

I press my finger to my lips. She doesn't say things as quietly as she thinks. The older she's gotten, the more careless she's become.

"That's what happens when people are on their own for too long," Helen told me once. "They lose their filters."

Fern lives in the house she inherited when her mother died. She worked as a schoolteacher for most of her life, which is what her mother wanted her to do. She's done well for herself. The house is neat and nicely decorated. She has a good pension. But I don't think Fern has ever been happy. She hides it well behind her wisecracks. The best thing for her would've been to get out from under her mother's shadow. But that never happened. Fern had to take care of her. And now that her mother is gone, I sense a growing anger in her. I think she feels cheated out of a life. Still, she's been good company for me over the years, especially since Charlie's death. We take comfort in our solitary status. When we're together, there's no talk of husbands or children or grand-children to endure. Just two older women, passing the time.

Right before the service ends, Fern and I make our way down to the basement. We're in charge of the dessert table. My date squares are still making me nervous, but I'm comforted by the fact that someone has brought the most horrible-looking lemon squares. I scoop my squares out onto a plate with an air of superiority. At one point dur-ing the luncheon, Arlene Disdale looks over at me and gives me the thumbs-up. I'm not joining her bridge club.

"Are my arms shorter or is my stomach bigger?" Fern asks later while we do the dishes. "I can't seem to get close enough to this sink."

I offer to wash if she wants to dry, but she says she'll get by. Her midsection is a wet, dark oval and she's elbow-deep in suds.

"What were you up to today?" she asks.

"I went for my hair. Then to see Mrs. Pender." I frown as I rub a plate dry.

"How is she doing?"

"Fine." I set the plate down. Pick it up. Set it down. "Can you keep a secret?"

"I'll likely forget it before I tell it."

"I found something in Mrs. Pender's drawer. An old Mother's Day card from Freddy. It said he was moving to Miami." I lean in closer. "He never lived in Miami. And the card had two sevens on it. As in the year."

"But didn't he die?"

"Yes. A long time ago."

"That doesn't make sense." She's talking more to herself than to me. Her eyebrows rise and fall.

"I saw something like this on *Dateline* once. This man faked his own death. No one knew for years. It was a fascinating story." She turns to me. "Where's the card?"

"Still in Mrs. Pender's drawer."

"We should get our hands on it. I'd like to see it for myself." She's washing the dishes faster now. Suds splash her blouse. "Do you think, Joyce, that Freddy might be alive? I mean, is it even possible? And even if he isn't, what kind of secrets is that woman keeping?"

We're interrupted by Arlene carrying two paper plates stacked with sandwiches.

"I've made these up for you girls. There's a mountain of food left. I tried to do an assortment. Do you want some squares?"

"Just freeze them until the next funeral," Fern says.

"It better not be mine," Arlene replies. "I deserve more than thawed-out leftovers."

Before I leave, Fern tells me she'll call me later. "To discuss the situation," she says under her breath.

———

For dinner, I have a quarter sandwich of egg salad, a quarter of turkey and a half of ham salad. I have rice pudding for dessert. It tastes like paste and I barely finish it. I take a pad of paper from the telephone table and a pen and write down the following:

Things To Do. (Moving)

Then I sit and stare at the sheet of paper. Several times, I touch my pen to the surface only to pull it away again. A cluster of blue dots stare back, spider eyes, waiting for me to make the first move. The pen goes down and I watch as lines begin to form. First across, then down.

77

I get up from the table and dial Fern's number.

As much as I knew I'd regret it, I called Helen after talking to Fern. Then we laid out our plan. I don't like driving at night, although it's more dusk right now than dark. I don't trust myself outside of daylight. I feel disoriented, even though I know these streets like the back of my hand. Still, one wrong turn and I could end up in an alleyway with a stranger's silhouette staring me down. Or hit someone and be vilified in the next day's paper. I can already see the capital letters of self-righteous forty-year-olds in the Letters to the Editor. Seniors shouldn't be allowed to drive! A DANGER to SOCIETY!

I shouldn't be doing this. *We* shouldn't be doing this.

"Helen and I will distract her and you get the card," Fern said on the phone.

"This isn't a good idea."

"See you at the Golden Sunset at seven-thirty."

I turn onto Bleeker Street. I should be in my housecoat right now. I should be in my glider, worrying about whether my stool will be loose tomorrow morning.

Fern is already in the parking lot. I pull up beside her. "I thought Helen was coming with you," I say.

Fern points towards an approaching car. "I offered to pick her up, but she insisted on driving herself."

"Am I late?" Helen yells out her open window as she pulls in beside me. She's wearing that hat again. "I had an awful time getting away." The three of us slowly walk towards the entrance.

Fern runs through the plan again. "We'll take her out of the room. While we're gone, you get the card and the book. Next time you visit, you bring the card back."

"This is ridiculous," I say. "She'll know something is up. The two of you have never come to see her before."

"She'll appreciate the company," Helen says.

"Have you *met* Mrs. Pender?"

It's deathly quiet inside the Golden Sunset. Most of the residents are in their rooms, preparing for bed. The hallways are deserted. There's one lone soul, an old woman, sitting in her wheelchair next to the nurse's station. She looks up as we pass her.

"Wonderful evening," Fern says with a nod.

She sticks her tongue out.

I'm almost expecting Mrs. Pender not to be in her room. I'm not sure why. But when we push open the door, she's there in her chair, next to her bed, just like always. Her head is down, her chin pressed against her chest. She's wearing a dull grey cardigan, but whoever put it on her didn't take the time to smooth it down in the back. It sits bunched around her shoulders, a puddle of wool. The light from the fading sun slips through the blinds, casting shadowy bands across the room. Mrs. Ogilvy is sleeping, her mouth wide open like a rabbit hole. There's a faint smell of urine in the air.

"My god, she got old," Fern whispers.

"She's ninety-seven." I step towards her. "Mrs. Pender?"

No response. For a moment, I think she's dead. But then I see the slow rise of her back. Sleeping. That's all.

"We should come back," I say.

"Mrs. Pender?" Helen calls. "Hello?"

I squeeze Helen's elbow. "Are you *trying* to give her a heart attack?" I look over just in time to see Fern open Mrs. Pender's drawer and take the card. She slips it into her purse with a quick wink in my direction, then tiptoes out of the room. Helen follows her. I'm left standing there, my eyes darting between Mrs. Pender's bent grey head and the night table. How did I ever let myself get talked into this? I sneak out of the room before Mrs. Pender wakes up.

When he was nine, my son informed me he was leaving the junior choir.

"I'm not a baby anymore," he said, his face stiff with solemnity. His hair was so thick. I couldn't stop marvelling at it. Where had it come from? Not my side.

"I'm sorry if that upsets you, Mommy."

"I'm not upset," I said and pressed my hand down on his crown of brown curls. I was both impressed and saddened by my son's decision. Not that I cared about the junior choir. He'd outgrown it and I never got on well with the director. I couldn't understand why Mrs. Carr refused to give John more solos.

"I can't play favourites, Mrs. Sparks," she said once.

"I'm not asking you to," I replied. "But you have to admit, he's the best singer you've got. Why not encourage true talent?"

She was a horrible dwarf of a woman with two moles like a colon on the side of her cheek.

"She smells like booze sometimes," John told me once in a scandalized whisper.

"And what does booze smell like?" I asked.

"Like disinfectant. I bet she's an alcoholic."

Where was he learning these words?

"Don't you repeat that," I said. "It stays between you and me."

The truth was, I suspected the same about Mrs. Carr. I noticed that her eyes were often unfocused, as though there were two of everything in front of her and she couldn't decide which version to look at. Apparently there was a failed stage career in her past. This explained why she tried to shoot down any genuine talent that crossed her path.

"I think John has a wonderful voice," Mrs. Carr said. "But this is the St. Paul's United Church Junior Choir, Mrs. Sparks. Not Broadway."

When she said those words, something sharp went down my throat.

"That's fine," I said. "It's just that John loves to sing."

"He certainly does."

I tried to encourage him. "Well, if you leave the choir, is there anything else you'd like to do? You should always keep busy, John."

"I don't know what else I can do."

"You're talented at so many things. You're good at singing. And drawing. And you help me make the best cinnamon buns in the whole wide world."

"Really?"

Although he enjoyed being in the kitchen, I was getting concerned. I'd noticed in the past few months that his belly had begun to protrude over his waistband and his thighs were getting rounder. I wasn't too alarmed. I knew that most boys went through chubby phases. But the more times I caught him rooting through the cupboards, the deeper my doubts became. It seemed like something else was quietly building. An undercurrent of frustration. Or boredom. Perhaps both.

He needed to be more active. I'd make a point to remind Charlie about this. In any case, I wasn't too concerned. And besides, whatever minor downfalls he had were eclipsed by his sparkling personality. My boy was special. I wasn't the only one who thought so. I heard it from other people: teachers and friends and parents. John was intelligent and sensitive and well spoken and courteous. He had an endearing way with people.

"You're putting him on a pedestal," Charlie would say.

"I'm building his self-esteem. There's nothing wrong with that."

"You watch, Joyce. He'll fall from your perch sooner or later."

"No doubt you'd get some kind of pleasure from that."

I was convinced in those days that Charlie was having an affair. I'd spend afternoons going through his pockets, his change drawer, searching for anything that might validate my suspicions. I even examined his underwear for starchy stains. But I found nothing. The more empty-handed my searches left me, the more convinced I was that something was going on under my nose.

"Why are you so hell-bent on this?" Fern would ask me. "Usually when there's no evidence, it means no crime."

"Not necessarily," I said.

It was true that Charlie had grown more distant than usual, spending most of his time in his workroom, repairing or building while the sawdust drifted up from the vents. He seemed to take more interest in his two-by-fours and tools than in me or—and this was what bothered me most—his son. But I wonder now who was avoiding whom.

The more distant I allowed my world to become from my husband's, the closer it became to John's. We were inseparable. He had a way of understanding me, of seeing me in a way that Charlie, or anyone else for that matter, didn't.

"I hate when you're unhappy," he said once, resting his head on my shoulder as we watched a matinee. My mouth dropped open. He always knew. I'd said nothing to him to indicate my unhappiness. In fact, I was doing everything in my power to convince him otherwise.

"Why would you say that?" I asked.

"I can see it in your eyes."

He was eleven years old. The images on the screen turned to blurs. How in the world did a child like this find his way to me? How had I managed to stumble upon this gift? I squeezed his hand tightly in the darkness.

"*You* make me happy," I told him.

"You make me happy, too," he said, squeezing my hand back.

After that, he became the husband I had always wanted. For Valentine's Day, he gave me a box of chocolates and a giant card made from red construction paper with a doily border. The morning of Mother's Day, I awoke to find John at my bedside, smiling ear to ear. His hair was slicked back and he was wearing one of his ties. I smelled Charlie's aftershave on him.

"Happy Mother's Day," he said and pulled a handful of wilted daisies and Queen Anne's lace from behind his back. "I made breakfast for you, too."

The kitchen was a complete disaster. On a plate in front of my chair sat a misshapen cinnamon bun smothered in icing.

"You made this?" I asked, afraid I wouldn't be able to stomach all that sugar so early in the morning.

He nodded.

"What time did you get up this morning?"

"Same time as Dad. I told him to wake me up before he left for work."

"I can't believe I didn't hear you."

"I tried to be quiet. It's Mother's Day, after all."

After I discreetly scraped most of the icing off and took a few bites of the bun, he placed a brightly coloured package on the table.

"I picked it out," he said. "Daddy helped."

Inside the box, resting on a thick bed of cotton batten, was a necklace.

"It's beautiful," I said, even though it wasn't my style. It was cut glass and silver. Something a movie star might wear. Is this what my boy thought of me? I wondered as he fastened it around my neck. He called me Elizabeth Taylor and I laughed and laughed. I wore that necklace for the rest of the day. In spite of its garishness, I was surprised by how I felt: glamorous, special. I was out of my element amidst my kitchen cupboards and self-hemmed curtains. I almost believed in a version of myself that had long since faded away.

"Well, what do you think?" Charlie asked when he came home from work and saw the necklace. "He wanted to get you a tiara, but I held him back."

"It's perfect," I said. "Made my day."

Charlie presented me with a new flannel nightgown. He must've seen the disappointment on my face when I opened the box.

"That's what you said you wanted."

"You're right," I sighed. "It's exactly what I asked for."

I kept that necklace, even after my relationship with John fell apart and there was no reason to hang on to the painful mementoes of the people we used to be. I still have it. It's in my jewellery drawer, buried under tangles of beads and earrings with no partners. I can't even bear to look at it.

"Let's recap everything one more time," Fern says. We've assembled in her car, parked in the empty lot of the public library. I'm holding the card gingerly in my hands, trying to spread as few fingerprints on it as possible.

"Freddy died in 1959."

"Correct," Helen says. Her finger makes a check mark in the air.

"We have a Mother's Day card with his name on it, dated 1977."

"Correct," Helen says. Another check mark.

"There's only one logical explanation," Fern decides.

"Correct." Helen turns to Fern. "What's that?"

"This is ridiculous," I say and open the car door. "Good night."

"Freddy didn't die," Fern says, her eyes wide as two full moons. The car begins to chime. I close the door.

"He's dead," I say.

"Lots of people fake their own deaths," Helen says. "I read about one just the other day."

"I'm happy for you, Helen."

"Why are you being so irritable?"

"This ends here," I say, putting the card into my purse. "Not a word of this to anyone. Helen, that means you. I'm ashamed of myself for letting the two of you talk me into this. We went into an old lady's room and stole a personal item."

"There's no reason to get wound up," Helen says.

"*I'm* not the one who's wound up!" I open the door again and step out. "*You're* the ones wound up."

I almost cry with relief when I finally get home and into my bed, but sleep doesn't come easily. I can't stop seeing that card, the handwriting inside. It simply isn't possible. There has to be another explanation. The dead don't come back.

I wake to the sound of tapping on my window. It's John. I must've locked the back door before going to bed. Why would I do something like that? He said he'd be late.

Tap . . . tappity-tap . . . tap . . .

My boy is trapped outside, freezing and burning. He's been sick for some time. Skin and bones. Fingers like pencils. Hair wet with sweat. Never mind. He's come home. I'll take care of him. I'll let him in.

"I'm here," I say through the window, and the sound of my voice rips me from my dream.

Morning has turned the walls to steel. Short red dashes of the clock next to me assemble like soldiers. My tongue feels like clay.

Every morning when I wake up, I need to remind myself that my son is gone.

My brain feels heavy, as though a wet sponge has replaced it. I manage to get into a sitting position. My varicose vein throbs under my skin. I exerted myself yesterday with all that commotion. I need to take things easy today. I'll do laundry and watch television. That's all. And if Helen or Fern calls and wants to rehash last night, I'll simply tell them, "I don't want to discuss it."

I go to the bedroom window and pull up my blinds. When I look across the street, I see that Mr. Sparrow's blinds are down. I glance at my alarm clock. It's 7:10 a.m. He's usually up before me. I look back and feel a jab of concern. I decide to give him and his blinds a bit more time.

My stool is fine this morning and I thank god for small mercies. I go into the kitchen, turn on the radio and pour myself a bowl of cereal. The announcer says we're in store for another scorcher today. With the humidity, it will feel like 40 degrees. I do the Celsius-to-Fahrenheit conversion in my head like I always do. That's over 100. My head falls into my hand.

At seven-thirty I get up from the table to check on Mr. Sparrow's blinds. They're still down. I go back into the kitchen and find his number in my address book. I listen as the phone rings five times. Then six. I take the phone into the hallway.

Eight . . . nine . . .

I open my front door.

. . . ten.

I hang up and hope that no one else is up at this hour. I throw my jacket over my nightgown and put on a pair of sandals. My hairy legs are on display for everyone. Never mind. It doesn't matter.

I walk up Mr. Sparrow's driveway, wondering if it's better to try the front or the back door. The back, I decide. I still can't get over the size of his garden. It takes up most of the yard. I don't know how he manages to do it all himself. It looks as though the corn is coming in now. I'll expect a basket on my front porch in a matter of days. I open the screen door and knock loudly. I wait for a couple of seconds, then press the bell. Nothing. I slide the key Mr. Sparrow gave me a few years back into the lock and take a deep breath. The door opens. A smell like wet newspaper greets me.

"Mr. Sparrow? Are you home?"

I step up into the kitchen. A saucepan sits next to the sink. Two tomatoes rest on the windowsill. Newspapers and envelopes cover the kitchen table. I shake my head. He needs to tidy up. A cellophane tube of crackers lies next to a magnifying glass. His refrigerator clicks and starts to hum. I stop in my tracks, trying to listen over the sound of it. I go into the living room, but he's not there, either. The next place to check is the bedroom. I turn to face the hall. I'm not sure I can do it.

"Mr. Sparrow?" It comes not as a question, but as a request. As though I'm the one that needs to be found. I take a step into the hall. A floorboard creaks under my foot. The bedroom door is open. I squeeze my hands together in a prayer formation and press them against my lips. I have to do this. I have to go inside. What if he's suffering?

"Mr. Sparrow?"

There's a noise behind me. I whip around and see a band of light shining under the bathroom door.

"Mr. Sparrow!" I yell, hurrying down the hall. "Are you in there?"

His voice is weak and low. "I haven't got any valuables, so you best be on your way."

I nearly collapse with relief. "Mr. Sparrow, it's Joyce. Are you all right?"

"Oh. Joyce. Is that you? There are some tomatoes in the kitchen for you."

"Never mind about the tomatoes! Are you all right?"

"Well, I seem to have fallen."

"*Fallen?*" I try the door but it won't open. "Is this locked?"

"Yes," Mr. Sparrow says.

"Why do you lock the bathroom door if you're the only one here?"

"I'm a private person."

"I'll have to pick it. Do you have a bobby pin?"

"A doggie pen?"

"A BOBBY PIN! To pick the lock!" I'm somewhere between laughing and screaming.

"Check the kitchen drawer by the sink. Every useless thing I own is in there."

I hurry to the kitchen and start rummaging through the drawer. It's filled with elastic bands and pens and bottle openers and other sorts of junk. I think of Mrs. Pender and her purse. But there's no bobby pin. I find a miniature screwdriver, hoping it will work.

"Are you in pain?" I yell as I wiggle the screwdriver into the lock.

"No more than usual."

The lock turns over and I open the door. There, in the

middle of the bathroom floor, lies Mr. Sparrow. He's dressed, thank god, wearing blue pyjamas and brown slippers. I'm struck by his smallness. He's no bigger than the bath mat. In his hand, he holds a toothbrush.

"You poor man." I bend down. "How long have you been like this?"

"I don't know. One minute I was brushing my teeth. The next, I was on the floor. What time is it?"

"I don't know exactly. A little after seven-thirty, anyway. I saw your blinds were down so I came over. I'm calling an ambulance. You stay here."

"You don't need to do that," Mr. Sparrow says. There's a slight panic in his voice, but I ignore it. When I return, he's sitting up, his back against the wall.

"I told you not to move!"

"Get me my bathrobe, will you? It's hanging behind my bedroom door."

"For god's sake, stay put!"

"I was going to have my bath this morning." He sounds as though he's talking more to himself than to me. "I guess I can scratch that off my to-do list."

"You shouldn't be taking baths," I say, returning with the bathrobe. I hold it out and watch him slip one thin arm in, then the other.

"I may be old, but I don't want to smell," he says. "I grab hold of the towel bar for support."

"I don't know how secure that is." I glance up at the bar, thinking of my own. "You should have someone here when you take your bath. I'll come over and watch TV until you're done. Or we'll get you one of those plastic chairs to put in the tub."

Mr. Sparrow sighs and ties the bathrobe belt around his waist. "Next you'll be installing one of those raised toilet seats. The beginning of the end." He reaches over and places his hand over mine. I think it's the first time we've touched.

"Joyce, you don't have to take care of me. I'm not your responsibility."

"You're no trouble at all," I say.

"You can see that I'm all right, can't you? No broken bones. Maybe a bruise or two, but that's all. I still have my wits about me. My name is Hal Sparrow. I live at 297 Marian Street. See? Tell me you know that I'm all right."

"I don't know that you haven't broken anything. But you seem all right to me."

"I can cook for myself, too. Last night, I had potatoes and sausages for dinner. And I keep a tidy house. I even cut my fingernails yesterday." He holds up a hand for inspection. Thick ridges run down his nails.

"Very nice," I say. "But why are you telling me this?"

He grabs my sleeve. "Because I have to come home again. I need you to tell the doctors that I can take care of myself. My garden, this house. It's all I have left in the world."

"Of course," I say, my eyes following a tear as it runs down his cheek. "You'll be back. I promise."

"An accident." Mr. Sparrow dabs his cheek with the square of toilet paper I pass him. "That's all it was. They happen all the time, Joyce. Don't they?"

———

The paramedic tells me it could have been a mini-stroke.

"It's hard to say at this stage," he says. He looks twelve. "But don't worry. Your husband is in good hands now."

"He's not my husband," I say. "He's my neighbour." I hand him a grocery bag with Mr. Sparrow's medications, his wallet, eyeglasses and anything else I could think of.

"Please water the garden," Mr. Sparrow says in a shaking voice as he's wheeled into the ambulance. "And keep the birds out of the fruit trees."

They're taking him to the hospital in Andover. Balsden General is full. The other paramedic asks if I'm planning to follow.

"I don't drive on the highway," I explain. "But I'll call to find out how he's doing."

"Any next of kin?"

"There's a nephew. I have his number somewhere."

I stand in Mr. Sparrow's kitchen and watch the ambulance pull out of the driveway. Across the street, my own house stares back at me.

CHAPTER SIX

"It's not good for him to be on his own," Mr. Sparrow's nephew says when I call him. His name is Gerald.

"We keep a close eye on one another," I say.

"Well, that's all fine and dandy. But Christ almighty. What is he? Ninety?"

"Eighty-seven," I say. I'm tempted to tell Gerald he doesn't sound like a spring chicken himself. His voice is wheezy. Must be a smoker.

"Well," Gerald says, "close enough."

He coughs and I swear I can feel his spittle in my ear canal. I should never have called this man but I had no choice. He's the only family Mr. Sparrow has ever mentioned. All Smoker Gerald is likely concerned with is how much money his uncle has in the bank. I'm surprised he hasn't asked me to send him Mr. Sparrow's statements. Gerald suggests that a "place" for his uncle would be the best option. I hear the quotation marks dangling around the word. Somewhere, he says, that they can keep tabs on him.

"Wild horses couldn't drag that man into a nursing home," I say. "He's too independent." I spot a fly making its way across my kitchen counter and reach for the swatter. "There's a lot of life left in him."

"Sometimes," Gerald says, "decisions need to be made. Difficult ones."

Mr. Sparrow told me once that Gerald has never come to visit. Imagine having your fate rest in the hands of a dimwit like this. I lose sleep some nights, thinking that Mark and Marianne may be making similar decisions for me.

"You'll have to discuss this with your uncle," I say. I stand poised with the fly swatter. Out of the corner of my eye, I catch sight of something black. I turn my body slowly. The fly is on the stovetop, running around in tiny circles. "He's not dead, you know. Or senile."

I raise the swatter and bring it down with a snap. The fly takes off for the window. It shakes itself angrily against the glass.

Gerald wants to know what the doctor had to say. I've already told him. Twice.

"The doctor said he can come home tomorrow. He just needs to take it easy."

"And who are you again?"

"I'm his neighbour," I say tersely, then add, "and friend."

"How is he getting home?"

The fly lands on the kitchen table. It's motionless, staring me down, a dot of metallic green. John's jacket. He loved that green jacket. I bring the swatter down, hitting the fly. It falls to the floor.

"*I'm* picking him up," I say defiantly before ending the conversation, knowing full well I can't drive all the way to Andover. Just the thought of taking the highway makes my stomach contract, but I'll find a way to get there.

I bend over and press the iridescent fly between the folds of a Kleenex and deposit it in the garbage.

He was late coming home from school that day. Something was wrong. I sensed it. I stood on the front porch and watched for him, dread building like storm clouds.

"Perhaps he stopped to talk to a friend," I reasoned, my hands working an invisible piece of dough. "Or the teacher asked him for help."

It wouldn't have been out of place. John's grade eight teacher, Mrs. Myner, often had him stay behind and help her with her bulletin boards or wipe down the chalkboards. She was all of four-foot-nothing and couldn't reach as well as John. He'd shot up in height right after his thirteenth birthday. I was startled one day to turn around and find myself looking straight into his eyes—hazel, the same colour as mine.

"John is very courteous," Mrs. Myner had said at the last parent–teacher meeting. "Sensitive, too."

I nodded and waited. But there was no talk of kitchen sets or games of tag. No comments about questionable behaviour. The only subject he needed to improve in was math.

"Oh?" I relaxed in the chair.

"He's trying," Mrs. Myner said sympathetically. "Perhaps it's something you could help him with in the evenings."

"I'm afraid I'm not very good at math either," I said and laughed. My belly shook and immediately I pressed my hands against the widening swath beneath my skirt. Where had this fat come from? I'd wondered as I stood in front of the mirror that morning, holding my midsection as if it was a fish. Is this what happens to women after thirty?

"Men tend to be better at math," Mrs. Myner said. "Maybe it's something Mr. Sparks could help with."

"Mr. Sparks—" I began, but I wasn't sure where my words were headed. In the past few years, the divide between my husband and son had grown wider. John seemed to have graduated from a general awkwardness around his father to visible disdain. They didn't speak to one another so much as utter syllables. I was certain I felt my son drifting away from me as well.

He'd continued to gain weight. It bothered me to see him standing next to his cousins. He looked so downtrodden, his physicality cumbersome and waterlogged. But he wasn't what you'd call fat. Just chubby. Husky. I'd see to fixing things if I felt his weight crossed a line. Still, my hands balled into fists every time I heard those kitchen cupboard doors open.

"*Do* something," I'd say to John.

"Do what?" he'd ask, holding his bowl of chips or a stack of cookies defensively against his chest.

"Anything," I'd say, and hold off what I really wanted to say: *Anything but eat.*

"I'll ask my husband to give John some help with math," I said to Mrs. Myner.

"Some students experience difficulty when they get to high school." I noted an edge of caution in her tone. "Just make sure the lines of communication are open between the three of you."

Her words came back to me as I took a step down from the porch. There was no sign of John. I stood on my tiptoes, angling to get a better view of the schoolyard, and wrapped my sweater tightly around me. The last of the winter was over, thankfully, but a dead chill lingered. Tree branches scraped the sky. I would've walked over, but there were cookies in the oven. Snickerdoodles. John's favourite. The other day, he'd placed second in the speech contest sponsored by the Optimist Club of Balsden, and I baked them in celebration. He had to write something under the theme of "My Responsibility Involvement." John's speech highlighted the importance of helping neighbours. He spoke about how he helped Mr. Sparrow rake his lawn after Mr. Sparrow had broken his arm.

"We all have a responsibility," my son said to the audience. "To our parents, our neighbours and most importantly, to ourselves. When we take care of others, our hearts take care of us."

I wept and Charlie passed me a crinkled tissue. His eyes had a faint sheen to them too, and when John stepped down from the stage, he clapped louder than anyone else.

John should've won. There was little doubt about that, but the judges picked a little girl in a pink dress and pigtails who talked about her grandfather dying in World War One. It was obvious the judges were partial to her because she was cute. Still, my son seemed pleased with himself when he went up on stage to accept his second-place plaque. I stood to get a better look, but Charlie pulled me down before apologizing to the couple behind us.

"It's my son," I explained. "He's been working on his speech for weeks."

Their placid faces told me their child didn't place. I asked John on the car ride home if he was disappointed about not taking first place.

"Not really," he said, his finger tracing the spot on the plaque where his name would go. "I'm happy enough."

"Well, you should've won," I said. "You were much better than that girl."

"Joyce . . ."

"It's true, Charlie." I turned around. "Your father and I are very proud of you."

Proud. I stepped back inside a house that smelled like cinnamon. It was a quarter after four. John should've been home a half-hour ago. I tried calling the school, but got no answer. That secretary was hopeless. I'd had run-ins with her in the past. I turned off the oven and grabbed my overcoat and hurried down the porch steps, walking as quickly as I could towards the yellow bricks of the school.

At first, I saw a patchwork of colours in the far corner of the schoolyard. Blues, reds, a square of yellow. Winter jackets. The backs of boys' heads.

They're playing a game, I thought, scanning the crowd for John's new green jacket. He'd picked it out himself the previous week, even though I thought it was too formal for school. It was three-quarter length with shiny brass buttons running along the side. It looked smart on him and he was in love with it as soon as he tried it on. He couldn't stop looking at himself in the dressing room mirror. So what if it was a few dollars more than what I was expecting to pay? So what if it was different? Charlie didn't need to know everything. We had our share of secrets, my son and I.

I made my way across the field, annoyed at my son's lateness but happy to see him with friends. I'd been after him for some time about making some. I was getting tired of seeing him mope around the house on Saturday afternoons, restless and looking to me for entertainment.

"I don't know what it is you want to do," I'd say, after running through a list of possibilities. Nothing interested him and I didn't care for his petulance.

"Grown boys don't sulk," I'd say to him. "It's not becoming."

"I'm not a sulk," he'd reply, but the whine in his tone was like nails on a chalkboard. His constant lingering got under my skin. I needed breathing room.

"Does Mark cling to you?" I remember asking Helen once. It was one of the few times I decided to reach out. I needed to talk to someone, if only to vent.

"Oh, god no," Helen replied. "I can barely keep him in the same room as me for two seconds. Welcome to the teenaged years. Why are you asking?"

"It's nothing."

"Is John clingy with you?"

"A little. He's more frustrated than anything."

"John is more emotional than Mark. Remember when the boys were young and we took them to that amusement park? We put the two of them on that merry-go-round." She laughed. "John howled throughout the entire ride and I couldn't get Mark off his horse at the end."

I had no memory of that merry-go-round, no memory of my howling son. I stepped into cold puddles and water crept into my shoes. I hadn't thought to wear galoshes. The field behind the school seemed bigger than I remembered. The boys were tucked away in the far corner. There were six or seven of them from what I could see at this distance. Around the field's perimeter was a wooden fence threaded with twisted wire. The wood was reddish brown. I thought of meat. Brisket. As I approached, the noises the boys were making shifted from sounds to words—words I hadn't heard in years, words that still shocked me with their brutality. My feet stopped dead centre in a puddle. The words grew louder. My ears began to ring. And then I caught a glimpse of something, or rather *someone*, in the centre of the circle of boys. But he wasn't standing. He was lying on the cold, wet ground, curled up into a ball. The other boys were kicking him with their boots and sneakers. I heard the swipe of old snow, slick as steel, under their soles. And I knew, even before I saw the green coat, that my son was in the centre of this circle, surrounded by these boys and their spiteful words.

I must've made some sound because a couple of the boys turned around. I began running towards them, puddles shooting up my calves. But I tripped and fell. My hands slid in front of me, burning, as though the grass was fire. The boys took off, each one running in a different direction. They were going home. Back to their mothers.

John was lying on his back. He was bleeding from a wound above his eye. A thin trickle of blood slipped down the side of his dirty face. His pants were ripped, exposing the delicate pink oval of his knee.

"John," I said and sank down next to him. "What happened?"

His eyes were not on me but on the sky overhead. "Why did you come here?" His tone was seething, as though I was the one who'd just done this damage to him.

I didn't understand his question or the anger behind it. I told him we had to get home. I helped him stand up and he put his arm around my shoulder as we clumsily hobbled our way across the schoolyard, back to our home and my half-baked cookies.

To this day, I play this scene over and over again. The field. The freezing puddles. Sometimes I'm barefoot. Sometimes the number of boys in the circle quadruples. My son's question hangs in the air, like fog.

Why did you come here?

It was only years afterwards, once he was long gone and I was left with a name on a granite tombstone, that I understood what he meant. If I hadn't left the house that afternoon, if I hadn't stumbled on that scene, if I hadn't heard him being called those names or hovered over him as he lay bleeding on the ground, John would've been able to preserve some scrap of dignity. The boys would've bored of him. They would've gone on to other targets. He would've eventually gotten up. He would've made his way home on his own that day. He'd have thought up a story to explain things. That he'd fallen. That he'd stepped in to help another boy. Anything but the truth.

I would've believed him with all my heart.

I call Fern to tell her about Mr. Sparrow, hoping that I'm not too transparent. I need a ride to Andover, after all, and Fern has no problems taking her car on the highway, or anywhere else for that matter. The only thing she refuses to do is parallel park, but I don't blame her. Her car is the size of a boat. She's had it since the '80s, when big cars were all the rage. She should trade it in for something more compact on account of the environment, but she says she can't be bothered.

"A woman has to have a lot of car around her to feel safe," she told me.

"There he was, the poor soul," I tell her, "sprawled out on the bath mat. He had no idea how long he'd been there."

"He must have been terrified," Fern says.

"They're sending him home tomorrow. I'm just not sure how to bring him back. I don't trust that nephew."

"I don't blame you. My car needs a good run. I'll do it."

I hear the *Wheel of Fortune* theme in the background.

"Are you sure you don't mind, Fern? I wouldn't want to interfere with your day."

"The only thing I have on my agenda tomorrow is changing the light bulb in my bedroom. I'm sure I'll be able to squeeze in a drive to Andover."

"It's so strange to look out my living room window and know he isn't home. I opened my front door this morning and there wasn't a single vegetable waiting for me."

"He's such a kind man," Fern says. "I don't know why you never considered taking things beyond zucchinis and peppers."

"I don't like him in that way. And I don't want the responsibility of looking after someone."

"But isn't that what you're doing already?"

She has a point. "No," I say.

"If there was a widower with a garden and no obvious signs of deformity living across the street from me, I'd get myself over there lickety-split with nothing on but a pair of pantyhose."

I laugh despite myself. "You would not! Don't even try that with me." I pause. "About last night . . ." But I don't know what it was I intended to say. What *about* last night? "There's a perfectly rational explanation for that card. I'm just not sure what it is."

Fern wants to know what I plan to say to Mrs. Pender. "This is somewhat sticky."

"I'll have to think this through," I say.

Fern tells me she'll pick me up at eight o'clock tomorrow morning. We hang up and I stare at the phone. I should call

Helen and tell her about Mr. Sparrow, too. If she learns about it from Fern and not me, I won't hear the end of it. But I can't bring myself to dial Helen's number.

I get up early, the memory of John still weighing heavily on my mind. I dress and go over to Mr. Sparrow's house to tidy things up. He'll appreciate coming home to a clean house. I put a change of his clothes in a plastic bag and place a chicken pot pie I got at the grocery store in his freezer. Back home, I put on my lavender pantsuit. I remember Mr. Sparrow complimenting me once on how nicely the colour went with my silver hair. Then I brush my cheeks with blush, trace twin lines of grey pencil above my eyes and put on some lipstick to match my pantsuit. The face staring back from the medicine cabinet mirror feels like a stranger's. The cold slap of time. These wrinkles, droopy eyelids, the pulled-taffy tendons of my neck. I can't believe I was ever young.

I'm not expecting to see my sister in the passenger seat of Fern's car when it pulls into the driveway, but there she is, waving and wearing that stupid straw hat again.

"I hope you don't mind me tagging along," she calls out.

"Mr. Sparrow won't be in a wheelchair, will he?" Fern asks. "I've got bags of sweaters in the trunk."

"Those aren't the ones for Goodwill, are they?" Helen asks. "You've had them in there for weeks. They're going to smell."

"I'm not dropping them off until the weather cools down," Fern says. "No one will be buying sweaters in this heat. Including the destitute."

"Mr. Sparrow won't have a wheelchair," I say. "At least, I don't think so."

Fern announces she's taking the old highway as there are fewer trucks to contend with. It will take us longer to get to Andover, but the scenery helps pass the time. I haven't been out this way in ages and I'm struck by how little has changed over the years. We drive through towns with soft-drink signs hanging over convenience store entrances. The view seems so peaceful from my air-conditioned back seat. I picture happiness. A simple life.

I think of Charlie, wondering how much of himself he'd left behind when he moved out East. We'd travel back to the Prairies every couple of years, load up the car and take the American route to avoid the long haul around the Great Lakes. Those summer afternoons in the car, windows wide open, John in the back seat, blinking against the swirling wind, and Charlie smiling at the road in front of us. A snapshot of a happy family. No room in that car for doubts. No mud-soaked jackets. Only the open road and a destination.

Helen announces she's always wanted to live in the country.

"Imagine how peaceful it would be. Just you and Mother Nature."

"You'd go bonkers out here," I tell her. "You wouldn't know what to do with yourself."

"That's not true," Helen says. "I'd find plenty to do. I'd probably be busier than I am now."

"Milking cows is time consuming," Fern says with a wink.

"And even if I wasn't as busy," Helen says, "I'd be more content. I really would. Life is getting the better of me these days."

My sister is silent for a few moments, her straw hat motionless in front of me. I'd ask about Dickie, but what would she say? He's fine. Everything was as well as could be expected. But I know she's terrified. What will happen to her when he goes? Will she stay in the house? Will she move to be closer to Mark and Marianne? Will she leave me alone in Balsden? I'm terrified as well. She's the only family I have left in the world.

The fields fall away as we reach Andover's city limits. Traffic builds, and Fern's hands grip the steering wheel tighter. Stores and subdivisions rise from the ground, big grey boxes surrounded by beige houses with no more than a couple of feet between them. I used to love coming to Andover. But it's not the same. Everything is built for convenience and minivans. I watch as we pass a Wal-Mart and try to imagine trees. The memory of a deer surfaces.

"My goodness, they've really built things up," Helen says. The brim of her hat scratches the car roof. "I hardly recognize anything."

Something falls. I look down. There's a small dark circle on my lavender thigh. My finger touches it. I scrounge through my purse, looking for a Kleenex.

"Joyce?"

I find one and press it against my eyes. I won't have this. Not now. This is supposed to be a happy day. Mr. Sparrow is coming home. But the deer. I can't stop seeing it—the brown liquid eyes, its velvet coat. I remember seeing it among the trees all those years ago, before the construction started behind our house. I was so young then. Charlie, too. John. There was so much life. Such promise. Where did the deer go when they cut down the trees? I need to know it made it to safety. I need to know it survived. I need to know that everything turned out all right in the end.

Two summers ago, Fern and I went on a cruise around the Thousand Islands.

"Is this where the salad dressing was invented?" she asked the tour guide, but she got a vacant stare in response.

The boat was one of those old-fashioned steamers that cater to tourists. It looked like it had seen better days, and I'd heard stories of boats capsizing on Sunday-afternoon trips, spilling people into the water.

"Those types of accidents only happen in the southern states," Fern said. "You have nothing to worry about."

I wasn't so sure. I never learned how to swim, which made me anxious about boats in general. Charlie had tried to teach me once, but I hated being in the water. I didn't like the feel of nothingness beneath my feet, the sense of suspension.

We sat for lunch with a couple from Montreal. They were celebrating their fortieth wedding anniversary.

"How nice for you," Fern said, giving my thigh a sharp pinch under the table.

Once the servers collected the dessert plates, a chubby man in a top hat came out and told us we were in store for a wonderful treat. He grinned broadly, like a children's television host.

"Please join me in welcoming the Steamboat Dancers!"

We clapped as four young men and women skipped to the centre of the room, wearing white pants with red sequined vests and matching bowler hats. They assembled in two lines while the chubby man sat down behind a piano and began to play "Swanee River."

"I haven't heard this song in ages," Fern whispered to me.

The dancers began their routine, arms jutting out this way and that.

They weren't very good, which might explain why they were performing on an old ship on a Sunday afternoon for tourists. But their mediocrity charmed me and I found myself drawn to one blond dancer in particular. He wasn't much better than the rest of them, but he did have a certain spark. It was as though this was his last chance to get things right. One never knew who was sitting in the audience.

White clothes. Young boy. How many Freddy Penders did this world churn out?

The song ended. I managed a smile and an agreeable nod at the Montreal couple. The dancers took their bows. Just as quickly as he'd come into the room, the young man danced away.

It was impossible to concentrate on anything after that. The woman from Montreal kept asking me questions. Had I ever been to Montreal? How far away was Balsden? How did Fern and I know each other? When I could no longer stand the small talk, I excused myself, claiming a headache.

"I need to get some air."

I went out on the deck. It was a cool July day. I stood at the railing, looking out across the water. It wasn't the first time suicide had crossed my mind. In the days and years following John's death, it was all I could do to keep the blood flowing through my veins. If it hadn't been for Charlie, for the presence of another devastated human in the house, I doubt I would've ever gotten out of bed in the mornings. I would've lain there forever, letting the worms work through my withering insides.

There were meals to cook and volunteer groups to attend and sympathies to receive from well-meaning acquaintances. There was a life—or rather, a semblance of one—that needed to be picked up and put back together. I'd sit at the kitchen table, day after day, week after week, trying to fit together what pieces I could, trying to recompose some familiar landscape. But all I ever managed were fragments: a piece of sky, half a window, the tip of a smile.

I curled my hands around the railing of that boat, overwhelmed by solitude, a tidal wave's wall gathering above me. There was no one left in the world. Everything I once held dear was gone. My foot stepped up onto the railing's lowest rung. It would all happen so quickly and quietly. Everything would fade to black.

I heard voices behind me and turned around. Two young girls came onto the deck. I realized they were in the dance troupe, although it took a few moments to place them because they were now in their street clothes. They went to the far end of the deck and huddled together, talking in whispers—speculating about him? Calling him names? One of the girls laughed, and if Fern hadn't stepped onto the deck at that moment, I would've marched right over to them.

"You don't know the first thing about anyone," I would've said.

"No one told me the Andrews Sisters were coming to pick me up."

Mr. Sparrow is sitting in a wheelchair, his bathrobe wrapped tightly around his small frame. He looks better than I expected, in spite of a bandage stuck diagonally over his right eye. Seeing him again is like claiming a small piece of home.

"We're here for our Boogie Woogie Bugle Boy," Fern says.

"I brought you a change of clothes," I tell Mr. Sparrow. "I didn't imagine you'd want to go home in your pyjamas."

"That's very kind of you." He takes the bag from me. "Excuse me for a moment." He slowly gets up from his chair and shuffles to the bathroom. I want to take his arm and help him along. I'm nervous about him falling.

"He should have a walker," Helen whispers.

The three of us stand in silence while Mr. Sparrow changes in the bathroom. I feel Helen's eyes on me, but I focus on the white walls. I managed to collect myself in the car, stopping the tears as quickly as they'd started. I won't cry here.

The door to the bathroom opens and Mr. Sparrow comes out dressed in the brown pants and striped shirt I'd picked out for him.

"Have they been treating you well?" Helen asks him.

"As well as can be expected," he says as he shuffles back across the room. (Has he gotten shorter?) "The food isn't as bad as they make it out to be."

Fern guides Mr. Sparrow into the wheelchair. "You're not taking this chair with you, I hope."

I watch with irritation as she lays a blanket across his lap. He doesn't need that. It's too hot out. I step over to the wheelchair, informing them that I'll do the pushing.

"Sure is nice to be going home," Mr. Sparrow says as we make our way down the hall.

A young nurse waves. "Take care, Mr. Sparrow," she calls.

"She was quite taken with me," he says once we're in the elevator. I'm still lost inside my own head. I stare down at the bandage on Mr. Sparrow's forehead.

Luckily, Charlie was working days. There was time to get my son cleaned up before his father came home. It was John who insisted Charlie couldn't know.

"I don't feel comfortable lying," I said, dabbing a wet facecloth against the gash on his forehead. He was sitting at the kitchen table. I had to hold his chin in my hand to keep his head up. He refused to look at me. A few damp tendrils of hair framed his face. Smudges of mud on his cheeks were hardening to grey. He smelled like something left in the rain. The wound above his eye was superficial, thankfully, in spite of its jagged redness. There was no need for hospitals, although I was still tempted to take him.

"Your father needs to know," I said, dipping the facecloth in the bowl of water next to me.

"No, he doesn't," John said. "He doesn't need to know anything."

I wrung out the cloth. My hands were shaking, still burning from my fall.

"You should've fought back, John. That's what your father would've done."

Silence.

"Sometimes, in life, we have to stand up for ourselves. People have to know they can't push you around, that you're not a victim."

Water dripped.

"You have to be tough."

His eyes remained downcast. He seemed weak. I needed to light a fire in my son. I was desperate for some sign of anger and rebellion. Something that would signal that we'd recover. Shake this off.

"Did you say something to upset the boys?" I asked.

He shook his head. "I don't even talk to them."

"Did you *do* something?"

Another head shake. His green jacket was curled up in his lap. He'd refused to let me take it from him. He clutched it as if it were a part of him.

"Did one of the boys say something to *you*?"

I didn't look at him then. I couldn't. Those ugly names I'd heard.

"No." The voice was small. "Are you going to tell Dad?"

I sighed and pressed the facecloth against his wound. "Why don't you want your father to know?"

"I don't want him to think of me like that."

I paused. "Like what?"

"Like I'm different."

"Your father loves you, John. He may have trouble saying it, but he does. You know that, don't you?"

"I don't want to embarrass him."

"Why would you think—?"

His hand grabbed my wrist. "Please don't say anything. Please."

His eyes brimmed with tears; his voice was thin with desperation.

"All right," I said quietly. "Let's think of a story to tell your father."

"He was walking home and slipped in the parking lot," I said when Charlie got home from work that night. I didn't look at him and pretended to be occupied by something in a magazine. "I just bought him new pants and now they have a rip in the knee. I don't know if I have any patches."

"Are you sure he's all right?" Charlie said, getting up from his chair. He went down the hall towards John's room.

"He's perfectly fine," I called out, hoping he didn't notice the twinge in my voice. I watched him knock softly on John's door. He stood there, his head down, hands in his pockets, wearing the same beige work shirt he wore for all his shifts. Inside the collar was a small strip of white tape with "C. Sparks" written on it. Direct. Simple. I made things that way. Easier for him. To think then, that at the end, he was the one who would embrace things far more complex than I ever could.

John's door opened and Charlie disappeared into the room. I shifted in my seat, uncomfortable with the two of them alone like that. So I got up and walked down the hall. I stopped just short of the doorway and listened.

"You're very lucky, young man. You got very close to your eye. Another half inch and you would have done some real damage. Does it hurt?"

"Not really." I heard a slight touch of bravado in my son's voice.

"You should put some ice on it."

"Mom made me keep a bag of frozen peas on it all afternoon."

"One time, when I was your age, maybe a year or two younger, I tripped over a rock in a field and blacked out. When I woke up, it was night. Pitch black, not even a star in the sky. I couldn't see anything around me. But I heard my mom calling my name and I followed the sound until I found her."

His voice was quiet, his tone a gentle one I'd often heard but never paid much attention to. I closed my eyes and leaned against the wall.

"She was pretty relieved when she saw me. I had a bump on my forehead the size of an egg for a week afterwards, but I got by all right. It could have been worse."

"I suppose."

I quickly tiptoed down the hall again to my seat at the kitchen table.

"I'm surprised you're so calm about this," Charlie said when he sat back down at the table. He blew on a forkful of scalloped potatoes.

"Boys fall," I said, breaking my snickerdoodle cookie into pieces. Charlie said nothing else during the rest of dinner.

Afterwards, while John and Charlie sat in the living room watching TV, I scoured my pan, working away at the blackened spots of fat. My son wasn't what those boys had been calling him. I scrubbed and scrubbed, trapped in a hell that would only deepen as the years progressed.

The next day, I kept John home from school. He wouldn't have to face those boys. For another day, at least. After a big breakfast of pancakes and eggs, I sat him down in the living room. I hadn't slept a wink all night.

"I'll make sure those boys never hurt you again," I promised.

"You said you wouldn't say anything."

"This problem needs to be fixed, John."

"You'll only make things worse! You always do!"

He stormed out of the living room and down the hall. I flinched when his bedroom door slammed shut.

Every day for the rest of the year, I walked him to school in the morning and met him at the edge of the schoolyard at the end of each day. He hated me for it, but I wasn't bothered. My son was safe now. He was protected. This was my job, whether he liked it or not. He refused to let us walk side by side. I respected that and kept my distance behind him.

It's a matter of pride, I thought as I watched him hurry away from me.

Helen wants to join Mr. Sparrow and me in the back seat.

"Just in case," she whispers.

"In case of what?" I ask.

"Something happens. Again."

"He's fine, Helen. You sit up front with Fern. Besides, you get carsick when you're in the back."

When we pull up in Mr. Sparrow's driveway, he makes a soft, choked sound. He reaches over and grabs my hand.

"You're home again," I say.

We help him out of the car, although he seems to be pretty steady on his feet. As soon as he's standing, he scurries up his driveway.

"Just want to check things out back," he says.

"I watered the tomatoes," I call out, hoping that nothing is dead. The drive back did me some good. When we reached the outskirts of Balsden, I could feel myself sink into the grey upholstery of the back seat. I was back on home ground.

I catch Helen's scrutinizing gaze. I look away.

Mr. Sparrow invites us into the house for tea. "It's the least I can do in return for your kindness."

"That's not necessary," Fern says, but Mr. Sparrow insists.

The air inside is thick with heat.

"I'm going to fire up the air conditioner in the bedroom,"

he says. "That should cool things off a bit." He disappears down the hall, leaving the three of us sitting around his kitchen table.

"I can't stay here," Helen says in a low voice. She picks a newspaper off the kitchen table and begins to fan herself. "It's unbearable."

"What's that smell?" Fern's nose crinkles up. "He didn't leave any meat out, did he?"

"Of course not," I say. "The house just needs a good scrubbing. I've been meaning to come over and give the floors a wash."

"Did I tell you I hired a cleaning lady?" Helen asks. "She started last week. I pay her ten dollars an hour, but it's worth it. She got my bathtub looking like new again." She leans across the table. "Forearms like rolls of deli meat."

"I wouldn't want a maid," Fern says. "I wouldn't feel safe."

"Don't be silly," Helen says. "Grace is the sweetest thing."

"It's not Grace I'd be worried about," Fern says. "It's the unemployed husband she goes home to after cleaning your toilet. *He's* the one to watch out for."

"You're getting more and more paranoid in your old age," Helen says.

A loud *bang* comes from the hallway, causing the three of us to jump.

"What on earth . . . ?"

"The air conditioner," I remind them.

Mr. Sparrow returns to the kitchen. "You should start feeling cooler air soon," he says, wiping his hands on his pants.

"Does it always sound like that?" Helen asks.

"Like what?" Mr. Sparrow says, which answers the question. He goes to the sink to fill up the kettle. "So, what have I missed while I was away? Anyone die?"

"It depends on who you ask," I say, holding the newspaper in front of my face.

"What do you mean?" Mr. Sparrow asks.

"Don't get all wound up again," Helen says.

I flip the newspaper down. "He's either dead or he isn't. Let's see what a reasonable man like Mr. Sparrow thinks."

"Who's not dead?" Mr. Sparrow sets the kettle on the stovetop.

"Freddy Pender," I say.

Mr. Sparrow's brow furrows in concentration. "Pender . . . Pender. You mean the one who drowned years ago?"

"Joyce found a card from him in Mrs. Pender's room at the Golden Sunset retirement home," Fern says. "Dated 1977."

"It doesn't *mean* anything," I say.

"You're acting like we've done something wrong," Helen says. "We didn't ask to find this out."

"*You* made me go back to the home."

"I didn't make you *do* anything."

"We stole a Mother's Day card from an old woman."

"Borrowed," Helen insists. "Besides, Joyce, you're the one who brought this on yourself. You didn't have to tell anyone about the card. You could have kept your mouth shut and we'd be none the wiser."

I snap up the newspaper. It's indecipherable, the words a blur of black and white.

Mr. Sparrow holds his hand up. "I'm having a hard time following this. Women talk so fast when they're together."

I put the paper down again and tell him about the card and the date on it. Helen and Fern's theories. The kettle comes to a boil. I get up from the table.

"What do you make of all this, Mr. Sparrow?" Fern asks.

"It does seem a little strange. Maybe the easiest thing to do would be to ask Mrs. Pender."

"Mr. Sparrow, you're a man who makes perfect sense," Fern says.

"I wish my wife were still alive to hear you say that."

He asks us to stay. There's a frozen pizza in the fridge. It'll take no time to warm up. "I've got Uno cards, too," he says. "You don't have to rush off."

But I'm desperate to get away. I can think of nothing but my bed. The silence of my house. I'll close my eyes to these memories that keep bubbling to the surface.

"You've had a long day," I say to Mr. Sparrow. "You need nothing more than to rest."

"But I've been resting at the hospital. Besides, I'll have plenty of time for resting when I'd dead."

"Don't say that." My tone is harsher than I mean it to be. "You're not going anywhere anytime soon."

"I never said I was."

At the foot of my driveway, Helen places a hand on my arm. "Do you want some company? You don't seem yourself."

"I'm fine."

"You're looking awfully tired," Fern says.

"It's been a busy couple of days. I just need a good night's sleep."

They look at me, unconvinced. My sister's mouth puckers. "What are you going to do about the card?"

"I'll have to bring it back to Mrs. Pender. I'll slip it into her drawer at some point. Maybe I can pretend to find it while she's in the room. I'd feel better about doing things that way. At least it seems more honest."

"That sounds like a good idea," Fern says. "Let us know if you want company."

"I think the three of us have done enough for now," I say.

Even though I'm not hungry, I heat up a pasta dish in the microwave for dinner. I push small mushroom cubes around with my fork. My thoughts bounce back and forth. I can't ask Mrs. Pender about Freddy. I have to ask Mrs. Pender about Freddy.

I get up from the table and scoop the remains into a plastic container. On the wall behind me, the clock chimes.

Television laughter floats out from the rooms of the Golden Sunset as I make my way down the hall. I'll tell Mrs. Pender I looked for the library book. Then I'll mention finding the Mother's Day card.

"There it was," I'll say with a casual laugh. "I'm sure there's a simple explanation for it."

She's asleep in her chair when I enter the room, snores ruffling the hair hanging over her face. Mrs. Ogilvy is propped up in her bed, working on a crossword puzzle. I mouth the word "Hello." I hadn't anticipated Mrs. Pender being asleep and contemplate waking her. I notice her cardigan. It's a beautiful cranberry colour.

"Whuh-whuh."

Mrs. Ogilvy is pointing at Mrs. Pender.

"It's a nice cardigan," I whisper. "Is it new?"

Mrs. Ogilvy nods and points to something over my shoulder. I turn to see Mrs. Pender still sound asleep behind me.

"Whuh," Mrs. Ogilvy says again, jabbing her finger in the air. My eyes follow the invisible line. She's pointing to the dresser.

I scan the top of it and see a white business card. "Is this what you want, Mrs. Ogilvy?" I ask.

She nods. "Whuh."

"The Seahorse Motel" is written in black script. The Seahorse? That's in Andover. I'm positive the card wasn't here the other day. Then I turn the card over. There's handwriting on the back. I bring it close to my face and squint. *Call me if you want to talk. I go back to Miami on Friday.*

Mrs. Ogilvy grunts. She's nodding again and pointing at something else on the dresser—Freddy's picture.

"That's her son," I say.

"Whuh." Mrs. Ogilvy touches her sleeve and stares at Mrs. Pender.

I feel a thousand pin pricks beneath my skin. "Are you telling me that's who gave her the cardigan?"

A wide, satisfied smile spreads across Mrs. Ogilvy's face. "Whuh," she exhales.

CHAPTER SEVEN

JUST BEFORE THREE, I get out of bed, defeated by my mind's relentless thoughts. Sleep will not come tonight. That's the only thing I know for certain. I wrap my housecoat tightly around myself and go into the living room. For the first time in a long while, I'm frightened of my house. The walls threaten to fall away, leaving me exposed and vulnerable to the night. In dark corners, animals wait to pounce. Things rattle inside boxes in the basement, wanting to be released. The central air comes on, sending the white sheers fluttering like phantoms. I stand in the centre of the living room, hands cupping elbows, trying to calm my racing heart.

I stood in this same spot many mornings, watching from the front window as John made his way to high school. He refused to allow me to accompany him when he started grade nine, which even I admitted would have been crossing a line. My mind understood that he needed to do things on his own, to be out there, in the world outside our front door. But my heart ached as I watched him go and there were many mornings when fears would overwhelm me and I'd burst into tears. I'd keep picturing that day in the field. What other dangers lay waiting for my son?

Still, I had hoped that high school was a new beginning, not just for John, but for me as well. I needed to let go. I wanted to feel clean, to rid myself of the constant dread that nipped at my heels. My son wasn't perfect. He had some problems. I knew that. But there wasn't anything *seriously* wrong with him. Nothing that couldn't be fixed. Growing pains, I told myself. All boys went through stages. He'd thin out. Make new friends. Join a sports team. Sign up for student council. I imagined the phone ringing with invitations to parties and championship games. All that was needed was a fresh start. It would only be a matter of time before I'd be laughing at my foolish worries.

So why couldn't I shake my fears?

At first, things seemed to go well. John said there were no problems with his classmates, and I believed him. He made a new friend named Ralph who sometimes came over after school. Ralph was as thin as a licorice whip with acne covering his face. He rarely looked me in the eye, but he seemed like a nice enough boy. The two of them would watch *The Lucy Show* or *Batman* in the basement. I'd bring them cookies and milk, even though John repeatedly told me not to bother them.

"It's embarrassing," he'd say.

"Ralph appreciates my thoughtfulness," I'd say. "It's too bad my son doesn't."

But Ralph disappeared midway through the year, leaving John to watch his TV shows alone.

"Did you get into a fight?" I asked.

"No."

"Well, what happened?"

"Ralph got weird."

So John had been the one to abandon the friendship. I was relieved.

"What do you mean by weird?"

"Just weird."

That was as much as I ever got. I never saw Ralph again.

I was thrilled when I noticed John cutting back on his eating halfway through the year. His pants got looser and he was perpetually pulling them up. One day, Charlie said, "Take this," putting two twenty-dollar bills on the table. "John needs a pair of pants that fit him properly." He turned to John. "Don't you think you deserve it?"

"I guess so," John said with a shrug.

He said he wanted jeans, so we went to Sears. A young salesgirl came by to help us. She looked only a few years older than John and I soon discovered they both went to the same high school.

"Isn't that something?" I remarked while John turned three shades of crimson. Her name was Janice and she was sixteen. Her mother worked in the jewellery department. While she went in search of jeans for John, I eyed her up and down. She seemed like a perfectly nice girl. I even noticed a gold crucifix nestled in the V of her neck.

"Do you know anything about her?" I asked John. I was considering making a run to the jewellery department to see if I could get a glimpse of her mother.

"Keep your voice down," John said. "She goes with a different crowd."

"What do you mean by different?" I asked.

"Different from me," he said. "She's part of a group. Please don't say anything more to her."

While John was in the change room, I mentioned to Janice that this was his first pair of jeans.

"Well, *teenaged* jeans," I said with a laugh. "He has to keep up with the latest styles."

Janice gave me a peculiar look. I wasn't sure if I liked her after all.

"He's recently lost some weight," I said. "He was a bit on the pudgy side, but I knew he'd grow out of it. He's always go, go, go. I can barely keep track of him."

Why did I care what she thought?

"His father was fed up with the way his jeans kept sliding off. Not fed up in an angry way. He was good-natured about it. He and John are similar in that way. Fathers and sons."

Janice glanced absently at another corner of the store.

"Maybe sometime you and John could get together. To study, of course. Or grab a bite to eat. He's extremely friendly."

"I have a boyfriend."

"Oh. I didn't mean—" I laughed and waved my hand. "Never mind. I'm just being foolish."

The door opened a crack. John's hand emerged, holding a pair of jeans.

"They don't fit right," he said quietly. Janice went off to find another pair.

When I stepped over to the change room door, I peered through the crack and saw a reflection of my son in the mirror. He was standing beneath the harsh fluorescent lights in his white briefs and sweatshirt, crying. My hand instinctively went to the door handle, but I managed, for once, to stop myself.

When he was sixteen, John signed up for the school band, which put me on cloud nine.

"He'll be the next Benny Goodman," I said to Helen, laughing. She'd called to express her concerns about Mark signing up for the football team.

For once, I felt superior. "John says the band goes on a trip every year. They're planning to go to Winnipeg in the spring for the national finals, if you can believe it."

"What did you say he's playing again?"

"The baritone."

"What is that? Some kind of trombone?"

"More like a tuba. A baby tuba."

"Oh."

When John brought his new instrument home the first time, I was perplexed. "Of all the instruments in the world," I said, "you picked this one?"

"I felt bad for it."

"You felt bad for an instrument?"

"No one wanted it. Everyone else wanted the clarinet or the trombone. The baritone was just sitting there by itself. So I took it."

"Is anyone else in band playing the baritone?" I asked. Maybe it would draw too much attention.

"I'm the only one," he said. "Isn't that terrific?"

Charlie asked him to play it for us.

"I don't know any songs yet," John said.

"That doesn't matter," Charlie said. "I'd like to hear how it sounds. Besides, you've got to get used to playing in front of an audience."

Charlie was still trying to make connections with his son. He would ask John questions about school, homework, life in general. But all he ever got were one-word answers and mumbles. As the years went by, John seemed to wind himself tighter and tighter, like a spool of thread with no visible loose end to unravel it.

I look back on those years now and can only imagine what my son was going through, what darkness his mind must've held. Demons chased him down the school hallways and the hallways of his own house. There would've been no escape, no safe haven to tuck into.

I clung to my hopes during his teenage years, always believing we were only one step away from the normalcy that I craved. A baritone, then. That would do it. It was the hobby my son needed.

Up until that point, the only things that had held John's interest were movies. Every Saturday afternoon, he'd ride his bike downtown to the Capitol Theatre. The previous year, he'd become obsessed with *Who's Afraid of Virginia Woolf* and took me to see it. He even paid my admission, which I thought was very generous. But it bothered me that he was drawn to such a dark film. I couldn't take all the screaming and drinking.

"This doesn't remind you of your father and me, does it?" I asked when we came out of the theatre.

"Elizabeth Taylor is the best actress in the world," he said. "I want to meet her someday."

I felt a pang of jealousy, I admit. It's hard for mothers to compete with film stars. He went to see the movie three times. Likely more, although I can't say for sure. I began to wonder how many of those Saturday afternoons he claimed to be at the library were really spent at the Capitol. And I couldn't help but be reminded of those Friday nights I'd spent with Freddy at the theatre.

So band was a welcome change and I was never so happy to hear those horrible sounds coming from his bedroom night after night. Before long those sounds turned into notes, and within a few months, I could detect melodies. I imagined him playing in an orchestra one day. Things began looking up.

Then came the trip to Winnipeg.

I fall asleep listening to one of those public television music specials and wake up just as morning is sliding across the neighbourhood. I slowly raise my head, wincing. My neck has turned as hard as cement. The wall clock reads 6:04. It takes me a moment to remember Mrs. Pender's cardigan and the "whuh" of Mrs. Ogilvy's confirmation and the plan I came up with in the wee hours of the morning. I need to get going. There's no time to lose.

I go to the kitchen and get my car keys from my purse. Then I unlock the front door and step onto the porch. I should change out of my housecoat, but I don't care who sees me. No one will be up at this hour anyway. Aside from Mr. Sparrow. I look over and see that his blinds are down. It's still early, I remind myself. No reason to get worked up. Not yet.

The stair railing is dotted with dew and cool to my touch. I walk to my car and get the map out of the glove compartment, then hurry up the front walk and back into the house.

I don't need the map. I know the way. But it calms me to think of planning out the route, to see things from a bird's-eye view, like God. I move the bowl of plastic fruit from the centre of the kitchen table and spread the map out, smoothing the creases with my palms. I squint at lines as thin as spider veins. I'm terrified by the idea of driving on the highway. But there's no other choice. I find Balsden eventually and, taking a ballpoint pen, dot the old highway to Andover with evenly spaced pinpoints.

"That's all you have to do, Joyce," I say. "Just drive from one dot to the next."

Everything looks so simple on paper.

In the den, I pick up yesterday's newspaper and open it to the weather forecast, even though I checked it last night.

Sunny with a high of 29. That's 84 Fahrenheit, a nice summer day. The humidity has broken and there's no rain expected. To be certain, I turn on the weather channel and sit in my glider, watching repeats of the same information. The springs of the glider click noisily beneath me. It's a hard sound, like bone grinding against bone. Still, no rain. Only sunny skies.

"All right, then," I say to myself, and at that moment, Mr. Sparrow's blinds roll up like a sailor's good omen. Everything, it seems, is falling into place.

I turn on the radio and try listening to the morning's news, but it's hard to concentrate. My cereal bloats in its milk lake. Pulp dries on the sides of my juice glass. The butterflies on my placemat reveal new patterns. Electric. That's how I feel, as though I could lay a finger on a lamp and it would turn on. Is this how people feel when they take drugs?

I take out the map again, my eyes surveying all the squiggly lines and the varying letter sizes of the towns and cities. The smell of the paper is comforting and reminds me of Charlie for some reason. I've missed him more than I ever thought I would. To think he was gone so soon after retiring. A life of shift work in exchange for a few short years of freedom.

I take my powder-blue pantsuit from the bedroom closet and pick out a yellow-striped blouse to wear underneath. In the bathroom, I smooth foundation over my face and spin small circles of blush on my cheeks. Then I go back to my bedroom for one final touch of perfume.

I grab my purse, the map and a couple of peppermints

from the jar on the kitchen counter. Then I step out onto the porch for the second time. The day is heating up. I consider going back inside to apply some deodorant.

"Well, hello there!"

Mr. Sparrow is standing in his front yard, garden hose in hand.

Damn it, I think, trying to jam the map into my purse. It catches on the clasp.

"Good morning," I call back and make my way down the front steps. "Looks like it'll be a warm one today."

"What's that?" Mr. Sparrow cups his ear.

"I SAID IT'S SUPPOSED TO BE QUITE WARM TODAY."

He shuffles down his driveway. I check my watch. I don't have time for this!

"Well, someone's all dolled up for a Wednesday," he says when he reaches the curb.

"I'VE HAD THIS OUTFIT FOR SOME TIME."

"Purple suits you."

Purple? Is he colour blind? "THANK YOU. IT'S ACT-UALLY BLUE. I SUPPOSE THERE'S A HINT OF PURPLE IN IT."

Why am I going on like this? He could've said it was plaid for all I care. I need to get going. "HAVE YOU BEEN ALL RIGHT?"

"Have I been on a bike?"

For the love of god. I stand on my tiptoes and cup my hand alongside my mouth. "HAVE YOU BEEN *ALL RIGHT*?"

"Yes, thank you. All things considered. The peaches are coming in nicely. I'll bring you over a basket."

"THAT'S VERY NICE OF YOU." I begin to walk backwards to the car. "TAKE CARE AND DON'T STAY OUT IN THIS HEAT."

I pop a peppermint into my mouth as soon as I get into the car. All that yelling has made my throat sore. Half the neighbourhood has probably heard our conversation. I'm just glad he didn't bring up Freddy. I slowly reverse out of the driveway.

Everything was Winnipeg. Winnipeg, Winnipeg, Winnipeg. I'd never heard the name so much in the months leading up to the band finals. I'd wake up in the morning with the word spelled out in thick black letters on my bedroom ceiling.

John's band needed to raise money for their trip, so the winter and early spring saw one fundraising gimmick after the next. I had to sort through our closets for yard sale contributions and make dozens of cookies for as many bake sales. I sold bricks of cheese to everyone I could think of.

"Why do I feel like I'm doing all the work?" I asked John.

"You're not," he said. "I sold three blocks of cheese to Mr. Sparrow the other day. He's a big fan of marble, although I had him pegged as an old cheddar sort of guy."

"How much more money do you need to raise? You're going to Manitoba, not Switzerland."

"There's a lot involved with this trip. Transportation, accommodations, new uniforms. This isn't amateur hour, Mother."

Mother. My new name. I hated the way he said it, through his nose with an air of formality. A condescension. Charlie, I noted, was still called Dad. How had he managed to escape John's disapproval?

I griped and complained about the efforts going into the trip, but I was happy for John. I hadn't seen him that excited for the longest time. He'd finally found his niche. A group of band members got together after school to practise—a boy who played the trumpet and two girls who played the clarinet. John seemed to hit it off in particular with one of the girls. A redhead named Angela. She was pleasant enough, although I thought her complexion was too pale and she had bad teeth. Soft. I could tell by looking at them. She certainly wasn't the type of girl I pictured my son with, although when I stopped to consider it, I couldn't think what type I *could* picture him with.

"Are you and Angela more than friends?" I ventured once.

John's mouth compressed into a tight line as he informed me they were just friends, thank you very much. I told him I bet my bottom dollar that Angela had feelings for him.

"I see the way she looks at you," I said, surprised by the twinge of jealousy I felt.

In the final days leading up to the trip, I became racked with worry. John hadn't been away from home before, at least not without Charlie and me. He was too young to make such a big trip. I was certain something was going to happen.

"How many guardians will be accompanying the students?" I asked the band director, Mr. Mandalay.

"We have six adults for forty-seven students. It was all outlined in the letter I sent home. Did John not give it to you?"

"Of course he did. But that's eight students per adult. I really don't think it's sufficient. You know how rowdy teenagers can get."

"'Rowdy' isn't an adjective generally used to describe band kids, Mrs. Sparks."

Charlie told me I was overreacting as usual. "Just be happy for him," he said.

"I am!"

"You can't control everything in his life."

"I'm not trying to."

The day of the departure, I drove John to the school parking lot in the dark hours of an April morning. We ran through the list of items he was taking, including the phone number of my aunt who lived in Winnipeg.

"She's expecting a visit," I said. "Be sure you call."

"I won't have time."

"Yes, you will. And I've already cleared it with Mr. Mandalay."

"Tell me you're joking."

There was a yellow school bus in the parking lot, surrounded by an assortment of cars. I saw students with suitcases and black cases, holding their instruments of choice. My son was with good people. Kind people. These were people who communicated with music, not fists. John asked me to pull over a fair distance from the school bus. He didn't want me to come any closer. I could live with that. I hugged him and kissed his cheek and told him to call me the minute he arrived in Winnipeg.

"You'll have a great time," I said as he opened the door. "And give my love to Aunt Eleanor."

I watched him as he crossed the parking lot, lit up by the twin beams of my headlights, his baritone case and suitcase alternately hitting the sides of his thighs. I parked in a far corner. His face was a blur in the window as the bus pulled away.

I went home and kept the radio on all day, listening for news of cars crossing medians or broken bridge railings. But there was nothing. The next evening, we received a collect call. He was fine. They were in Winnipeg. The hotel was nice. He hadn't called Aunt Eleanor yet, but promised he would. I pressed the telephone receiver tightly against my ear, trying to eliminate the distance between us.

A few days later, Aunt Eleanor phoned.

"When did you say John was coming?"

"He's there now," I said. "He hasn't called?"

"No. And I've got a ham in the fridge."

I called the hotel. There was no answer in John's room. It was seven o'clock. What was the time difference in Manitoba? I couldn't remember. I called Charlie at work, embarrassed by my worry.

"He should've called Eleanor by now, Charlie."

"There's no point getting worked up. I don't know why you insisted he visit her in the first place."

"She wanted to see him."

"Only after you told her he was coming."

"What if she saw him on the street?"

"She's never met him, Joyce."

The more I thought things through, the more I realized John had no intention of visiting Aunt Eleanor. My nails dug into my palms. I'd ground him the minute he stepped off the bus. I called Aunt Eleanor back.

"I'm awfully sorry, but I'm not sure John will be able to visit you. They're very busy with the competition. I hope that ham won't go to waste." I told her to call me if she heard from him. She never did.

The day of his return, I got to the parking lot earlier than needed. I sat there in the car, my arms crossed. This wasn't like him. John was always courteous and polite to a fault, especially around relatives. When I'd told him that Aunt Eleanor had six cats and was a pack rat, his interest had perked up.

"You like strange old women," I teased. "Why is that?"

He shrugged. "Most of them don't care if they're strange."

Eventually, the yellow bus pulled into the lot. I couldn't prevent the smile from spreading across my face. My son was home. It had been a week, and I'd missed him terribly. I'd found myself pacing the floors, uncertain what to do without him.

But my delight was short-lived. The second he got into the car, I knew something was wrong. I could smell it.

"Did you win?" I asked.

"We didn't even place," he said. "Some band from Kamloops won. I've never even heard of Kamloops."

"Did you have fun, at least?"

An uncertain nod.

"Aunt Eleanor called me."

"I didn't have time."

"She was expecting you, John."

"I didn't have time."

When we got back home, he went straight to his room and stayed there until I called him for dinner. I'd made his favourite—tuna casserole. He trudged down the hallway and pushed his food around his plate.

"Are you all right?" I asked. My thoughts immediately went to Angela.

"I'm fine," he said. "Just tired. It was a long bus ride home."

I assumed that, whatever the cause, his bad mood would clear up within a few days. But it didn't. If anything, his mood seemed to darken. When he looked at me, his eyes were unfocused. I was competing for attention against an enemy I couldn't see.

"Something happened," I whispered to Charlie. "In Winnipeg."

"Girl problems," Charlie said. "The redhead must've done something."

"He told me they're just friends."

"That's what all boys say."

John moved from one day to the next, seeming more and more distant as time went on. He refused to acknowledge that anything was wrong and insisted he was fine. As soon as he came home from school, he'd lock himself in his bedroom and practise his baritone. The sounds were so mournful. I'd press my ear against the door, hoping for some insight, some spoken fragments, but there was nothing. My panic rose with each passing day.

I turned to the only person who might have an answer. I found Angela's number in the phone book.

"Please don't tell John I called you," I said. "I'm worried about him. He's different since he got back from the trip. Do you know if something happened?"

"Not that I know of," she said slowly. "I didn't see him all that much."

"You didn't?"

"No. At least, not after we lost in the first rounds."

"Where did he go?"

"Nowhere. He was still at the hotel. But there were a lot of people at the competition. It was hard to keep track of anyone."

She paused. I wound the phone cord around my finger.

Then, very carefully, she said, "He made a new friend, from Quebec. A trumpet player. I don't know what his name was. The two of them really hit it off."

A jingle for a mattress store booms through the speakers. Why does everyone have to scream to be heard these days? I reach over and turn the radio off. I need to focus all of my concentration on the road ahead. I'm afraid something will dart in front of me. I know I'm supposed to keep driving, even if it means hitting it. That's what Charlie always told me.

"Never swerve. It's either your life or the raccoon's."

"I'm fine," I say aloud. "I'm perfectly capable. I just need to maintain a straight path. That's all."

People travel on highways every day. Thousands of them. Even this paltry stretch of road I'm on right now. Not even a highway. Just a two-lane road, no different from the one I take to the hairdresser or to the mall. I'm just going a little faster.

I clear my throat and grip the wheel tighter. In my rearview mirror, a transport truck shimmers to life. Within moments, it'll be right behind me. I'll make out the angry expression on the driver's face. He'll honk his horn. I'll press my foot down on the gas pedal to appease him. But it won't work. I can't go fast enough for him. I'll start to lose—

Stop.

I give my head a quick shake. Enough. I'm getting worked up over nothing. I'm on the highway to find out if Freddy Pender is alive and well and staying at the Seahorse Motel. This is insanity. It can't be real. I must be inside a dream.

I sometimes wondered what would've happened had Freddy stayed in Balsden. Would I have convinced myself that someone like him could've fallen in love with someone like me? Would we have had a relationship? Gotten married? Impossible. I knew it even back then. Freddy had his sights set on other things besides Balsden or me.

This, perhaps, is what upset me the most when he left. Not that he hadn't liked me, but that he found a way out. He escaped and left me standing on the sidelines.

My fingers grip the wheel. Why am I doing this, risking my life on this highway to confront a man I haven't seen in over fifty years? I'm not the person I used to be, so he won't be the same either. Freddy Pender can't make everything all right again.

There are only two cars in the parking lot at the Seahorse: one red, the other silver. No white limo. I pull into what seems like a discreet spot beneath a large maple tree and wait for my heart to return to its regular rhythm. My mind jumps to the drive home. The highway will be busier by that time, filled with trucks like lumbering dinosaurs. I take the compact from my purse and anxiously blot the shine from my nose.

Behind me sits a U-shape of red bricks and blue doors and the white backs of curtains. Is he in one of these rooms right now? Or is it all just a misunderstanding? I start to doubt myself again. Maybe I should've just gone back to Mrs. Pender and asked her directly. Would she lie about her own son's death? Never mind. I'm here now. I step out of the car, squinting against the sun's glare, and walk to the motel office, keeping my head down and my purse tight against my stomach.

A chubby girl with glasses is sitting behind a desk in the small office. She's watching a talk show on a television suspended from the ceiling by a pole. I hear someone yelling accusations, followed by audience applause.

"Can I help you?" Her eyes dart between the television and me.

"I'm looking for someone who might be staying here."

The girl moves over to her computer. "What's the last name?"

"Pender. Fred Pender." It feels surreal saying it.

The girl begins to type the name and I notice her dark roots running down the centre of her head. On TV, someone is told that the DNA results confirm that he's the baby's father, followed by a chorus of boos. When did stupidity become entertainment?

The girl blinks slowly. "No one here by that name."

"You're sure? Perhaps he might have checked out already."

The girl looks over my shoulder at the television. "No one here by that name."

"Thank you," I say as politely as I can.

Outside, the humidity slaps me like a damp washcloth. The asphalt beneath my sandals is a burnt crust. A car horn honks in the distance but I don't look up. It's not meant for me. I've already made myself a fool too many times today.

"Table for one," I tell the girl in gingham at the café across the street from the Seahorse. She takes a menu and leads me through a waist-level cloud of grey and white heads. We're everywhere, it seems. Seniors. We congregate in coffee shops with our bran muffins and decaf. We clog up lines at banks and drugstores. We smile from behind volunteer desks and ask if the question can be repeated. What nuisances we are.

I order tea and a muffin and sit back to scan the faces around me. Mouths pucker and stretch. Heads tilt. Fingers fumble with foil lids of butter packets. I thought things would be different at this stage of my life. I thought I might have some wisdom in return for sticking it out, some guru-on-the-mountain insight not found in people whose lives rolled out as perfectly as pastry. But there's nothing I can claim. No answers found. No riddles solved. Time moves from one tiny dot to the next, as it always has.

Cruel the way life cuts down hope. Seems to me the only way to cope is to have no hope at all.

There. That's my insight.

"Here we are."

The gingham girl places my muffin in front of me, a fat spaceship.

The morning after my phone call to Angela, I watched John eat his breakfast. I'd gotten up earlier to make him oatmeal with brown sugar.

"Busy day ahead of you?" I asked.

He shrugged. "I have a geography test this afternoon."

"You never mentioned you had a test."

He looked up from his bowl. "I didn't think it mattered."

"You hardly talk to me anymore. I never know what's going on in your world." I looked down at my red-flecked nails and decided to paint them that morning. John might like that. Did I still have a chance of being "pretty mommy" again?

"There's not much to tell."

"Oh?"

"Nothing interesting." His eyes narrowed. "Why are you bringing this up?"

"No reason. Just an observation." I took his empty bowl from him. "I suppose it's to be expected. You're getting older."

I set the bowl in the sink and turned on the tap. "Certainly too old to be mothered. You'll be out of here in no time."

"Not for a couple of years. I want to get my grade twelve."

"And then?"

He got up from the table. "I don't know."

"Not the refineries, John. Even your father doesn't want you doing shift work."

"There aren't many other choices in Balsden."

"I think you'd make a wonderful teacher."

"I don't."

"Or a social worker. You're so good with people."

"I likely won't stay in Balsden."

I felt a tremor in my knees. "You say that now."

"There's nothing here for me."

I stood at the living room window, watching him walk down the sidewalk to school. *There's nothing here for me.* When I couldn't see him any longer, I immediately went to his bedroom.

I shouldn't have let him go on that trip, I thought as I tossed sock balls from his dresser onto the floor. My hands slid between sweaters. I was certain I'd find something. A note I could confront him with. Hard evidence of what he was hiding. Who was this trumpet player? I'd demand. And what exactly happened on that trip? Don't you lie to me. I got down on my knees and opened the bottom drawer of his dresser. Next, I'd check his closet. And under the mattress. I knew a thing or two about hiding places.

"What are you doing?"

I glanced sideways and saw my son's shoes in the doorway.

"I was reorganizing things," I said, using the open drawers to help myself stand up again. "Why aren't you at school?"

"I forgot a book." He took a step towards me and I took a step back. "What are you looking for?"

"I told you what—"

He tried to snatch the jeans I had in my hand. "Drugs? Stolen goods?"

"I wasn't looking for anything. I was tidying up. Honestly, John, you're the messiest—"

"Don't lie to me! You're always lying to me!"

I took another step backwards. "I'm not lying."

"You're a hypocrite. You make me out to be the greatest son in the world and the second my back is turned, you're snooping through my stuff. You have no idea who I am."

A fuse lit inside of me. "I know plenty about you, mister. How is your friend in Quebec doing?"

There was a brief flash of confusion on his face. Then fear. Then rage, red as hot coal.

"You don't know anything. You're an idiot."

"Don't you talk to me like that!"

"You're a horrible, selfish person."

"John!"

"I can't wait to get away from you."

He grabbed a book from his desk and tore off down the hall. I heard the front door slam. I stood there in the silence, balled socks at my feet, a pair of lifeless jeans in my hands, and tried to catch my breath.

———

That morning in John's bedroom was the beginning of the end. A line had been crossed. Which one of us betrayed the other first? I think about these things sometimes, when I'm lying in bed at night or sitting in a café, a picked-apart muffin and a cup of lukewarm tea in front of me.

"Can I get you anything else?" gingham girl asks.

I shake my head. "Just the bill," I say.

I walk back to my car. My key touches the door lock and stops.

I'll take my life today.

The thought comes from nowhere. There's a bottle of pills in my dresser drawer. Charlie's painkillers, remnants from the final stages of his cancer. I've held on to them all these years. Expired, no doubt, but they'll do. Now everything falls into place. A feeling sweeps over me. A warm tide. A surrender. I'm ready to let all of this go. The key slides into the lock.

As I'm getting in, a white car pulls into the parking lot. It swerves into a spot farther down. I spin around to see the driver, holding my breath. No, I remind myself. He isn't here. Freddy's dead. Nevertheless, I dig through my purse to find my sunglasses and slide them on. I hear a car door open. Slowly, I turn my head. It's a man. From this distance and angle, I can't see his face. But he looks short. And chubby. He closes the trunk and walks towards a blue door.

I don't remember Freddy as short. No, he was taller than

me, I'm sure of it. But still. People shrink with age. Damn these sunglasses. Everything looks like dusk.

The curtains remain closed. I count to ten before slowly making my way across the parking lot, keeping my head down. What I wouldn't give for Helen's straw hat. I reach the back of the white car. I let my car keys fall from my hand.

"Silly me," I say, in case someone can hear, but there's no one in sight.

My knees crunch as I kneel down to pick them up. Placing my hand on the back bumper to steady myself, I focus on the licence place. There's a circle between the numbers. I take off my sunglasses and squint. An orange. Beneath it are two words in green letters.

Sunshine State.

- - - -

I'm in no mood for parties. I don't know how many times I need to tell Hilda this, but she's not getting the point.

"I don't care for music," I say. "Especially those tin drums. How is anyone supposed to enjoy that racket?"

"They're steel pan drums," Hilda says. "The band has travelled all the way from Toronto to play for the residents today." She frowns at me, as though I'm a naughty two-year-old. "It would be a shame."

Today is the annual Chestnut Park gala and all the chubby volunteers have descended on the home like seagulls on a bread crumb. All morning, I've been watching them hang pennants in the parking lot. Last year's gala theme was Italy Fest, and I couldn't go anywhere without bumping into green, white and red balloons. The volunteers scurried around with kerchiefs tied around their heads, saying things like "mamma mia" and "bunjurno" as they served us plates of mushy pasta and chicken cutlets sprinkled with oregano. Dessert was spumoni, which I've never been fond of. You're either a candied peel person or you're not.

Imagine the confusion among the residents when it came time for the entertainment and a dozen Ukrainian dancers came skipping out in their brocade vests and flowered headbands.

"The Italian singer we booked came down with laryngitis," Hilda told me later. "Thank god I still had the number for the Stoyko Dance Ensemble from last year."

This year's theme is "A Taste of the Caribbean." The Filipina nurse is wearing a T-shirt with "Jamaica . . . Yeah mon!" in scrawling letters across her tiny bust.

Hilda asks me to consider changing my mind. She'd hate for me to be sitting up here all alone while the party goes on.

"It might do you some good, Joyce," she said, placing her hand on the arm of my wheelchair.

I feel a hot flush of shame. I know what she's trying to tell me. I'm an ornery old woman, stuck in the misery of my own making. A wrinkled ball of harshness. I imagine the music of the steel drums sweeping over me, transporting me, awakening something inside I haven't felt for years.

I keep my hands in my lap and stare down at the grey smoke rolling out from the barbecue. Hilda tells me they're cooking something called jerk chicken. I manage to hold my tongue. If I see Timothy, I may go down. It would be rude not to say hello.

As if reading my mind, Hilda says, "Timothy won't be there. He didn't respond to my email."

"I'm fine right where I am," I say.

Ruth is still in the hospital. It's been three weeks now and they won't tell me anything. Not even the hospital where she's staying. I'm bothered by thoughts of her lying terrified in a strange bed wearing that green mask. Does she know if she's coming back here? Does she understand that people are concerned about her?

"Maybe I can help," Timothy had said.

"How?"

"I'll visit her."

"They won't tell you where she is."

"Sure they will. It's Ruth we're talking about, not Jimmy Hoffa. Just give me one second."

His hand grazed my shoulder. It was the first time we'd touched. I noticed a silver ring on his middle finger. He's a nice young man. Kind. There aren't many people like that in the world. I want to ask him things, personal questions, but I can't. All I can manage is what I asked him last week:

"Why do you come here?" This was after we had a lengthy discussion about the woes of rheumatoid arthritis. "Don't tell me you enjoy listening to old people complain."

He shrugged. "I think of it as a matter of insurance."

"In what way?"

"That when I'm old, someone will visit me."

"You don't have children." I meant this as a question, but it came out as a statement.

"Just a schnauzer."

"You should bring your dog in sometime. I'd like to meet him."

"He'll likely pee on the floor."

"Then he'll fit right in."

Timothy was soon back in my room. "Well, that took all of three seconds. She's at Our Lady of Mercy."

"The *Catholic* hospital?"

"I'll go tomorrow afternoon and then stop by here."

"You don't have to do this."

"I don't mind. Now. What do you want me to tell her?"

"Tell her . . ." I looked over at the photograph of John on my dresser. "Tell her I'm waiting for her."

After he left, my energy evaporated. My arms became heavy and my hands started to itch. In the past couple of days, I'd felt my heart pause, deciding whether it should keep beating. I looked up to see a woman reflected in the window. She startled me. Her hair was a pulled-apart cotton ball. For a moment, I thought it was Mrs. Pender. But of course it wasn't. She's been dead for years.

"Me," I decided.

It's almost a week since the gala, and I'm anxious for Timothy's arrival. I putter around the room, rearranging the plants on my window ledge. When did he say he was going to the hospital? I don't remember.

When noon rolls around, I decide to opt out of lunch and wait in my room.

"I'm not hungry," I tell the fire-headed nurse.

"Nonsense," she says. "It's Spaghetti Saturday."

She wheels me into the dining room, parks me at my table and ties a blue-and-white-checked bib around my neck before I can say a word of protest. I'm left staring at the vacant faces of my tablemates.

"Henry, let me switch sides with you," I say. "I want to keep an eye on the hall. I'm expecting company."

He looks confused and perhaps he has good reason. The only other thing I've ever said to him is "Hand me the ketchup." But he pulls back from the table and, with some considerable manoeuvring, we manage to switch places. Irene stares at me. There's a piece of spaghetti stuck to her chin.

"Nothing wrong with a change in scenery," I say, reaching for a roll from the basket.

Timothy doesn't come until mid-afternoon.

"How's Ruth?" I ask before he even has a chance to sit down. He's wearing a smart jacket. It's black with grey stripes. John used to like jackets as well. Charlie did, too, now that I think about it. Did they notice the things they had in common?

"Tired, but good," he says. "I had to put on a gown and a mask and gloves. I'm not sure she even knew who I was."

"Did you say hello to her for me?"

He sits down on the bed. "Yes. I said you were waiting for her."

"Did you speak with a doctor?"

He shakes his head. "The nurse wouldn't tell me any-thing. I'm not family, after all. But I saw no reason why she wouldn't be leaving soon. They're likely keeping her there as a precautionary measure. I'm sure she'll be back within a week. Guaranteed."

"There are no guarantees in life," I tell him. Then I pause. "You did a very nice thing. Not only for Ruth, but also for me. Kindness is hard to find. Especially in this day and age."

"You really believe that?"

"You don't?"

"I think what goes around, comes around. Maybe you have some acts of kindness owing to you."

I nearly laugh. "That couldn't be further from the truth."

He wags his finger at me. "You're too hard on yourself, Mrs. Sparks."

"Call me Joyce. And you don't know the first thing about me."

"I beg to differ," he says.

CHAPTER EIGHT

It was a Tuesday in April, a few weeks after John's return from Winnipeg. Charlie was working days. I listened to him get dressed in the darkness of the bedroom that morning. The clank of his belt buckle. His dresser drawers sliding out. The floorboards creaking beneath his socked feet. Sounds so familiar to me after all those years. When we were first married, I'd get up to have breakfast with him. I believed it was important for us to share those early-morning moments. But not anymore. I kept my eyes shut and the covers wrapped around me, waiting until I saw the flash of the headlights on the bedroom's far wall.

How sad for Charlie, I think now. To get up in that darkness, morning after morning. I imagine him on those drives into work, a lunch box beside him (one he'd packed himself, as I stopped doing that years ago as well), perhaps the radio news to keep him company, if news was even broadcast at that hour, the oil drums rising in the distance, the dull humming of machines, the smell of crude oil wafting in through the vents of the car. What a landscape compared to wheat fields.

I got out of bed and went into the hall. John's door was closed, as usual. I'd wake him for school in a half-hour. He'd become so lethargic in the mornings, moving from bedroom to bathroom to kitchen like someone dragged into existence. I ate toast, listened to the radio and brought in the milk when I heard the delivery truck pull away. By then it was seven o'clock. I went down the hall and knocked on John's door.

"Time to get up," I called and opened the door. His bed was empty. I tried to remember if he had band practice that morning. No. He had practice on Wednesdays and Fridays. Had he mentioned a school meeting? Then I saw the piece of paper on top of his pillow. I knew then. My son had left. I turned on the light and read the letter with shaking hands.

Mom and Dad. I'll call you when the time is right. Don't worry about me. John.

Somehow, my fingers managed to dial Charlie's work number. When had he left? It must've been in the middle of the night. My boy. What have you done?

"Where would he go?" Charlie asked.

"I don't know." But I had my suspicions. Was John hitch-hiking his way towards Quebec at that moment?

"We'll find him," Charlie said.

I called Angela as soon as I hung up with Charlie. Her mother answered the phone.

"Angela's in the bathroom," Mrs. Dawber said. "Who's calling?"

"It's Joyce Sparks. John's mother. I need to speak with Angela. My son has run away."

"Oh, dear. Hold on, Mrs. Sparks."

I heard the hard bounce of the phone landing on the floor. This couldn't be happening. John was playing a joke. A trick to get back at me for looking through his things.

"Mrs. Sparks?"

"Angela, John has run away. I found a note on his bed. Do you know anything about this? You have to tell me. Did he say where he was going?"

"No. He didn't tell me anything."

"Are you lying to me?"

"No, Mrs. Sparks. Honest. I haven't even talked to John for the past week."

I brought the phone close to my lips and lowered my voice. "Is he with the trumpet player? Don't be embarrassed to tell me."

"The trumpet . . . ? I don't know what you mean."

"Did he tell you what happened between him and the trumpet player? In Winnipeg? Tell me, Angela."

I heard muffled noise followed by a brief pause.

"Mrs. Sparks, it's Mrs. Dawber again. Angela says she doesn't know anything. But if she hears anything from your son, I promise we'll contact you right away. You'll have to excuse us, but Angela has to get ready for school. Goodbye."

Helen assured me he'd be home in a day or two.

"Wild oats," she reasoned over the phone. "I told you about the time I found alcohol in Mark's bag, didn't I?"

"Helen, my son has *run away*. We're not talking about a few sips from a vodka bottle. I'm going crazy with worry. Charlie is driving the streets as we speak."

"Joyce." She spoke my name as though it was something painful in her mouth. "I know there are certain things we don't discuss. Sometimes I wish we talked more. We're sisters, after all. I'm always here for you."

Why was she saying this? I had no time for her sentimentality. I looked up at the kitchen clock. Thirty minutes had passed since I discovered John was gone.

"I know, Joyce. About John."

"You know what?"

"I don't feel comfortable saying it. So I won't. But you know what I'm talking about. And I'm not blaming you. You've been a good mother. I can see that."

"I don't know what you're talking about," I said. There was a mark on my kitchen wall, just beside the oven. How long had it been there?

"John isn't right, Joyce. Even Mark and Marianne know that. They told me he gets picked on at school. They say John brings it on himself. That he acts different."

The mark on the wall looked like a hand. A little red hand.

"Have you ever tried seeing someone? A doctor, I mean. For John."

"You mean a psychiatrist."

"Yes. Or not even. Maybe all he needs is to talk to a school counsellor. Or a friend. I'm sure Mark or Marianne could give him some advice. They care about John. We *all* do, Joyce."

John had told me once that Marianne showed him a line of hickies on her stomach and that Mark was barely scraping by in most of his classes. They were the last people my son needed advice from.

She cleared her throat. "Mark told me that John tried to kiss him once."

"What?" I laughed but felt my stomach twist.

"It happened a long time ago. When they were kids. Obviously, it upset Mark a great deal. He looked up to John. Don't say anything. I promised Mark I'd never tell."

"That's ridiculous. Mark is telling lies."

"Why would he lie about something like *that*, Joyce?"

I suddenly felt naked and wrapped my bathrobe tighter around me. How could my sister say that? No one knew John. Especially not Helen. Especially not her *children*. Had things slipped past me? Had I lost my grip? *He gets picked on at school.* That's what she'd said. But it wasn't true. Couldn't be. John had never said anything of the sort. Besides, he had band. He had friends. He'd just gone to Winnipeg. He was my son, for god's sake. I knew him better than anyone.

"You've got no right speaking about John this way," I said. "Especially at a time like this."

"I'm sorry. I shouldn't have said anything."

"It's too late for apologies now."

I hung up the phone and attacked the mark on the wall with my fingernails.

———

There's a small gash on door number 12 of the Seahorse Motel. I try to ignore it and instead focus on the peephole staring back at me. If it's Freddy, it might take him a second or two to recognize me. It's been years, after all. Oh, god. I look nothing like the girl I once was. In any case, it's best to attempt a friendly face, even though I'm not sure I have the strength to hoist up the corners of my mouth. I knock once on the door and step back, shivering in spite of the heat.

Seconds tick by. I knock again, this time more loudly. He could be hard of hearing. It was number 12 that he went into, wasn't it? I step back from the door to look at the other numbers. Yes, it was 12. Or had it been 13? No, it was 12. Definitely 12. I turn around to look at the car again. It's big and white. I think of Mrs. Pender waiting for a white limousine. Had it finally arrived?

The deadbolt clicks behind me. I swing around. The door opens a crack.

"I don't need housekeeping, thank you." The door closes.

"Wait!" I say, knocking again. "I'm not the maid. I'm Joyce."

"Pardon?" The door opens again, slightly wider this time. Now there's an eye between the door and the frame. Half a nose. "You're *whom?*"

"Joyce Sparks," I say. "Conrad, I mean. Joyce Conrad." My words spill out. Oh, god. Is it him? It can't be. "I took the highway. I never drive— Well, I do, just not— Are you . . . ?" I take a step closer. "Is that you, Freddy?"

The eye widens and the door shuts. I hear the chain rattle. The door swings open.

The man standing in front of me is chubby and short. Although he looks to be around the same age as me, there's a too-thick mass of dyed auburn curls covering his head. He pushes a pair of gold-rimmed glasses up his nose with a stubby finger. I see a flash of rings. It's not him.

"I've made a mistake. Excuse me." I turn and start to walk away.

"Wait!" I hear. "You knew Fred?"

My feet stop dead in their tracks. I turn on my heel. "Fred?"

The man puts a hand on his hip. He's wearing a black shirt with orange and green geometrical shapes. "Well, that's what you said, wasn't it?"

"Yes. That's what I said. Fred."

"I thought so." The man steps out from the dark room and into the sunlight. He shields his eyes with his hand. "What did you say your name was?"

"Joyce. Sparks is my married name, but Conrad was my maiden name. Who are you?"

"I'm Walter Clarke." He says this as though I should know.

"Oh," I say. "Have we met before?"

"Not that I'm aware of."

"I see." This is shaping up to be one of the most confusing moments of my life. "But you know the Freddy I'm talking about?"

"Quite well, as a matter of fact. Fred was my partner. I don't mean business partner. I mean life partner. The word 'lover' leaves less room for interpretation, but I don't like the connotation. As though all you do is feed each other grapes. It's lucky you caught me. I just got back from visiting Freddy's mother at the Fading Sunset."

"You mean the Golden Sunset?"

"Fading, Golden, Final." He rolls his eyes and swats the air. "Call it what you like. The place smells like piss and plug-in air fresheners. It's nasal rape. I'm sorry I didn't answer the door right away. Truth is, I'm a little on edge." His voice drops to a hoarse whisper. "Motels make me nervous. I hear a knock and I jump fifty feet in the air. I've watched too many horror movies. Fred said this was the only decent motel in the area. But there must be *something* closer to Balsden. I'm so sick of the drive. Did you work at the ice cream shop?"

"Yes. How did you know?"

"Oh, he told me about you." He peers over my shoulder. "This is the first time I've been here. To Ontario, I mean. It's quite charming, really. Lots of trees. And fields. Fruit stands, too." He frowns. "I haven't seen a moose, though."

"Freddy mentioned me?"

"That's right. He talked about his life in Balsden on occasion."

What did he say about me? I want to ask. What did I mean to him? I feel like a jilted teenager all over again.

"When did you arrive?"

"Monday."

"From Florida?"

"Miami. I own a restaurant there. Have you ever been?"

"To the restaurant?"

"No, to Miami."

"I don't think so."

He crosses his arms. "You don't remember if you've been to Miami?"

"No, I've never been to Miami." My head is spinning. I need to sit down.

"It's a wonderful city."

"I don't know— This isn't—"

He takes a step towards me. "You don't have a heart condition, do you? I had a feeling this wouldn't go well."

"What wouldn't go well?"

"Coming here." He pushes his glasses up again. "To Fred's hometown. What a mess she made of things."

"Who?"

He looks at me with an expression somewhere between annoyance and pity. "Do you want to grab a coffee, Joyce? You're looking a little pale."

He retreats into the motel room. I turn around to face the parking lot, pressing my hand against my forehead. What on earth is happening?

He comes out wearing a pair of black sunglasses that swallow half his head. We make our way across the parking lot towards the café.

"On the drive up here, I saw a goose," he says. "A Canada goose. Fred told me they shit something horrible. They migrate between the north and the south, don't they? Like seniors."

We find a table in a corner.

"Doesn't it seem like the worst restaurants are always the closest?"

He sighs and flips open the menu. My eyes scan the café for familiar faces. I'm embarrassed to be sitting with him. The last thing I need is to be seen with a strange-looking homosexual.

Fred was my partner. That's what he said. It can only mean one thing. Freddy was a homosexual. *Was.* That means Fred isn't alive. I notice a couple at another table look over with a sly smile. What are they thinking? I want to get away from this man, but I can't. I need to know what's going on. I need the truth.

Gingham girl does a double take when she comes to our table. She must think I'm crazy. This time I order a blueberry muffin and an orange juice.

"Are the sausages pork or beef?" Walter asks.

"Pork," she says. "I think. I can check with the cook."

"No, don't bother." His hands fly through the air. I've never seen so many rings on a man before. There's a ruby the size of a postage stamp on his pinkie finger. He glances over at me. "Why am I even asking about sausages? It's like shopping when you have no money." He turns his attention back to the waitress. "Is it possible to get an omelette made with egg whites?"

The waitress scratches her head with the tip of her pencil. "I suppose?"

He removes his glasses and massages the bridge of his nose. "My dear, make it a bran muffin and a coffee."

He leans across the table after she walks away. "Is it just me or are people getting stupider? I blame it on television."

I clear my throat and lay my hands flat on the table. "Just so I'm clear, Mr. Clarke. Freddy isn't alive, correct?"

"No. He died two months ago of cancer."

"Two *months* ago . . . You mean to say he didn't jump from the deck of a cruise ship?"

"Oh, god. She could have at least made him disappear by doing something heroic. Rescuing someone from a fire, or taking a bullet for a nun. Even a car accident." He picks up the salt shaker and squints at it. "I never understood why they put rice in the salt. There must be a reason."

"It absorbs the moisture," I say. "Who's the 'she' you're talking about?"

"Mrs. Pender, of course."

The waitress comes back with our order. I stare dumbly at the muffin she places in front of me.

"Fred never forgave her for those lies." He splits his muffin and spreads a thin layer of butter across each half. "Not that you'd ever forgive your mother for killing you off. But a *suicide*." He shakes his head. "Even in death, she stripped him of any dignity. Fred would never have killed himself. He'd been through some hard times, mind you. But give me a break."

He takes a bite of his muffin. Crumbs land on his geometrical shapes.

"She's a psychopath. I really believe that. How else could you explain it? Not that *my* mother ever accepted me. But she never threw me off a ship."

I'm acutely aware of everything around me, as though I've suddenly developed superhero powers. I hear Walter's teeth clicking together as he chews. The sugar landing at the bottom of his coffee cup. The rustling of his nose hair as he exhales.

"I suppose you can tell we've never gotten along. Mrs. Pender and I, that is. I tried to find a way to relate to her, especially during those early years. I complimented her hair. Asked how she maintained her figure. Blah, blah, blah. You know—what women like to hear. But she wouldn't have it. I was the evildoer, you see. I had corrupted her son."

He swallows and I hear a glob of muffin glide down his throat. I feel nauseous.

"Not that Fred hadn't been corrupted long before me." He winks. "I often wonder if she has a heart at all. Sometimes I try to picture it. But all I can ever see is a small grey fossil tucked behind her rib cage. It doesn't beat so much as rattle. I can't believe she's lived this long. God must be avoiding her." He stops and looks down at his muffin. "This tastes like a barnyard."

"Mine tastes fine," I say, before realizing I haven't even taken a bite. "Will you excuse me for a minute?"

I take my purse and hurry to the bathroom. I lock myself into a stall, pull out my teeth and vomit into the toilet bowl. This isn't happening. It's not possible. But there's the swirl of my vomit in the water. And a man I didn't know ten minutes ago is sitting out there, saying things that can't possibly be true. I flush the toilet and sit down on the seat. Freddy was alive all those years. And to have this Walter person, this complete stranger, sit across from me and speak about his life without an ounce of discretion, without any regard for . . . talking so matter-of-factly about his relationship—if you can even call it that—with another man. I'm certain people at other tables overheard him. They'll assume things about me. I'll have to endure their whispers. The horizontal slide of their eyes. The pointed fingers. I can't go back out there and face all of that. I'll wait in here until the café closes. Until they've all gone home. The back of my throat burns. My teeth stare back at me in my hand, a lipless smile.

After three days away, my son called home.

"Where are you?"

"I'm fine," he said. "I'm not telling."

"You come home. Immediately."

"Not yet."

"Why did you go, John? Did something happen?"

"I need some time on my own."

"Where are you? Tell me that at least."

"No. Not now."

"I've been so worried. Do you have any idea what you've put your father and me through?"

"This isn't about you."

Two nights later, Charlie and I were sitting at the kitchen table eating dinner when we heard the front door open. My fork paused mid-air. I looked at Charlie. He looked at me. And then our prodigal son was standing in the doorway.

"I'm back," he said to the kitchen curtains. Then he walked down the hall to his room and shut the door. Charlie and I ate the rest of our meal in silence. I think we were afraid that if one of us spoke, the mirage we'd just witnessed would disappear into the air.

Later, after Charlie had gone to work, I made up a plate of food and went to John's room. He was sitting on his bed, his arms wrapped around his shins, his chin resting on his knees.

"I thought you might be hungry," I said and placed the food on his desk. I sat down on the edge of the bed. "I won't ask you where you went or who you saw. I don't want to know."

He looked at me, his eyes wide with disbelief.

"I don't *need* to know," I said. "No one needs to know."

"But I want to tell you. I have to tell someone."

I couldn't allow that. Not after all these years of trying to set him right. "No you don't. You don't have to tell anyone anything."

"If you only knew half the things that go on in my mind. Nothing ever seems right with me. Everything is so wrong."

"Saying something out loud makes it real. And what you're going through isn't real, John. It's an illusion."

"If I don't say it, I'll go crazy." He was sobbing by this point, and it took every ounce of strength not to reach out and take him into my arms. I needed to be strong.

"John—"

"I met him on the band trip. I wrote to him when I got back and he said he'd meet me in Ottawa."

"Please keep quiet."

"We met up at the bus station and we drove to a hotel."

"You don't mean this. This never happened." I closed my eyes. Inside me, a sound began to build. A hum.

"I felt sick afterwards and threw up in the bathroom. He took me back to the bus station. He didn't even say goodbye."

"You have no idea—" The hum was building in its pitch. I'd worked so hard. I'd given everything to fix this. *Everything*.

"I couldn't come back home. I wandered around the city for days. I was so tired and afraid. Why didn't he stay with me? He was nice in Winnipeg. What did I do wrong?"

This was not happening. I was not hearing my son say these words.

"I got lost, Mom."

Mom. My eyes sprung open and I grabbed his wrist. "You're home now. You're safe. Tomorrow morning, you'll get up and go to school and soon, it will be like Ottawa never happened. We will never talk about this again. Do you understand?"

He shook his head. "But it *did* happen."

"That doesn't make it true, John."

"It *is* true. How can you say it isn't? I'm different. I know that. I'm like a jigsaw puzzle where none of the pieces fit together. There are parts of me I hate, but there are parts of me I like. I don't know how to sort it all out." He looked at me then, so young in that moment. Younger than I ever thought I'd see him again.

"It's not natural, John. It's not the way things go. You need to take control. You have to change."

He looked away. Then asked in a voice so quiet I barely heard the words, "But what if I don't want to change?"

I rose from the bed. "Stop being selfish! It's not always about what *you* want. Think of your father. What if he found out about you? His only son. You should be ashamed of yourself."

He started weeping again. A low, mournful note. I thought of his baritone. I'd found his Achilles heel. I told myself I'd won this round and brushed the dirt from my hands.

"Eat your dinner," I said and left the room.

I wipe my mouth with a square of toilet paper and step out of the stall. I need to get out of here. I can't go back to the table and sit with that man while he talks about omelettes and salt shakers and his perversion. I set my purse on the ledge of the sink and examine my face in the mirror. Lipstick. I need lipstick. I root through my purse.

I'd stood on Mrs. Pender's front porch after I learned about Freddy's death. I'd made date squares. She'd looked at me with such incomprehension. Such loss. How could she take those squares from me? How could Freddy allow me to believe he was dead?

I find my lipstick and run it across my lips, but my hand won't stop shaking and I have to keep wiping the colour away with my square of toilet paper. This is some kind of joke. A trick. I look around the bathroom, convinced I'll see a camera lodged in the paper towel dispenser or a television host peeping out from under a stall. I've been duped. They think it's so easy to fool a woman like me.

I finish applying my lipstick and walk out of the restroom. I don't stop. I walk right past Walter. I walk until I'm out the door and into the steely shine of the morning sun.

———

My son died twice. I used to believe the first time he died was in the schoolyard that day, as he lay in the centre of that ring of boys, muddied and bloodied in his green coat. But that was me taking the easy way out. It was simpler, less horrific if I could point the finger at anyone else except myself.

But time won't let you get away with much. Not for long. And eventually, that finger began to shift like the arrow of a weather vane and I found myself staring at the black, pointed head of the truth I'd been avoiding for most of my grown life.

The real moment of that first death, the true one, took place in a bedroom with a crying boy and a mother walking out.

The click of the door shutting behind me could've been the shot of a handgun for all it mattered. My son had asked for help. And I cut him down. I believed I was doing the right thing at the time. I thought I knew best, the way all mothers think they know best, especially when it comes to their children. But they don't. Mothers know only what's best for them.

What would he have said to me if I'd let him? That he'd fallen in love with a boy? How would I have responded? What *could* I have said? There was no place for that answer in the world. No room. Not then. Nothing but a silence so heavy you could feel its weight in your palm.

The parking lot at the Golden Sunset is half empty at this time of the day. A few residents sit on the wraparound porch, blankets over their laps in spite of the heat. I scan their faces, but Mrs. Pender isn't one of them. She never goes outside. She may be having a mid-morning nap. No matter. I'll shake her until she wakes up. I'll tell her there's a strange man in town. That he's telling lies about Freddy. Then I'll hand over the Mother's Day card, take the library book, and never set foot in her room again.

I mount the front steps, avoiding the faces of the people I pass. Someone says "Good afternoon" but I pretend not to hear. I pass the nurses' station. More residents line the halls, and I think of garbage cans on curbs, waiting for pickup. My heart is a fist. Vomit rises in my throat again and I swallow it down.

Up the stairs. Up to the second floor where she lives. The woman in the shoe who had so many children, she didn't know what to do. As my feet take the steps, I notice the carpeting for the first time. It's thick and dusty white. I should've replaced the carpet in my house. It's all buckled now. Ridges so high I trip on them if I'm not careful. Whoever buys my house will no doubt tear it all up to reveal the hardwood beneath. I bet it's a young couple. Perhaps they have a child. A son. I'll leave a note for them on the kitchen counter.

Hold tight to everything.

Mrs. Pender's door is partly shut. The paper acorn dangles. It's moments away from falling. I push open the door.

She's sitting beside her bed, wearing that cranberry cardigan. She looks up at me and in the flash of the moment, she looks happy to see me. Her face widens. Wrinkles soften. Her mouth falls open, about to speak.

"Whuh, whuh, whuh-whuh." Mrs. Ogilvy waves from her bed. I nod in her direction, but I can't take my eyes off Mrs. Pender. I don't move from the doorway.

"I'm glad you're here. I found that book." Mrs. Pender points towards her dresser.

"You've lied," I say, my voice flat. "All this time, you've done nothing but lie."

"I don't know what you're talking about."

I take a step into the room. "Freddy never killed himself. He never jumped off a ship. You made it all up."

She's quiet for a second, but when she speaks, her voice is a screech. "Don't you come in here talking like that!"

"All these years, your son was alive."

"I'm going to call the nurse if you keep this up."

"You're a sick woman."

"Mrs. Ogilvy, pull the cord."

"You should be ashamed of yourself."

"Pull the cord!"

"There's no need for that, Cruella."

I turn around to see Walter standing in the doorway, his forehead glistening and chest heaving. He wags a finger at me. "You, my dear, owe me three dollars and forty-four cents. Plus gas."

"How did you know where to find me?" I ask.

"Women's intuition," he says.

"I told you I didn't want you back here!" Mrs. Pender yells at him. "I've got no more business with you."

"Is that any way to talk to your favourite son-in-law?" He

steps into the room. "Perhaps Mrs. Ogilvy might appreciate that new cardigan more than you do."

"Whuh."

"You've got no right to follow me," I tell him. I open my purse and begin fumbling for my wallet. "If it's the money you want, I'll give it to you. Then you need to be on your way."

"I'm not here for money, Joyce. I'm here because you looked like death warmed over at the café. You were as white as a sheet when you walked out. I was worried. This must be very troubling for you."

"Troubling?" I laugh at the absurdity of his words. "I'm not troubled. *She's* troubled." I point at Mrs. Pender.

"I'm troubled by many things," Mrs. Pender says. "Laziness. Greed. The shirt he's wearing."

"Fred always said you'd have to pay the piper one day," Walter replies, stepping towards her.

"I've been paying the piper for ninety-seven years now." She turns her head. "Mrs. Ogilvy, pull that cord!"

Something explodes inside of me, sending tremors through my bones, blurring my vision. I march over to Mrs. Pender. "I sat here and listened to your misery. I pitied you because you had no one, because you'd lost a son. But you had him all along. What kind of a mother would lie about the death of her own child?"

"I know about you, Joyce," she says quietly. "Word gets around in a place like Balsden. Nothing stays a secret very long. You had a son, too."

"Don't you dare bring John into this!"

"He lived in Toronto, didn't he? I remember hearing he was a chef at a fancy restaurant. Never married. No children. An early death. I read the notice in the paper."

"Be quiet!"

"No cause of death given, from what I remember."

"He had cancer!"

"Joyce—"

Something sounds in the distance. An electronic pulse. Mrs. Ogilvy has pulled the buzzer. I feel a hand on my arm and yank it away. "Don't touch me. Don't anyone touch me!"

The buzzer bleats.

"Perhaps we had things in common," Mrs. Pender says, her mouth a crooked slash. "Things we never talked about. Mother to mother."

"I have nothing in common with you!"

"Is everything all right in here?"

I glance over my shoulder and see a woman in a uniform.

"Everything's fine," Walter says. "I think."

And before another word is said, I rush out of the room.

Rushing. Rushing. Panic always rising inside me. I had to keep watch over my son. I couldn't let him get away. Couldn't let him escape again. The words of that kindergarten teacher had haunted me: *Keep a close eye on him.*

So long as John lived in my house, within my walls, he'd be safe.

And for a time, things were fine again. He came and went to school. He got a part-time job working as a stock boy at Dove's

Grocers. I'd wait for him in the parking lot at the end of his shifts and watch him walking towards the car, tugging at the black bow tie around his collar. He was getting older. Taller. There were bristles on his chin. He was becoming a man.

"Everything will turn out," I promised myself and him. John was a good boy. He'd find a nice girl to settle down with. They'd have children. Charlie and I would go over there on Sunday afternoons for dinner. I'd tell John's wife stories about when he was younger. She'd look lovingly in his direction, wondering how she ever landed someone as special as him. And I'd laugh in such a carefree way as I passed the mashed potatoes or played hide-and-seek with the grandkids. I'd been so silly. There hadn't been a thing to worry about. It had all worked out in the end.

A few months before he graduated from high school, John told Charlie and me he was planning to go to college. "For chef training," he said.

"When did this all come about?" I'd been holding on to the hope that he might go to teachers' college. It would be a safe and respectable career.

"I've been thinking about it for a while. I could make good money, although I'd be working mostly evenings and weekends."

"Sounds good to me," Charlie said.

"I didn't know they had a chef course at Balsden College," I said.

"They don't. But the college in Andover has one. I could get a diploma in two years' time. Mark is planning to go there too, for engineering. We've talked about sharing an apartment."

"Mark?" I asked, casting a sideways glance in Charlie's direction. My sister's revelation had been burned into my mind. Neither of us had mentioned it again. But something was different between us. There was a noticeable shift. I resented her for observing something that I'd worked so hard to keep secret. I hated her suspicions about John. At times, I'd catch her looking over at him, her verdict written all over her face. It galled me. Her children weren't perfect. It wasn't as though she was living some charmed life.

But if Mark was really that uncomfortable around John, as Helen had claimed, why would he agree to share a place with him? And why would Helen agree to let the two of them live together? Still, I didn't like the idea of John being so far away.

"It's a forty-minute drive," Charlie said later that evening. "We'll see him once a week."

"Andover is a much bigger city than Balsden," I said.

"My work would give him a scholarship," Charlie said, completely bypassing my worries. He looked genuinely excited. I couldn't remember the last time I'd seen him like this. "His grades are good enough. I'll talk to the administration person tomorrow."

"The boys have their differences," Helen said the next day. I noticed an edge of caution in her voice. "But they're family. Besides, I feel better about Mark staying with John rather than a bunch of strangers. Don't you?"

Yes, I did. But the only way I could control things was if John went to the college here and lived at home. The moment he was on his own, away from me, bad things would happen. He needed to be monitored.

"You have to let them go sometime," Helen said. "God help us mothers."

When late summer rolled around, we packed up the car and moved John to his new apartment. I was silent on the drive, my thoughts heavy. Mark, Helen and Dickie were at the apartment when we arrived. Helen had sewn curtains for the kitchen, and both of us packed the boys' freezer with foil-wrapped dinners. Dickie looked ragged, a hollowed-out souvenir of his younger self. I don't know how Helen had managed throughout the years. He made a joke about the number of women who'd be coming through the front door and we all laughed. Helen playfully hit him in the arm with a tea towel.

"These boys need to keep their priorities straight," she said, pointing her finger at John and Mark. "School, school, school. No girls. There will be plenty of time for that once you graduate."

I glanced at John and he looked away.

Charlie and I drove home in silence. As we turned onto our street, he reached over and took my hand. "He'll be fine, Joyce."

I said nothing.

"My son is a college student." He shook his head, a half-believing grin on his face. Charlie had only gone as far as grade eight. I realized that underneath my layers of worry, I was proud of John, too. My son was going further than his father and I ever had. Still, I couldn't shake the dark thoughts that hovered above my head in the weeks that followed. I would take precautions.

"I don't want you spying, of course," I told Mark a few weeks later. "It's not that I don't trust him. I do. But John can be too nice for his own good. Gullible. There's a chance he could fall in with the wrong crowd."

"I don't see much chance of that happening," Mark said. "He hardly ever goes out."

"He's shy," I said. "Just keep an eye on your cousin, Mark. If you see anything that alarms you—anything at all—let me know."

"Aunt Joyce, are you talking about drugs?"

"No," I said. "Not drugs." I bit my lips as I mapped out my next words. "You're a good nephew, Mark. I'm glad you're with John. It makes me feel better. But I need your help. *John* needs your help, even if he doesn't know it. If you see anything that doesn't seem normal, you let me know right away, all right? You need to call me, Mark."

"I will," he said. "But to be honest, John's always been a little weird."

I lightened my tone. "Do you have a girlfriend, Mark?"

"A what?"

"A girlfriend. Someone you go out with."

"Not really."

"If you do meet someone, she might have a friend. Then you and John could go on double dates together. That would be fun, wouldn't it?"

"I suppose," he said, but the words came out sounding like a question.

I usually spoke to John twice during the week and on Sundays. We'd talk about his classes and how they were going and if Mark was getting under his skin and if he was eating well.

"I'm fine," he'd say. "Everything is fine."

Fine. A four-letter word. I hated hearing it because it told me nothing. I'd ramble on about the mundane details of my life: what we'd eaten for supper the previous night, who I ran into at the grocery store, the colour I was thinking of painting the living room. Looking back, I think I believed that so long as I kept talking, nothing would go wrong. There wasn't enough space between my words for problems. How he must've hated those phone calls.

"Have you met any friends?"

"A couple of people in class. I don't really have time to socialize much. The workload is heavy. More than I imagined it would be."

He came home for Thanksgiving with a sack of dirty laundry over his shoulder and hair that hung over his forehead. He'd lost weight and looked tired. When I mentioned it to him, he said I was overreacting. I piled his plate up with mashed potatoes and gave him an extra dollop of Dream Whip on his pumpkin pie. He ate everything and raided my pantry for canned goods that he rammed into his laundry sack amongst the jeans and shirts I'd washed, ironed and folded so neatly. And then he went back to a life I knew nothing about.

———

After leaving the Golden Sunset, I drive in circles around Balsden, turning down streets I've known my entire life. I pass the house where Helen and I grew up. I stop in front of my old high school, the church where Charlie and I got married. The hospital where John was born. Then I pull over on some no-name side street, lean my head against the steering wheel and cry.

I drive to the grocery store, anger building in me now. How could Mrs. Pender have lied like that? I leave my sunglasses on to hide my red eyes and accidentally bring down a display of toilet paper at the end of an aisle.

"I'm sorry," I say to the stock clerk and hurry away. I find daisies in the florist section. The white petals and mustard-coloured buttons call to me. I need their simplicity.

The flowers are sitting next to me on the passenger seat, wrapped in brown paper. They won't last more than a day or two, but I don't care. I usually buy artificial roses in the summer, but not now. This time, I want something real.

I've seen other women, tending after graves the way you would a house. They water the grass. Plant flowers. Decorate the tombstones with trinkets and candles. I used to watch them as I sat on the bench next to the plot that John and Charlie now share.

"What comfort can a slab of stone give you?" I wanted to ask those women.

I don't come to the cemetery very often anymore. Not like

I used to. But I make a point of changing the flowers in the stone vase every season. Neither John nor Charlie cared much for flowers, so I don't spend too much time fussing over which ones to get. Poinsettias in winter, tulips in spring, roses in the summer, tiger lilies in the fall. It makes me feel better knowing the flowers are here. Perhaps a stranger walking past the tombstone will notice them and know that the people resting here were loved. The last time I came here was the end of May. I brought a bouquet of roses with plastic dew-drops on their petals to replace the purple tulips that I'd placed here in March. Since my son's death, spring has always been the hardest season. New beginnings abound. But not for all. Some hearts will always be stuck in winter.

The cemetery road is a snare of twists and narrow turns. I crank the steering wheel this way and that until I see the familiar oak tree. The day is warm, but there's a cool under-current in the air that cuts through. Fall is on its way. Bus trips and sweaters. Thanksgiving at Helen's. I'll nod my way through dinner, listening as she talks about her grand-children. Three of them are in university now. It's so hard to believe.

I'll stick a fork into my mouth.

The roses are more pink than red. The sun and rain and heat have bled the colour from their silk petals. But the dew-drops are still there. Frozen tears. There's no reason I can't come out here more often or plant real flowers like other people do. Why have I been so neglectful? What kind of a mother and wife am I? I tear the plastic from around the daisies and, after pulling out the roses, stuff the stems inside. The sight of them makes me feel even more terrible. My good intentions have only worsened things. I seem to have a habit of doing that.

He was slipping away. His visits home became less frequent. I'd call the apartment, but no one would pick up. School was busy, he'd remind me. I had no idea the kind of pressure he was under.

"Of course," I'd say, embarrassed. "I'm sorry."

I told myself it would be only a matter of weeks before he graduated. Then he'd come back home to find work.

"They're building apartments in the east end," I told him. "Quite spacious, from what I hear. And I was in the Sears restaurant the other day and noticed a Help Wanted sign. You should apply."

"I didn't take two years of chef school to make Jell-O cubes."

"It's a perfectly good restaurant. It's always busy."

He paused. "I'm not coming back to Balsden when I graduate. There's nothing for me there."

"What do you mean?"

"I need to be someplace else. Somewhere I can grow."

Grow. "Is this what they do in school? Puff up your ego?"

"What restaurants in Balsden serve foie gras?"

"I don't know even know what that is. But there's no reason you couldn't—"

"I'm not coming home, Mom. My mind was made up even before I left."

My fingers went to my throat, trying to pry free the invisible hand clamped around it. "You never told me that."

"If I had, you would never have let me go in the first place."

"What do you think of me?" I asked, my voice suddenly small.

But there was no answer.

Later that evening I stood at the sink, feeling like I was at the edge of a cliff, as though the floor had broken away on the other side of my slippers. He was older now, I reasoned. He had a good head on his shoulders. He was bright and personable and had a caring soul. I needed to stop doubting him. I needed to hold my breath and watch him go, fingers crossed behind my back. I'd done everything in my power. The rest was up to him. Children left home all the time. It was natural. What did I expect, anyway? For John to live around the corner from me? What kind of life was that? What sort of happiness could he find attached forever to his mother? He needed to be a man. His own person.

Keep a close eye on him.

I saw my son in the shadow of a suicide. I was petrified he might take his life one day, the way that I thought Freddy had taken his. Ironic, then, that what took my son's life was a scythe neither of us saw coming.

CHAPTER NINE

A WHITE CAR is parked in front of my house, but no one is in it. The backyard is empty. Nothing waiting for me except twin laundry-line poles. My eyes narrow. I toss the cellophane wrapper that held the daisies into the garbage can before unlocking the back door. The cool air inside immediately calms my nerves. I step out of my shoes, hang my jacket on the back of a kitchen chair and deposit my earrings and necklace on top of the stove. The answering machine is blinking. I hesitate before pressing the play button.

"Hello. This is the Balsden Public Library calling."

For crying out loud.

"You have one overdue book. Please return it to us as soon as—"

I delete the message and go to the living room window and stare at the car. How did he find my house? And who does he think he is, following me here? The wall clock says it's been an hour since I left the Golden Sunset. I call Mr. Sparrow.

"Joyce!" he exclaims when he finally picks up. "I thought you left town. You were all dolled up in purple this morning."

"Blue," I say, impatiently. "I just got back."

"Do you see the big white car parked in front of your house?"

"That's why I was calling—"

"There I was, sitting on my front porch, when this car pulls up. I watch this fellow get out and start knocking on your front door. I thought, 'If it's not those goddamned Jehovahs coming back again.' When this fellow didn't get an answer, he goes around to the back. Jehovahs don't usually try the back door. So I went to investigate."

"Mr. Sparrow, you shouldn't have done that."

"You weigh your odds at my age. I go around to the back of your house and there he is, standing at the door. 'What are you up to?' I holler at him. Oh boy, he jumped. He says he's looking for you. I say, 'Well, if she was here, don't you think she'd answer the door?'"

I can't help but smile as I imagine the scene. Mr. Sparrow—my unlikely protector.

"Then he asks me who I am. I say, 'Never mind who *I* am. Who the hell are *you*?' So then he says, 'I'm Walter,' as if I should already know that. I've never seen this man before in my life. He tells me he's a friend of yours. I tell him you're not the type to receive gentlemen callers. He says it's never too late to start."

I massage my forehead. "Do you know where he is?"

"In my washroom."

"*He's at your house?*"

Mr. Sparrow tells me he invited Walter to wait for me over a cup of tea. "We've been having a nice chat about Miami. He's American. Why don't you come over? I was going to pull a pie out of the freezer."

"I'm not feeling my best at the moment."

"I'll tell you what—I'll send him over. It's not me he wants to see, anyway."

"That's not a good idea."

"Bye, Joyce."

He hangs up and a squeaking sound escapes my throat. I don't want to speak to that little man. He's got no business coming here, to *my* house, talking to *my* neighbours. I want to erase this day. This week.

"I won't answer the door," I tell myself. "He can knock all he wants."

I tiptoe into the living room and slip behind the curtains. A few seconds later, he emerges from Mr. Sparrow's, wearing those bug sunglasses and carrying something in his hand. What is it? I step closer to the window to get a better look. He sees me and waves. I move away, mortified. There's no escape.

"I hope this isn't the first time you've had a strange man on your doorstep," he says when I open the front door. "Especially when he's packing one of these." He extends a zucchini at me. "Mr. Sparrow gave it to me. I have absolutely no clue what someone would do with this."

"Muffins," I say. I keep my feet on the step, my arms crossed, my hip pressed against the screen door. "You make muffins with them."

He lowers his sunglasses. "Do I look like someone who makes muffins?"

"I don't know what you look like," I say.

"I don't blame you for being upset."

"I'm fine."

"You don't look fine."

"You followed me to the Sunset. Now you've followed me home. How do you even know where I live?"

"Phone book."

"Look, I'm sorry that I left you at the café holding the bill. I offered to pay you back but you declined. I don't know what it is that you want."

"Who was the one who first came knocking on *my* door?"

"That . . . that was different," I stammer. "I had a moment. A very foolish moment."

"Life is lived one foolish moment to the next."

"What is it you want from me, Mr. Clarke?"

He looks at me with the saddest face, and a picture forms in my head of what he must've looked like as a child. My heart twitches.

"Your help, my dear," he says.

Once inside, he can't stop talking about my butterfly kitchen. "Your attention to detail is almost militant," he says, his head pivoting this way and that.

"The wallpaper border was first," I explain. "Then I got the curtains. I found the tablecloth in Paris."

"Isn't France wonderful? Fred and I went there in '82."

"Not *that* Paris," I say. "Paris, Ontario."

His hand goes to his chest. "Now that's just cruel."

I offer him a seat and debate whether I should put on some coffee or tea. Why should I go out of my way for him? I don't know what kind of "help" he wants, but I'm not anxious to hear it.

"How long have you lived here?" he asks. "In this house?"

"Fifty years."

"And you're here by yourself?"

"My husband died eight years ago."

"My condolences. And also for your son."

My backbone presses against the spindles of my chair.

"Mrs. Pender didn't know my son." I'll say nothing more. It's none of his business and I can't bear the idea of someone like him pitying me.

"Fred always wanted children," he sighs. "He would have been a fantastic father. Especially considering he lost his own father at such a young age. You know about Mr. Pender, I'm assuming."

"He was struck by lightning and fell off his roof."

"That bothered Fred something terrible. Not just the death, but also the manner in which it happened. He struggled with it for years, especially the older he got. You'd think the reverse would be true, but it wasn't. It was a sensational story. You don't hear of death-by-lightning all that often. There was a mythical quality to it, wouldn't you say?"

233

I shrug, even though I'm in agreement. "I suppose."

"That's what got under Fred's skin—the fact that his father's death overshadowed his life. Funny how something you have absolutely no control over can define you in the eyes of everyone else."

"I'm still confused," I say. "About everything you told me."

He presses his hands together as though he's about to pray. "Mrs. Pender didn't approve of Fred's sexuality and he wasn't willing to hide it. Not that you could ever be *open* about it in those days. The world was a different place for our generation. There were rules in place, most of them ill conceived. Fred wasn't willing to go into *denial*. That's a key difference. She'd put him on such a pedestal his whole life. Her up-and-coming movie star. Of course, it was all over-compensation. She offset what she saw as his flaw by making him perfect in every other way. Some mothers tend to do that."

I get up from the table. I don't want to look at him anymore. Why did I let him in? I open one of the kitchen cupboards and pull out a package of digestive cookies.

"She killed him because she couldn't control him," he says. "Told that horrible lie about him jumping off a ship. What kind of mother—?"

"I don't know," I say, trying to neatly arrange the cookies on a plate, but my hand is trembling.

"They made up eventually, although he never really forgave her. She'd come out to visit every few years. Needless to say, I didn't enjoy her company. I hated her for what she'd done to Fred. But, as he pointed out, she'd done more damage to herself. She created a world that left her utterly alone."

I set the plate of cookies between us. "And Fred never came back here? To Balsden?"

He shakes his head. "The dead can't come back."

"What sort of help do you want from me, Mr. Clarke?"

"Call me Walter." He reaches for a cookie. "My god, I'm starving."

"Do you want a sandwich? I've got some cold cuts in the fridge." I offer it up before I can even stop myself.

He bites into the cookie and waves his hand. "No, no. What I meant was I'm *always* starving. I'm dieting." He says this as though he's divulging a secret. "I've been eating non-stop since Fred died. It's not healthy, I know. But we all have our coping mechanisms. I'm what you call an emotional eater. Happy, sad, scared, bored. You name the feeling and I'll eat myself through it."

He sighs and places the cookie down in front of him, a brown half-moon. "Fred was always better with self-control than I was. He was the responsible one. Did all the banking, took care of the dogs, ran the business. I don't know how I've managed to get through these past few months without him. I feel as though I have one of those ear infections that affect your balance. I teeter this way and that." He looks down at his cookie. "When the doctors told Fred he had only a few months to live, he asked me to come back here. To see his mother. He worried about her. I often think the people who hurt you most in life are the ones you carry closest. Fred liked this part of the province. He often talked about the summers and the trees and the snow forts he and his father used to make in his backyard."

I don't want to hear about fathers and sons. The telephone rings, startling both of us.

"Excuse me," I say. I get up from the table and hurry down the hall to the den. I don't want him listening in on my conversation.

It's Fern. "Do you have a plunger?"

"A what?"

"It's not what you think. I dropped my deodorant down the toilet."

I cup the receiver with both hands. "I can't talk right now."

"Why? What's going on?"

"There's someone here."

"Who?"

"I can't say."

"Joyce, if you're in any danger, I want you to say the word 'cutlet' right now. I'll have the police there in ten seconds."

"He didn't die, Fern."

"What?"

"Freddy. He didn't die. Well, he did. But not until recently."

"What are you talking about?"

"I don't have time to explain."

"Who's at your house?"

"Walter Clarke. He was Freddy's . . ." My words falter. "Friend."

"What's he doing *there*?"

"He says he needs my help."

"Help for what?"

"If you let me get off the phone, I could find out."

I promise to call her the minute he leaves. When I return to the kitchen, two more cookies are gone. There's a scattering of crumbs on the table.

"I'm sorry about that," I say, uncertain if I should offer him more to eat. "Where were we?"

He shifts in his chair and the wood cracks. "I want to do something for Fred. Here, in Balsden. He needs to be properly commemorated in his hometown."

"You mean a funeral?"

"Nothing as sombre as that. Fred would never approve. More like a party with his friends."

I don't know what to say. There aren't many people left who'd remember who Fred was, let alone want to attend a memorial for him. And I'm not even sure he had many friends in the first place.

"It's only fair," Walter says, and I notice a shine in his eyes. "Fred had something taken from him. His dignity. He deserves to get that back."

I reach for the box of tissues on the shelf behind me and pass it to him.

"It was cancer that took him," he says before blowing his nose. I can't help but feel sorry for him.

"I lost my husband to cancer," I say.

"And your son, too."

"Yes."

"Fred had a brain tumour. We were out for our usual morning walk one day when all of a sudden, he starts talking gibberish. The doctor thought it was a stroke. Things were fine for a while. He got some of his speech back, but not all of it. A few weeks later, he couldn't move his right arm. A week after that, there were problems with his vision. When his leg went, I called the ambulance. The spectacle humiliated him. Those flashing lights in the driveway, all the neighbours watching. I still hate myself for that. I could have driven him. But I wasn't in the right frame of mind.

"Once the doctors realized there was a tumour growing inside his brain, they removed some of the fluid around it to ease the pressure and to help bring back some of his motor skills. I remember walking into his hospital room after the surgery and there he was, sitting at his bedside table, his chin resting in his cupped hand so matter-of-factly. He could speak, too. Not more than a few words, but it was something. And he could move. To anyone else, it would have seemed he was getting better. But I knew. And he knew, as well. We were in the eye of the storm. I'd give anything to have that moment back again."

I pull another tissue from the box, this one for my own eyes. John and Charlie hover behind me. I've never forgotten a single detail of their demise. Not one.

"It wasn't long before the fluid came back," Walter says. "Everything happened so fast. I'm not sure I was any use to him." He presses the tissue against an eye. "He died while I was at home. He was alone at the end. I've never forgiven myself."

I get up from the table again. "Would you like a coffee? I should warn you, it's always too strong or too weak. I need a new coffee maker."

"My taste buds are shot. You could use a dirty sock as a filter and I'd be none the wiser."

After I pour him a cup, I clear my throat. "About this memorial . . ."

"I don't have grandiose expectations, Joyce. Just some crust-less sandwiches. Lemonade. Teacups. Something quaint and small-town."

"Balsden is hardly small-town, Mr. Clarke."

"How many shopping malls do you have?"

"One."

"It's small-town."

I put my annoyance aside and try to think of a possible venue for him. "The Holiday Inn puts on a good brunch with live jazz on Sundays. You might consider that. There's also Smiley's, if you're looking for something outdoors."

"It would be so nice to meet some people who knew Fred back in the day."

"That restaurant downtown is supposed to be good. What's it called again?"

"I'm sure there are lots of stories people could share."

"Cedarwood Grill."

"Having your help would mean so much."

My head tilts. "Pardon?"

His eyes grow large. "You don't expect me to do this on my own. How will I know whom to invite?"

"You want me to help?"

"Of course. You knew him, after all."

"I can't."

"Why not?"

My mouth opens and closes, opens and closes as I try to think of an excuse that doesn't sound like an excuse. "I'm going on a bus trip to Turkeyville. And I have to start packing. I'm moving. Into my sister's place. She has an apartment in her basement."

"And leave your butterflies?"

"I can't manage this house anymore. The winters are so hard. I'd be happy to help you if things were different. I hope you understand."

He gives me a tight nod but says nothing.

"Can I get you more coffee?"

He covers his mug with his hand and tells me he's fine. "I should be on my way. I've had a very long day. I'm sure you can relate. Thank you for the coffee. And the cookies."

I walk him to the door and remind him not to forget his zucchini. "When are you heading home?"

"Tomorrow, I guess," he says.

"What about the memorial?"

"What about it? My expectations were too high. Serves me right. I'll head out in the morning."

"It's a lonely journey back to Miami driving all on your own."

"All journeys are lonely, Joyce." He steps out onto the porch and turns around. "Thank you for your hospitality. Fred had kind things to say about you."

"He did?"

"He told me you could have been the girl he ended up with if he'd been less honest about himself."

"I hope your move goes well."

I watch him walk down the driveway, zucchini in hand. I wave when he pulls into the driveway to turn around, but he doesn't wave back.

I can't call Fern and go through everything. Not now. I gather up the coffee cups and dump their remains down the sink. I've got no time for anything, let alone to help a complete stranger organize a memorial for someone I last spoke to fifty years ago. I take two Aspirin and go to my bedroom. The coverlet is cool to the touch and I lie down. I'm stiff, inflexible as plastic. All I can hope for is sleep. I turn onto my side and stare at a blue patch of wall until my eyelids grow heavy.

My son never lived at home again. A few months after graduating, he got a job as a station chef at a private club in Toronto.

"It's where the rich people hang out," he told me. "I'll be cooking for millionaires."

He was excited, naturally. I tried to be excited for him in return.

"What do millionaires eat?" I asked.

"Anything they want."

"They're paying you well?"

"More than I'd make at the Sears restaurant in Balsden."

He was taking the bus to Toronto the following weekend to look for an apartment.

"Angela lives there now. Remember her?"

Yes, I remembered. My frenzied call the morning of his disappearance. Did she ever tell him? Did he have any idea about the wretched things his mother had done over the years in the name of protecting him?

"She's married now to a lawyer. He's a member of the club. That's how I found out about the job. They're trying to recruit younger members, so they want to mix things up a bit. Update the menu. Apparently, they've been serving jellied beef consommé for years. Can you imagine? She's meeting me at the bus station and we're going to look at a few apartments."

At least he knew someone in the city.

Later that evening, I looked down at the mushy casserole on my plate and thought about the time John had come home to cook dinner for Charlie and me. I knew that he was desperate to please us, to show us what he was learning in school. There was a chilled soup with a design as intricate as Chinese letters etched in the surface. A chicken breast stuffed with asparagus and cheese in a cream sauce. Potatoes whipped so mercilessly, they seemed more like clouds than food. Charlie had never been a fan of rich foods. He often suffered from indigestion. I watched him slide tiny pieces past his lips, trying to disguise his distaste. When John set out a pecan tart on the table, I was certain Charlie was going to faint.

"My goodness," I said. "How do you eat like this and not explode?"

"This isn't everyday dining," John said hastily. He must've

been disappointed by the leftovers on Charlie's plate but said nothing.

"We'll have to go and visit him," Charlie said when I told him about John's new job.

"It's a private club," I said. "They don't let people like us inside."

"What if we wore our good overalls?"

John found a small one-bedroom apartment on the third floor of a complex in what he referred to as "midtown." The grounds were well cared for, he said, and there was a fountain. His apartment faced the opposite direction, though, and overlooked the subway tracks. I couldn't imagine having to live with that constant racket.

"You'll never be able to open your window."

"I won't notice after a while," he said.

We rented a van and moved him on a bright October morning. He didn't have much: a sofa, a mattress and a dozen or so boxes. I wanted to give him our old kitchen table and chair set, but there wasn't room in the van. We'd have to bring it down another time. The apartment was clean but small. I listened to the trains rattle by every few minutes as I unpacked the boxes of newspaper-wrapped dishes and copper-bottomed pans and jars of spices labelled with names I'd never heard before. After lunch, we drove downtown past the building where John would be working. It was stately, with a turquoise eavestrough and ornate white bars on the windows—exactly the sort of place I imagined where rich people made small talk and nibbled on hors d'oeuvres no bigger than quarters. This would be my son's world now. He'd be associating with people on a very different social level from his father and me.

"There's a racquetball court in the basement," John said. "And seven fireplaces. Did I tell you the Eaton family comes here?"

I looked out the car window at the blur of faces, wishing I could be happier for him. Why couldn't this new job, this new apartment, this new city be the most wonderful thing to happen to him?

Back at the apartment, we finished most of the unpacking. John told me to leave the boxes marked "Bedroom."

"I'll take care of those," he said.

Charlie and John went to the grocery store to stock up on a few things. By then I'd finished all the other boxes. I walked around the apartment for a final inspection. The boxes in the bedroom were pushed into the corner. There were only a few of them, along with three garbage bags, which I assumed contained his clothes. I started with the bags first, and carefully folded his undershirts and underwear into neat little squares. After those were done, I looked down at the boxes. One in particular caught my eye. It was bound with silver duct tape, not clear tape like the others. I nibbled the inside of my cheek.

I knelt down and carefully peeled back the strap of tape from the top of the box. Inside, there were cookbooks. There was also a black travel bag with toiletries inside. Beneath that, a set of pillowcases. And beneath the pillowcases, magazines.

There were a half-dozen of them. Muscle magazines. I felt nauseous as I picked up one called *Male Pix*. The cover featured a young man in a skimpy bathing suit. I flipped past page after page of scantily clad men in various poses, each one wearing an expression between sultriness and stupidity. This excited him? This parade of male sexuality? My hand went to my mouth, revulsion running quickly up my throat.

I was ashamed that my own fingerprints were now on those pages. I put everything back in its place: the magazines, pillowcases, travel bag, books. I pulled the tape back over the flap so that it looked untouched. He'd never know the difference. But then I pulled back the tape again and left it dangling down the side of the box, an upside-down question mark.

I hurried Charlie out the door as soon as he and John got back. I said something about driving at night. Nerves. I had things to do in the morning. My lips grazed the side of my son's cheek and in that moment, even I felt the coldness emanating from me.

"You're awfully quiet," Charlie said as we drove back in darkness, save for the glow of the van's dashboard. I imagined the road before us was a conveyor belt, pulling us back to the safety of home.

"Am I?" I said, knowing full well he was right. I'd barely said a word since we left John's apartment.

"You're nervous for him." Not a question from Charlie this time. A statement of fact.

"In some ways."

"What ways?"

I was expecting one of his usual responses: *Don't worry. There's only so much you can control in life, Joyce. Everything will work out in the end. Have a little faith in him.* I glanced over, although I couldn't make out Charlie's expression in the dark. How much did he know? He must've noticed things over the years—behaviour that would've caused him to question John. He would've compared his son to other boys as I had done and noticed the glaring discrepancies.

What ways?

Charlie, I wondered, what would you say if I told you? What would you think if I unloaded everything into this cargo van?

Things had gotten better between Charlie and me. We'd sunk into our routines in John's absence. We started enjoying one another's company in a way that was both new and familiar at the same time. The other night, we'd made love on the living room sofa. I couldn't remember the last time we'd done something so spontaneous. And his retirement wasn't that far off anymore. We talked about going to Hawaii next year with Helen and Dickie. And a trip out West to visit his sister. There were things he was looking forward to.

I took a deep breath. "You know me," I said. "Always worrying."

I felt his hand brush my thigh, his way of telling me that everything would work out.

A noise. My eyes flutter behind my lids. My hands are numb and curled up against my chest. The telephone. My eyes open to fog. I blink a few times and the fog lifts. The red numbers of my clock come into focus. It's 3:03 p.m. I've been asleep for an hour. My mouth feels frozen. The phone rings again and I fumble for it.

"Joyce."

It's Mrs. Pender.

"Hello? Joyce, is that you?"

I prop myself up on an elbow. "I have nothing to—"

"Oh, you *are* there. You need to speak up a little more when you answer. My hearing isn't that good anymore and it's difficult for me on the phone. The other day, I was speaking to a man for a good ten minutes before I realized he was trying to sell me a newspaper subscription. 'Why do I want to read the newspaper?' I asked him. 'Life is depressing enough.'"

Her words bounce along like tiny balls. This must be her attempt at cheerfulness.

"Don't call here ever again," I say.

"Please, Joyce! Don't hang up!"

Her voice is so desperate that I don't. Instead, I lie back on the pillow, one hand pressed against my forehead. I wait. I hear a sob, followed by muffled words. I make out the word *lying*. Or is it *dying*? Either way, the word is one and the same if it's coming from her mouth.

"I never meant it." Her voice is damp. "Freddy left me all alone. He said he'd come back for me. That was his promise. And he never did. Five long years I waited. Nothing. I went to New York to check up on him and the situation was much worse than I thought. Freddy had made *friends*, Joyce. All of them, running around my son's apartment on their tippy-toes. Fussing over one another like schoolgirls. I told Freddy to come back home immediately. He said I was crazy, there was nothing left in Balsden for him. 'What about me?' I asked, but he didn't answer. It was the coldest silence I've ever felt."

"So you came back here and told everyone he committed suicide?"

"Not everyone. Just Evelyn Rogers. She was always asking about Freddy. I was so sick of covering for him that I made up a lie of my own. The next thing I knew, everyone was at my door with baked goods. What could I do?"

"You could've told people the truth!"

"He wasn't coming back. And I didn't want him back. Not after what I'd seen in New York. I was sick to my stomach thinking about it. I always knew Freddy had those tendencies. When he lived with me, I could keep his behaviour under lock and key. But I let him escape. In the end, everyone was better off believing the lie."

"How can you *say* that?"

"I had to protect him."

"You're a fraud."

"I've got a heart that won't stop beating. I'm at the mercy of people who see me as nothing more than a piece of furniture. I'm tired, Joyce. I'm so tired of everything. I want to die, but even death won't have me."

"At least your son had a *life!*" My words hit the walls like rocks. As soon as I say this, I want to pull it back.

A sound comes through the receiver. It's a low, broken moan. I've heard the same sound come from my own lips. A mother's cry for all the things she can't fix.

"I never told Freddy I was sorry. He died and I never told him. I can't live—"

I hang up the phone. Then I get up from my bed and pace the floor, trying to shake off her words. But they stick to me like flies to flypaper.

Freddy was alive all these years and my son was dead. I can't bear this weight. The phone rings again.

Two years ago, in early July, there was a parade in downtown Balsden. It wasn't the usual sort of parade with marching bands and clowns and floats on flatbed trucks. It was a gay parade. There had never been one before in Balsden. A young man named Philip Cooper was organizing it. He had moved to town the previous year from Toronto and saw no reason why a city this size couldn't have some sort of celebration.

"We need to recognize the gay and lesbian people within our community," the *Examiner* quoted him as saying. "Balsden needs to get in step with the times."

There were letters to the editor, of course. People quoting Scriptures about Sodom or using the parade as their opportunity to discuss everything they saw wrong with the world.

"Once we cross this line," one man wrote, "we'll never be safe again."

Other people wrote in defence of the parade. One woman had a lesbian daughter. There was no reason, she said, that her daughter should be denied the same basic rights as everyone else. In regards to those Christians, she said they'd make excellent tailors the way they customize everything to their own liking.

The Letters to the Editor section grew and grew. People shouted back and forth via newsprint. In a show of support, homosexuals from Andover and neighbouring cities planned to march as well. Buoyed by the support, Mr. Cooper decided to extend things beyond the parade. The Balsden Pride Committee would also host a fundraising dinner and a picnic the following afternoon.

"We won't be stopped," he said in an article. "Our opposition only makes us stronger."

The paper ran a picture of him this time. He looked back at me from the page—a young man with bushy eyebrows and a downturned mouth. Harmless. Sad, almost. Where was his mother? I wondered.

The morning of the parade threatened rain but the clouds departed shortly before noon. I got into my car and drove downtown, making sure to take my sunglasses and hat. I parked three blocks from Parker Street where the parade would be ending and found an inconspicuous spot in the shadows of the library. If I were spotted, I'd say I was running errands and had just stopped to see what the fuss was about. I fidgeted with my purse straps while I waited for the parade to make its way down the street. Before long, a clamour grew. The dozens of onlookers along the sides of the road clapped and craned their necks. And then I saw the tops of heads as people walked down the street and banners with the names of community groups from across the province. A truck went by with two shirtless skinny boys waving from the cab. I heard whistles. Some people had giant water guns that they sprayed across the crowd. Then the whistles gave way to cheers, and I stepped a few feet closer, wondering if it was the mayor. He'd been noncommittal about his participation. But it wasn't him. I saw a man and a woman walk by, holding hands. They wore rainbow-coloured scarves around their necks. Other couples were walking with them, wearing buttons and waving flags. One of them carried a sign: "We Love Our Gay Kids."

I thought my heart had shattered to pieces years before, but an intact fragment cracked in that moment. I stood there, in the shadows, on the other side of that wall of people.

There were no parades for John and me.

My son and I became strangers. He led a life in a different city—a life I couldn't see, nor could ever know. I couldn't grasp what he was doing at any given time or the people he was associating with. He said he enjoyed living in Toronto and working at the club, although it was stressful at times. By the time he was twenty-seven, he was promoted to second chef.

"They say I'm a breath of fresh air," he told me. "The younger members love what I'm doing. The older ones don't. They'll keep slurping their lobster bisque until they croak."

Charlie and I were happy for him. I called Helen right after I hung up with John, eager to brag to her about John's success. I'd heard enough about the lacklustre accomplishments of Marianne and Mark over the years.

"He's certainly moving in elite circles," Helen said. "All he needs to do now is marry one of the society ladies he serves. Then he'll be set for life."

I laughed, even though I suspected her comment was meant as a dig. I longed for the telephone call when John would tell me that he'd met a special girl.

"We really hit it off," he'd say, unable to keep the enthusiasm out of his voice. "I think this might lead to something."

I'd insist that he bring her for dinner the next weekend. I'd make a pot roast and steal a few minutes alone with her in the kitchen to talk about my boy.

"He keeps to himself," I'd say. "But he's got a heart of gold. You won't find a better man. Hang on to him tightly."

But there were no pot roasts or mentions of future daughters-in-law during our weekly phone calls. I once asked him if he was seeing anyone.

"No," he replied stiffly. "I don't have time for that. I'm too busy at the club."

"Do you have friends?"

"Of course I have friends. Why would you ask something like that?"

There it was. That sharpness in his tone, a blade making tiny cuts in my ear. I assumed it was fatigue from work, from a life lived in a bigger, more complicated city. But I see now that it was anger at the questions I asked and the answers he couldn't give.

As time went on, his words became fewer and our phone conversations became nothing more than me listing off my week's activities. I'd bought some turkey pot pies at the church bazaar yesterday. I was thinking of redoing the kitchen. Charlie's back was giving him trouble. We needed a new roof.

So many words and not one of them amounted to anything. Endless loops of the same conversation. Nothing had changed since his days at college. Occasionally, I'd ask him to come home for a visit.

"You haven't been back to Balsden in months," I'd remind him. "I almost forget what you look like."

"I work on weekends."

"Then come during the week."

"I don't have a car."

"Take the train. I'll pay for your ticket."

"There's nothing for me to do there." Had our home become such a terrible place?

"You don't have to *do* anything, John. We can relax and talk."

"I'll look at my calendar and get back to you," he'd say.

Eventually, I stopped asking. "The more you nag, the more he'll resist," Charlie said. "Stop asking and he'll change his mind."

"Since when do you know him so well?" I snapped.

I was still smarting from Charlie's visit with John a few weeks before. I'd gone on a bus trip to Stratford one Saturday with Helen and Fern. Charlie had the day off and was planning to clear out the shed in the backyard. When I got home that evening, he was nowhere to be found. Instead, there was a note on the kitchen table.

Decided to visit John. Should be back by night.

Visit John? By himself? Initially, I considered it a thoughtful gesture. I think I even said "How nice" out loud. But why hadn't Charlie told me? He could've at least waited for a day when both of us were available. Why all this secrecy? And what would the two of them have done together? They barely spoke.

I immediately called John. He told me that Charlie had left an hour ago.

"He should be home soon," he said. "Provided he didn't get caught in traffic."

"He didn't tell me he was going to visit you," I said, trying to sound casual. "I would've come otherwise."

"It was a spur-of-the-moment thing. He called me this morning and I didn't have anything on, so we figured why not?"

"Why not?" I repeated. "And what did the two of you do all day?"

They grocery shopped. Charlie fixed the screen door that led to the balcony. They watched an afternoon movie on TV. John cooked his father lunch.

"What on earth did you make?" I said with a laugh. "Your father is such a fussy eater."

"Minestrone," he said. "Dad really liked it. He's bringing the recipe back with him. Said he's tired of casseroles."

"I see." My husband had never complained about his dinners. "And did the two of you talk?" I asked, wincing as soon as I said the words.

"What do you think?" That sharp tone again. "Of course we did."

"Well, I'm happy."

"You don't sound happy."

"I only wish I could've been there."

I wanted to see my son again. I needed to see his face. I missed the boy I used to take to matinees, the one who'd help me in the kitchen, the boy who gave me a necklace fit for a movie star. I had trouble convincing myself that we'd ever had that relationship. Now, here he was, spending the day with his father.

Most of my anger had faded to cool jealousy by the time Charlie pulled into the driveway.

"You could've said something," I said to him.

"You already had plans."

"I would've cancelled them. He's my son."

"He's my son, too. Or have you forgotten that?"

One Friday evening as I was clearing the dinner dishes, the phone rang. It was John. He said he was coming home for a visit. "Tonight."

"Tonight?" I practically screamed back. "Why? What's going on?"

"You don't want to see me?" His voice was playful and warm again. The John I used to know. Hope surged inside me.

"Of course I want to see you. This is so sudden. I haven't prepared anything."

"I'm bringing someone with me."

My heart skipped. "Oh?"

"A friend. We're driving."

"At this time of night?"

"Mom, it's eight o'clock. We'll be there by ten. See you soon."

I hung up. Who was this friend? A girl? Could it be possible? I called Charlie at work.

"I'll set up the cot in the living room for this friend, so don't make too much noise when you come home in the morning."

"How long is John staying?" Charlie asked.

"He didn't say." I didn't like surprises, but hoped that at least this was going to be a pleasant one. I hurried from room to room, tidying up as best I could, and threw two sheet sets into the washing machine. Then I searched through my cupboard drawers and pulled together enough ingredients to make a batch of chocolate haystacks. The front door opened shortly before ten.

"Hello?" John called out. "Anyone home?"

He stood in the hallway with a duffle bag over his shoulder. He looked heavier. His face was fuller, rounder. He'd grown a moustache that hid his mouth. His jeans were stretched tight across his thighs. I couldn't help but notice a shape like a fist at his groin. Behind him stood a man with reddish hair and a pug nose. He looked away when our eyes met. I couldn't believe John would be this bold.

"Come in," I said quickly, hurrying behind them to shut the front door.

His name was Kyle. The two of them sat at the kitchen table while I arranged the haystacks on a plate. I offered them milk, but John asked if we had any wine.

"I think I have a box," I said, bending over to peer into the fridge. "Your father bought it a few weeks ago."

"Told you," John said under his breath. I saw him nudge Kyle with his elbow.

"Told you what?" I asked as I took the wineglasses from the china cabinet.

"Nothing," John said.

I was somewhat relieved to find out that Kyle and John worked together. Kyle was a waiter at the club. Perhaps I'd been too quick to draw conclusions.

"John's been telling me about Balsden for weeks now," Kyle said. "I just had to come and see it for myself." His eyes roamed my kitchen.

"The new movie theatre just opened up," I said.

John raised an eyebrow. "How exciting."

"A lot has changed since you were last here."

"I'm sure."

I showed Kyle where I'd set up the cot and passed him a folded towel with a washcloth. I left them sitting in the living room watching television and listened to the faint muffle as I lay in bed. What had John told Kyle about Balsden, about Charlie and me? From the looks the two of them exchanged, I imagined it was nothing complimentary. No doubt they were making fun of me at that moment. I tossed and turned in bed, my resentment growing. Why couldn't John have come alone? At least we would've had the chance to talk.

I woke when Charlie slipped into the bedroom and sat on the edge of the bed, unbuttoning his shirt.

"Did you see John?" I whispered.

"His door was shut."

"And his friend?" I sat up in bed. "Was he in the living room?"

There was a split second of a pause. "Of course," Charlie said, pulling his shirt off his shoulders. "Where else would he be?"

The boys got up shortly after eight. I pulled out cereal boxes and put a bunch of bananas on the table.

"If you'd given me more notice, I could've cooked a proper breakfast," I said to a bed-headed John before turning to an equally bed-headed Kyle. "John always liked porridge in the morning. Did you sleep all right last night? I hope the cot wasn't too lumpy."

"It was just fine," Kyle said.

They decided they'd go to the mall that morning and then take a drive around to see the sights. While Kyle was in the shower, I took a piece of paper and started to write out the directions to the mall.

"Mom, I know how to get there," John said. "I grew up here, after all."

"Right," I said, feeling foolish. "Just be back in time for dinner. Your father goes in at six tonight, so we'll eat at five. I know he wants to spend some time with you."

"We were planning to head out before dinner."

"But you just got here."

"Kyle has to work tomorrow."

"Then Kyle can go home and you stay. Your father is off tomorrow. He'll drive you back to Toronto."

"I don't want— I need to get back as well. I've got a pile of things I need to get through tomorrow."

I banged the cereal bowls in the sink. "Why did you even bother coming, then? You haven't been home for months."

"What's the big deal?"

"The big deal, John, is that it's not fair to do this to me. I'm busy too, you know. Contrary to what you might think, I don't sit around all day pining for you to visit us, let alone with some stranger."

"He's my friend."

"Don't think I don't know about the two of you. Laughing about my wine. I don't need you coming in here with your superior attitude. You think you're too good for this place, for your father and me, with your private clubs and your members and your lobster beak."

"Bisque."

"Whatever. I don't deserve this." My voice was loud, much too loud, but I couldn't stop the train barrelling down the tracks. "I'm your mother. Not the manager of a hotel. I deserve more than this."

"No, you don't. You don't deserve anything."

"Don't you talk to me like that! You, of all people."

Over John's shoulder, two heads came into focus. One was Kyle dressed now, his hair wet and pressed against his forehead. The other was Charlie in his maroon-and-grey-striped pyjamas.

"What's going on?" he asked.

"The usual," John said. "Good morning, Dad. Kyle, we're leaving. This was a complete mistake."

"John," Charlie said, "there's no reason to go. You can stay until tomorrow. We'll go for breakfast when I get home from work."

"Thanks, Dad, but no thanks," John said, brushing past him.

Charlie looked over at Kyle. "You're welcome to stay, too. Both of you."

"It's up to John," Kyle mumbled apologetically.

That was the last time John slept in our house. I often wonder about that night. Sometimes, I imagine John sneaking out of his room and tiptoeing to the cot where Kyle slept. I imagine sheets pulled back and hushed laughter and the embrace of that redheaded stranger. The thought of this midnight tryst comforts me in a way I never expected. I'd feel better if what happened to John took place within our home, rather than in the bedroom of a stranger. This way, at least I was close to him.

It's possible that nothing went on that night. The two of them might've been nothing more than friends. I have no way of knowing. I never heard of or saw Kyle again. He's likely dead, too, leaving his mother behind with her own mountain of grief.

■ ■ ■

I wake to the sounds of strangers' voices. I look up to see a gurney in the middle of the room. Panic takes hold. Has it come for me? I'm just about to pull the cord attached to my purse when one of the orderlies speaks.

"You're home, Mrs. Schueller."

I see fingers point towards the ceiling and the flash of a silver medic bracelet around a thin forearm. They lift Ruth onto her bed. After considerable fussing, they get her settled comfortably enough and then, just as suddenly as they appeared, the two orderlies leave. I reach for my bed control and raise the mattress to get a better look at her, but she's lost in the darkness.

"Ruth," I say. "Ruth."

I think she hears me, but I can't be certain. She lies motionless.

"It's good that you're back," I say. "I sent that fellow to check in on you. Do you remember him? Timothy."

Silence.

"They wouldn't even tell me which hospital you were at. But Timothy and I worked together like a couple of spies. They weren't any match for either of us. I'm glad you're back," I say again.

The reply is a snore and that's good enough for me.

My relief doesn't last long, though. This morning, when I wake up, I get a better look at her. She's lost weight. It's as though someone has let the air out of her face. Her jowls hang from her jaw. The bags under her eyes are smudges of melted lilac wax. Her eyelids flutter as though they're keeping something at bay.

"You're looking well," I call out. "It was pneumonia you had. Did you know that? I'm not surprised. Not in this place. Germs everywhere."

When breakfast time comes, the Filipina nurse wheels me to the dining room. Ruth, she tells me, is getting breakfast in bed.

"The rest of us should be so lucky," I say as she deposits me at my usual table. I hurry through my scrambled eggs and bacon. I don't like the idea of Ruth being in there by herself. When I return, she's sound asleep, her breakfast untouched. The fire-headed woman comes in to take her tray away. She stops and looks sympathetically at Ruth. Then she looks over at me and shakes her head. What is that supposed to mean?

I'm relieved when Timothy drops by after dinner. He immediately goes over to Ruth's bedside.

"Hello, Mrs. Schueller," he says. "It's nice to see you."

She blinks back at him, a blank canvas.

"She's not well," I tell him. "Look how gaunt she is."

"It will take a while to get her strength back," he says. "She was very ill."

He sits down next to me and opens his knapsack. "I brought something for you."

He hands me an apple-shaped cookie in a Baggie. It has red icing and a sugared mint leaf at its stem. My initials are written on it in white icing. The cookie is almost the size of my hand.

"I'm something of an amateur baker," he says with a shrug. "Probably nowhere near as good as your son."

"You made this?"

"I saw a picture of them in a magazine and couldn't resist. You don't have to eat it. I know that people are on restricted diets around here. I don't think I'm even supposed to be passing out homemade food. You'd mentioned the apple cake your son once made and I thought . . . well, I don't know exactly what I thought. Only that you might enjoy something sweet. Hope you don't mind."

I don't remember the last time I received such a simple gift. Tears form in my eyes. My finger traces the raised script of the J and S.

"Can I ask how your son died?"

I turn the cookie over in my hand. How many times have I been asked this over the years? The well-meaning faces. The sympathetic hands. The downturned mouths. Such concern and curiosity. Never once did anyone get the truth. But now, this moment, this cookie, this young man who has come to mean more to me than he'll ever know.

"John died of . . ." Why can't I say the word? Even after all this time. "My son died from what a lot of young men died from in the '80s."

Timothy looks at me, then looks down.

"I see." He clears his throat. "I don't want to make assumptions, but perhaps I should mention that I'm gay. I'm assuming you'd figured that out by now. About me. Most straight men don't pass out apple-shaped cookies to senior women."

"Why is that?" I ask, looking at him for what feels like the first time.

"I don't know. Maybe they don't see the value in it."

"And you do?"

He shrugs. "I like old people."

"Do your parents know? About you?"

"I told them when I was eighteen."

My god. Just a child.

"You must've given your mother a heart attack."

"She was fine. Said she knew all along."

"Most mothers do."

"She had a boyfriend in high school who turned out to be gay. They still keep in touch."

"Imagine that," I say.

After Timothy leaves, I gently set the cookie on my night table, next to the picture of John. I won't eat it. It's too precious. And if anyone asks me where I got it, I'll play dumb and pretend I don't hear the question. It's no one's business.

I pull my buzzer cord. I want to get out of this chair and lie down. My back is bothering me. I've got no cartilage left in my spine. Bone grinds against bone. It's agony and the pills they give me don't do any good at all. I don't know how many times I've asked for something stronger, but the nurses stare back at me as though I'm speaking another language. The light outside our door begins to flash and beep. God knows when someone will arrive. I glance over at Ruth. She looks no better than she did this morning.

I wheel over to my window and wait. The wind kicks up outside. Fall is on the way. I watch as leaves scuttle across the pavement like crabs. Soon, the trees will be bare. Branches like stiff arteries. There's a residence for college students across the way. A few days ago, I watched a procession of cars pull up in the circular driveway, depositing boys and girls who seemed far too young to be left on their own. I remembered John at that age, living in that apartment with Mark. I was so afraid to let him go. I thought I had good reason. Perhaps I did. I watched the awkward hugs, the cars heading home with the back seats empty. I was never happy for John. Not really. That, perhaps, was my biggest crime.

"What is it, Mrs. Sparks?"

A nurse appears at my door. She's fairly new. An unfortunate rear end, but pleasant enough.

"I want to lie down," I say.

"Are you sure? It's only eight o'clock."

"My back is on fire. I can't take it anymore."

She positions my chair next to the bed and hooks her arms under me. "On the count of three."

When she lifts, the pain shoots up my spine. It's so bad that I holler. "Watch what you're doing. Oh! None of you know how to do anything."

I feel the softness of the bed beneath me. She takes my ankles and swings me around. "There we go," she says, but it's barely above a whisper. I should apologize. It's not her fault. But it's too late now.

During the night, I dream. Two figures come into my room. They're dressed in white, but they don't have wings. I hear faint murmurings. The sounds are comforting, a gentle current in the room. How nice to have angels here, I think. Finally some qualified staff. I watch them out of the corner of my eye. They flutter about the room, taking care of the dusting and cleaning. They make hardly any noise at all. I doubt their feet are even touching the ground. I want to reach out to them, to thank them for coming, but my arms remain at my sides, stone-heavy. I hear a few clicks and then a wave of white covers the room, peaceful snow, and I fall back asleep.

In the morning, I discover it was no dream. Ruth is gone.

"Back to the hospital?" I ask one of the aides.

My answer is a slow shake of the head.

It's been two weeks since Ruth has died and they still haven't replaced her. I've heard rumours that it might be Rose Dunlop from down the hall. Her money is running out and her family can't afford a private room anymore.

"Have you seen the amount of stuff she has packed into that room?" Mae asks me. "She's a hoarder through and through. I saw a documentary on TV about it. They don't throw anything away. It's psychological."

"Can you be an emotional hoarder?" I ask, but Mae has turned her attention elsewhere. She reaches for the arm of a nurse walking by and asks to be returned to her room.

I don't want Rose in my room. I don't want to have to share with anyone anymore. I want to be back in my house. I want my old mattress. My bathroom with the brown furry bath mat. I want my butterfly kitchen. But all of that is gone. Strangers live there now. They've likely torn up the carpets. Steamed off the wallpaper. Painted the walls and patched up the holes where I hung my pictures. I don't even want to think what they've done to John's old room.

Timothy brings in Ruth's obituary notice from the newspaper. It says she was eighty-four.

"I thought she was eighty-two."

He shrugs. I'm not as sad about Ruth's death as I thought I'd be. I have Timothy now. The service will be held at the funeral home on Tuesday, followed by a luncheon.

"Look at all these names they wrote in here. 'Dearly missed by' my arse," I say. "I've never seen one of these relatives walk through those doors. Not one. I don't intend to eat your cookie."

His eyebrows shoot up. "You don't?"

"It's too nice. If I ate it, I wouldn't be able to look at it and you did such a nice job. You should sell them."

"I don't think there's a lot of money to be made in cookies."

"Tell that to Mr. Christie."

He laughs, and the sound makes me close my eyes. It feels like I haven't heard laughter in years. He tells me he won't be coming next Friday. He's going away for the weekend. Back to Toronto.

"Oh," I say, hoping I don't sound as disappointed as I feel. "Anything special?"

"Just visiting friends. I haven't been back since the spring. I miss it sometimes."

"Do you drive?"

"Yes, I have a car."

Then it comes to me. A wish so old, it's fraying around the edges. "May I ask a favour?"

He nods. "Of course."

I'm not sure if it's right to ask. But I'm more afraid of *not* asking.

He leans in. "What is it?"

"My son is buried at Lakeside Cemetery. My husband, too. I don't remember the last time I was there. There's a vase on top of the stone. I used to put flowers inside. People might think that no one cares."

"You'd like me to take flowers to the cemetery?"

"No," I say. "I want you to take *me* to the cemetery. I'd like to visit." *One last time*, I think.

He exhales and slowly slides his palms down his thighs. "Joyce, I'm not sure I can do that. You're in a wheelchair—"

"It folds up."

"—and I doubt the home would let me—"

"Lots of people go on day trips. There's no rule against it."

"It's not . . . it's not as simple as it seems."

I look down at my hands. "I see."

"I would if I could."

"I shouldn't have asked."

A heavy silence closes in. I've crossed a line.

"Have a nice time in Toronto," I say.

CHAPTER TEN

I HAVE TO get groceries. Walter consumed all of my cookies. My cupboards yawn back at me. When I open the front door, I'm ashamed to see Mr. Sparrow standing on my porch. Since his return from the hospital, I haven't dropped by or asked him how he's doing. He's holding a pint of peaches and wearing a blue baseball cap that reads "Don't Forget My Senior's Discount!" in white letters.

"How was your visit with that fellow?" he asks.

"Fine," I say, taking the peaches from him. "Strange. But fine."

"He was a little ornate, if you don't mind me saying."

"I don't mind you saying." I consider filling him in on the situation, then think the better of it. I don't want to say the word *homosexual* in front of Mr. Sparrow. It doesn't fit within our talks of weather and vegetables. "Excuse me for a moment." I slip back inside and set the peaches on the chair in the hallway. I need to get to the grocery store before it closes. When I step back out, I lock the front door behind me, hoping he gets the message.

"You changed," he says, gesturing at me. "You were wearing that nice outfit before."

"I'm on my way to pick up a few things. Would you like me to get anything for you?"

"I'm good. But thanks. I'm assuming he's gone home by now."

"Who?"

"Walter. Said he was driving back to Miami. I asked why he didn't fly and he said he didn't like his feet leaving the ground. I can appreciate that."

I pause. "Did Walter tell you? About Freddy . . . and him?"

He turns to face the street. He takes so long to answer me, I think he may not have heard. "I had an older brother up north. Earl. He worked in the forestry business. Never married. He'd come to visit every couple of years or so. Maybe you met him."

"I don't think I did."

"Eileen and I always believed he was of a particular persuasion, so to speak, but he never said anything to confirm our suspicions. Earl and I never talked about it. That bothered me. Not that I cared one way or another if he was that way, but the silence got to me. Eileen was always after me to ask him, but I never did. That's what happens. When you don't talk about things, you're left forever making up conversations in your head."

Mr. Sparrow places his hands on his hips. "He died a long

time ago. Going on twenty-five years now, I guess. Heart attack. Seems a shame to me that all those years went by between us."

He turns back to me. "Walter said he was going to ask you to help him with a party."

"He did."

"You said no."

"It's not that I don't want to help."

"No need to defend yourself."

"I don't know him at all."

"You know him a little."

"It would be so much work."

"Maybe not." He stands there, blinking. "Well, I won't keep you then." He adjusts his ball cap and begins making his way down the front steps, slowly, one at a time. "Those peaches should ripen up in a day or two. Put them in a paper bag. I find that always helps."

He shuffles down my front walk, his brown pants hanging off him. My hand massages my forehead. Damn it, Mr. Sparrow. Damn your peaches and your sad stories.

"Mr. Sparrow!" I call out. "If I do this, you have to come to the party."

"With bells on!" he calls back.

I call the Seahorse Motel as soon as I go back inside. If I put off doing it, I know I won't go through with it.

"Walter Clarke's room, please," I say, hoping that he may have checked out.

The line clicks. I consider hanging up, but push myself on. "Hello?"

"Walter, it's Joyce Sparks."

"You're not outside my door again, are you?"

"No, I'm home. I'm calling . . ." I don't want to do this. I don't *have* to do this. I just want this man to go away. I want all of this to go away.

"Joyce?"

"I'm sorry. I'm a little scattered. The past couple of days have been difficult ones. I'm not used to dealing with these sorts of . . . things."

"Is there a particular reason for your call?"

I squeeze my eyes shut. "I'd like to invite you to a potluck lunch tomorrow at my house. It may not be exactly what you had in mind, but I'll invite some friends who knew Fred. Not that anyone was close to him. But they're people who knew him. My sister. And my friend Fern. I'm also inviting Mr. Sparrow."

"I don't know what to say, Joyce."

"Say you like meatballs because that's what we're having."

I keep checking my list as I circle the grocery store aisles. Onion flakes. *Check*. Minute Rice. *Check*. Tomato soup. What aisle is the soup in? I squint at the overhead signs. I can't remember the last time I actually cooked for someone other than myself.

I hold a package of ground beef in each hand, debating how much I need. When did I last make porcupine meatballs?

I put both packages into my shopping cart and add a third. Then I add a fourth for good measure. I'll freeze the leftovers. It'll do me good to get away from those packaged dinners that are far too easy to toss into the microwave.

I had to run Walter's story by Fern three times before she got it down.

"And Freddy never came back to Balsden?" she asked. "Not even once?"

"How is he supposed to come back if he's dead?"

"It's not like anyone would've recognized him. Let's face it, Joyce. None of us look the same as we did at seventeen. What can I bring for lunch?"

"How about that broccoli salad? The one with the cheese."

"I'll have to go out and get ingredients."

"I'm sorry about the short notice," I said. "Everything came up so suddenly."

"No need to apologize. I'm a woman of the United Church of Canada. I can make a salmon loaf standing on my head in thirty seconds."

Helen kept her opinions to herself. "I'll bring scalloped potatoes. And something for dessert. Maybe squares. I'll see what I have on hand. Is this man Jewish? The potatoes call for bacon."

"I never thought to ask. Why would he be Jewish?"

"Why wouldn't he be?" She said she'd leave it out to be on the safe side.

Something catches in my throat and I start to cough.

"Are you all right?" Helen asks.

"I'm fine. Relatively speaking. It's been a lot to digest in the course of a day." I don't tell her about the cemetery. There are things Helen and I don't discuss.

He coughed during one of our Sunday-afternoon phone calls. I remember that moment distinctly. It was Victoria Day, 1984. We'd had a terrible rainstorm the previous day and water had seeped into the basement. Charlie had spent most of the morning going up and down the stairs carrying cardboard boxes and setting them to dry out in the backyard. I'd been telling John about Marianne's upcoming wedding. It was taking place in September. John was to be one of the groomsmen. I was looking forward to seeing him in a tuxedo, knowing that it might be the only time I'd ever see him in one. I had almost given up hope of his ever getting married.

"Helen said Marianne is already over budget," I was telling him. "And she hasn't even bought the dress yet. Helen wants her to go traditional, but you know Marianne. She has some peculiar tastes. Apparently, she wants all the bridesmaids in burgundy."

Then it came. A sound as dry as cracked clay.

"Are you sick?"

"Just a bug," he said. "I've been off work for a few days."

"Have you been to a doctor?"

"No. And don't start. It's a cold, nothing more."

I'd been hearing the odd thing in the news, snippets about an illness that was affecting men ... well, gay men. The term *gay* was foreign to me, too distant from my vocabulary. My son was not one of *them*.

I told him to get his rest. When he came home at the beginning of June for Charlie's birthday, he seemed fine. A little thinner, but nothing alarming. I was happy to see he'd shaved his moustache off. He said he was in the running for executive chef at the club.

"If I get this," he said, "I'll be the youngest executive chef they've ever had."

"We'll keep our fingers crossed for you," Charlie said.

But a few weeks later, during another Sunday phone call, the cough was back. Only that time, it sounded looser, more jarring. Stones rattling.

"I thought you said you were over that cold."

"I am. It's just taking a while to fully clear itself out."

"You should see a doctor. This isn't the time of year for colds."

"Everyone at work is sick right now. I'll see one if it gets worse."

"Promise?" He often said things I wanted to hear.

"Promise."

"I don't like the idea of you being alone. I can come for a visit. I'll take the bus."

"Mom, I'm thirty-one. I can take care of myself."

I made him swear to call me the minute he came down with fever or if his cough got worse. "I'm serious, John. You can't take these things lightly."

"Yes, Sergeant."

I called back two days later. He said he was fine. I called back on Sunday. He admitted that he'd come down with a fever a few days before, but it had been mild. He said he was feeling much better. I wasn't to worry. He planned to go back to work the next morning. On Tuesday, I received a phone call.

"Mrs. Sparks? It's Angela Dawber. John's friend from high school?"

Panic raced through me. "What's wrong?"

"I took John to the hospital last night."

"The *hospital*?"

"He's fine now and back home. He was feeling short of breath."

"He's had some sort of cold," I said. "He hasn't been able to shake it."

"I think you should come to Toronto if you can. Just for a few days. John could use a little help, although you'd never hear him say that. You raised a stubborn son, Mrs. Sparks. Marty and I can't get to him as often as we'd like."

"Marty is your husband?"

She paused. "No. He's John's friend. I don't think you've met him. Anyway, the two of us have been checking in on him. He's lost some weight on account of being sick. Not too much. But some. If you stayed with him, you could fatten him up. Home cooking and all that."

"Yes, I'll come," I told Angela. Why did I have to hear this news from someone else? Why couldn't John have told me himself? I informed Charlie that John had taken ill and I'd be on the train to Toronto the next morning.

"I'll stay until he's on the mend. Maybe a week. There's a lasagna in the deep-freeze and some stew. Don't touch the squares. They're for the bake sale. And I'll know if you take one and try rearranging."

"I should come," Charlie said. His brow was lined. The overhead kitchen light accentuated a head of hair that had gone half grey. When had that happened?"I'll take some holiday time."

"One of us is all that tiny apartment can handle. I'll call you every day. He'll be fine, Charlie. Really."

I said whatever needed to be said. There was no point getting Charlie all worked up. But once the train reached the outskirts of Toronto and began to slow down, I couldn't shake the feeling of dread inside me. Although I would not, *could not* consider the possibility of the illness I'd read about, I felt the word's proximity, its cold shadow. I closed my eyes and vowed I wouldn't allow anything to harm him.

The train pulled into the station shortly after noon and I hopped in the first cab I found. Everything seemed so chaotic. The cars, the people on the streets. What was it about this city that had drawn John to it? We came to a red light close to John's apartment and I saw two men standing in front of a bank. One had his hand in the other one's back pocket. He caught me looking and waved, his fingers tinkling in the air like piano keys. I turned away.

John answered when I rang the buzzer."Uh-oh. Looks like the good times are over now." He said the door to his apartment was open.

He was lying on the couch, a blue blanket covering the peaks of his thin frame. Knees. Elbows. Toes. When he met my gaze, my worst fears were confirmed. He looked away. He knew that I knew. His expression took me back to a cold field on a March day and a burning question from many years before.

Why did you come?

He said he'd been running a fever since the morning. I wanted to take him back to the hospital. "There's no need," he said. "It will break. They always do."

I ran a washcloth under the kitchen tap, squeezed it out. The kitchen was a mess. Plants wilted on the sills. Sweatshirts lay on the floor like puddles. I'd have to clean everything once I got settled. I pressed the washcloth against his forehead, covering the top half of his face. I could see only a scrap of nose and a pair of lips sticking out from the scruff around his face.

"Why didn't you tell me you were sick?" I asked, more angry than concerned.

"I did."

"Not sick like this."

He propped himself up on his elbow and lifted the washcloth slightly. I saw a flash of eyes. "I can't be sick for much longer because I've booked a trip to Mexico."

"Mexico? Why on earth would you want to go there?"

"I'd let you come with me, if you thought you'd survive outside your ten-mile radius around Balsden."

"Don't be smart. I've been lots of places. I certainly don't need to add Mexico to the list. Besides, there's nothing in the world that you can't find in your own backyard."

"Is that so?"

"Yes, that's so."

"Well, I'd still like to go to Mexico. And I think you'd enjoy yourself, too. You could put on a bikini and do tequila shots on the beach."

"Don't be ridiculous."

He'd lost his job. He told me that the second day I was there. The manager had pulled him aside and said that some of the staff were concerned. It wasn't appropriate for him to be handling food. The members were nervous.

"They can't fire someone over the flu," I shot back. "Did you talk to Angela's husband about this?"

"I'm not getting him involved. I was getting tired of that place anyway. There are few things in life more demeaning than catering to the wealthy. They gave me three months' salary, which will do me for the time being. I'd like to find a place where I could really cut loose. Express my creativity. Someplace that doesn't serve lobster beak."

He smiled and I know I should've smiled back. But I couldn't. I went to the bathroom to get the thermometer from the medicine cabinet.

"If you're out of work, there's no way you're going on vacation," I called. "You'll just have to wait. Why all this sudden talk about Mexico, anyway? What's there that you can't get here?"

"Warmth," he called back, and I nearly crumpled. It was the end of June.

He had friends. They'd call in the evenings and John would excuse himself to his bedroom to talk. I listened at his door a few times, trying to pick up some of the conversation. Who were these people? What was he telling them that he wasn't telling me? But I could never make out specific words, only his quiet tone, slipping out from under the door.

After I'd been with him for a week I still didn't know what to think. He was sick. There was no doubt about that. But he was still able to get around. He wasn't incapacitated. We even went for a walk one day. I couldn't believe how expensive the houses were when John told me. It was ridiculous. They weren't much bigger than our place in Balsden.

"There's no way you can live here," I said. "How will you ever afford it?"

"I get by okay," he said as we started up the driveway in front of the apartment building. "I'll make it. Don't you worry."

Worry! How could I not? I heard him in the bathroom at night, wincing at some of the sounds. And yet, in the morning, he'd be all action, refusing to sit still. He needed to be out, he said. Doing things. My presence made him feel restless.

"Well, you don't have to worry about my presence for much longer," I said. I needed to get home to take care of a few things. I'd be gone a few days. Then I'd be back.

"Do you have someone?" I asked him the morning I left.

He looked up from his bowl of cereal, startled. "Someone?"

"You know what I mean. When I leave, is there someone to take care of you?" I waited. Would he mention this Marty? It felt like a dare.

"Yes. I have friends, Mom."

"Are any of them sick as well?"

"Some." He slipped a spoonful of cornflakes in his mouth. A teardrop of milk lodged in his beard. This has stuck with me over the years, this memory of milk in my son's dark beard.

"Come home with me."

This is what I should've said. If I had been a good mother, I would've insisted that he pack a bag and come back with me to Balsden. His father and I would've taken care of him. I'd have cooked his favourite meals. We'd just got a VCR and could watch old movies in the afternoons. Perhaps that *Virginia* movie he loved so much. We'd tour around Balsden. I'd show him what was new. He'd go back in a few weeks, find another job. We'd make plans for Mexico.

Come home, John. Come home.

But I couldn't bear the thought of people seeing him like this. They'd suspect more than the flu. Conclusions would be drawn. They'd think things that weren't true. Judge my son. Judge me. Charlie. I couldn't have that. He was better off in Toronto, with his friends, in his own apartment. Tucked away in a big, anonymous city.

So I didn't say the words. Instead, I looked past his shoulder and commented on how pretty the sky was that morning.

"Like a painting," I said.

He turned around slowly and said, "Ocean blue."

He offered to come with me to the station.

"I'm not crippled, you know," he said. "It might do me some good to get outside."

I refused and told him I'd call when I got home. "I'll be back in a few days." I looked down at the hallway tiles. "Your father will want to know how you're doing. He'll likely want to come back with me. I know he doesn't say it, but he loves you a great deal, John. What do you want me to tell him?"

"Nothing."

"I have to tell him something. He's your father."

"Then tell him I'm sick but I'm on the mend. Promise me you won't say anything more than that."

"I can't—"

He grabbed my arm. "Please promise me. He's . . . Dad's been good to me. I can't do this to him. He can't know."

Another secret. Another wound.

"All right, John. All right."

"I'll be fine," he said.

"But you're all alone."

"No." His voice turned angry. "You not being here does not make me alone. Do you understand that?"

"But I never meet anyone, John. I hear them call but no one ever drops by."

"You have no interest in meeting any of them, Mother. So stop pretending otherwise."

Mother. We were back to that. The ocean had receded.

I downplayed things to Charlie as John had asked. I told him that John had a bug but it didn't seem serious. In telling him this, I could partially believe my own words.

"What kind of a bug?" Charlie asked. We were sitting at the kitchen table. I'd made my cabbage roll casserole. It was Charlie's favourite, but I hated the way the smell hung in the air for hours afterwards.

"A flu bug," I said, pushing around the remains on my plate. "He's lost some weight and his energy is down, but he thinks he's on the mend."

"Has he seen the doctor?"

"Yes. He's on some kind of prescription. Don't ask me to repeat the name. I won't get it right."

A sharp inhale. A holding. Then a slow exhale. "I see."

"He had to leave work," I said. "They gave him three months' severance, which I think is reasonable. He said he was ready for a change."

Charlie looked up, weighing this new piece of information. He opened his mouth. Then closed it. His eyes slowly circled the room, looking for something.

"His spirits are good," I said quickly. "You know John. Can't sit still. He wants to go to Mexico when he gets better."

"He shouldn't be alone."

"He's not."

Charlie's eyebrows inched upwards. "That friend he came here with?"

"Of course not. Angela from high school. Do you remember her? There are others, too. They call to check up on him. He has a life there."

Charlie reached for his napkin and slowly wiped his mouth. His voice shook ever so slightly. "He should come home."

"I asked him to, but he wants to stay where he is. It's where he's most comfortable. I'll be going back in a week."

He put his napkin down. His eyes met mine. "I'm coming with you."

"You can't. You're working."

"I'll take vacation time."

"Don't be foolish, Charlie. It's not necessary. He's fine. Really."

"My son is sick. I want to see him. End of discussion."

I called John twice a day. Sometimes, the phone would ring through to his answering machine and I'd leave a panicked message, telling him to call me as soon as he got in. What if he'd fallen or was too sick to answer? Once, he didn't call me back for seven hours. I was beside myself and was about to tell Charlie we were driving to Toronto that night when the phone rang.

"Where have you been?" I cried.

Out. With friends. To dinner and then a movie. "You need to stop this, Mom. You're driving me crazy. I'm fine."

"No, you're not," I said. "You're not fine and you know it."

"Don't tell me what I know."

I sensed Charlie hovering around the corner. I lowered my voice.

"You can't blame me for being worried, John."

"I wouldn't blame you if there was something to worry about. I've been better these past few days. Tonight was the first time I've gone out in weeks. I was in a great mood. And then I come home to this."

"I'm sorry. It's just . . . when you don't answer, I start thinking things."

"Well, don't think."

He told me there was no need for me to come back to Toronto. He'd call if anything came up. "I'm fine. Scout's honour."

I'm not sure if I believed him or if I just *wanted* to believe him. Perhaps both. He agreed to Charlie and me coming down for a day within the next couple of weeks. He said he'd take us out for dinner at his favourite restaurant.

"Nothing too fancy," I said. "You know how we are."

"All too well," he said.

I cut my calls back to once a day, scrounging every ounce of self-control not to pick up that phone more than once some nights. Other times, Charlie called him, although he'd never tell me. He seemed to want to keep those conversations a secret.

"Are you taking vitamins?" I heard him ask once as I was coming through the back door. "Someone at work told me you should take them with your dinner. Not in the morning. They don't get into your system the same way. I'll send you some . . . No, it's fine. No trouble."

He went to the drugstore that night and bought two packages of multivitamins. I watched as he sat at the kitchen table and carefully wrapped them both in brown paper. He addressed the package in small capital letters, the way he wrote everything. The next morning, he was at the post office as soon as it opened.

"He'll be fine," I told Charlie when he got back, the irony of our role reversal not lost on either of us. "Everything is fine."

Until one day, it wasn't. Two weeks after my stay in Toronto, I got a call one afternoon from a man who introduced himself as Marty. I froze. He told me that John wasn't well. He'd been taken to the hospital a few hours before.

"He's been running a fever for the past week," the man said.

"But I was speaking with him the other night. He didn't say anything."

"There's a lot John doesn't tell you."

I hung up without saying goodbye.

There's no time to think. No time for me to get trapped in my head again, caught in endless memories. Only meatballs. I squish the cold ground beef between my fingers. It leaves a pinkish residue on my hands. I worry that Walter won't like them. He's probably used to finer cuisine than this and I'm reminded of John again and all the dishes he never got to make. The year after he died, I bought a gourmet cookbook. There was a recipe in it that was similar to the stuffed chicken breasts he made for Charlie and me that time. I was desperate to recreate them. I don't know why. I bought all the ingredients and pounded my chicken breasts until they were paper-thin but when it came time to roll them up, my fingers fumbled and the filling kept falling out. I ended up sticking a dozen toothpicks in each one to hold it in place.

"These look like sea creatures," Charlie said when I handed him his plate. I couldn't stop crying after that, even though he kept apologizing.

Once I place all the meatballs in a serving dish, I pour two cans of tomato soup over them and put them in the fridge to set overnight. Then I look around my house, wondering how I'm going to manage everything. I'll have to clean and dust and wash dishes I haven't touched in years. Do I even have napkins?

"I've got a package somewhere," Fern says when I call her. "They might have poinsettias on them, though."

"That's fine," I say. "Anything is better than paper towels."

"You didn't invite Mrs. Pender, did you?"

"No. I suppose I should. But I can't bring myself to do it, Fern. Every time I think of what she did, it makes my blood boil."

"I'm not going to tell you what to do. God knows you have your reasons for not inviting her. It's just that . . . he was her son, Joyce."

"I'm not sure she can even leave the home," I say. "She's in a wheelchair."

"There's your escape route. She can't come into your home if you don't have one of those ramps. Maybe you and Walter could drop by afterwards with leftovers. Make her feel like you haven't forgotten her."

I glance at the clock. It's just before nine. She's likely in bed, which means there's a good chance she won't answer the phone. I hang up with Fern and flip through my address book until I find Mrs. Pender's number. I'll give her four rings and then I'll—

"Hello?"

"Oh. Mrs. Pender. It's Joyce."

"Did you get your phone fixed?"

"I've invited Walter to lunch tomorrow and I'd like to extend the invitation to you as well. Walter wants to . . . commemorate Fred's memory. In his hometown. Meet some people who knew Fred. You probably won't be able to come as I don't have a ramp in front of my house."

"A ramp? Why would I need a ramp?"

"For your wheelchair."

"I can walk."

"You *can?*"

"I have legs, don't I?"

"I've only ever seen you in the chair or in bed."

"I'll have that American bring my walker. He'll give me a hand with the stairs."

"Will the home let you go?"

"They don't keep me chained to the bed, Joyce. I hope you're not serving ham. I never liked it. Freddy didn't, either."

"No ham." I massage the bridge of my nose.

She clears her throat. "I'm sorry about what I said earlier. I had no right to speak of your son. I've done too many things I regret in my life. Your hospitality means a great deal to me. And to Freddy."

"We'll see you tomorrow, Mrs. Pender."

CHAPTER ELEVEN

I'M HALFWAY INTO my pantyhose when the doorbell rings. I look over at the clock. It's 11:31. I invited people for noon. I wrestle on the rest of my clothes. I haven't even had a chance to put on makeup.

Mr. Sparrow is standing on my porch wearing a tweed fedora with a red feather tucked into the band, a suit jacket that looks two sizes too big and a yellow bow tie.

"Don't you look dapper," I say. My pantyhose are crooked. I'll adjust them later.

"Please take this," Mr. Sparrow says, holding out a pie. "It's peach. I made it myself."

The crust is haphazardly pieced together. It looks like a scorched quilt.

"You didn't have to bring anything."

"No trouble at all." He steps into the front hall and takes off his hat. "I don't believe in free lunches."

"Still," I say, trying to pry my fingers from the sticky under-side of the pie plate.

"I think it's a good thing you decided to have this party," he says. "You'll feel good about it afterwards."

I'm not betting on it.

We go into the kitchen and Mr. Sparrow compliments my table setting.

"My mother gave me those dishes when I got married," I explain, setting the pie on the counter. "She told me to use them only for special occasions. I think I've used them twice in all these years. Seems a shame."

Mr. Sparrow points to his bow tie. "Case in point. I bought this back in the '70s."

"I always wanted new water glasses," I say, picking one up to scrutinize it for spots. "I suppose it's too late now."

"It's never too late," Mr. Sparrow says.

I ask him how he's feeling. "I'm sorry I haven't been over since you got back from the hospital."

He settles himself into a kitchen chair. "Joyce, you don't have to take care of me. I do just fine on my own. I made that pie without having to call in the Armed Forces, didn't I? Besides, I hate the idea of being anyone's burden."

"You're not," I say. "I wish I could be more independent like you. I don't look after my house. I haven't watered the grass once this summer. At least you have your garden."

"You've got nothing to be ashamed about. Charlie would have been real proud of you for sticking it out as long as you have in this house."

Charlie, proud of me. If Mr. Sparrow only knew the truth. I feel a hard lump in my throat and swallow it back down. This would be a good time to mention selling the house, but I'm not sure how to do it. He has to find out sooner or later. And better he hears it directly from me than from a For Sale sign posted in the front yard.

"Maybe it's time for a change," he says, beating me to the punch. "You could move to an apartment and not have to worry about the lawn or the snow."

I sit down across from him. "I was thinking about that, actually. My sister has an apartment in her basement. She says she won't charge rent, although I wouldn't feel right staying there for free. Helen thinks the real estate market is 'hot' right now, whatever that means. She's been after me for months to move ahead with things. But before we do, she says I need to clear things out. I don't think there's much to do, really. Just empty the shelves in the basement. And whatever I don't take with me can go to the Goodwill or one of those rehabilitation places for drug addicts."

I stop when I see the soft curve of his lower lip.

"That's all future talk, though," I say quickly. "Nothing is confirmed. It might not happen. We'll see."

"Sounds pretty confirmed to me," he says with a slow nod. "Everything comes to its end sooner or later. Remember when you first moved here, Joyce?"

"Can you believe that was fifty years ago? In my mind, it was last week."

"Eileen and I were here a few years before you and Charlie,

when the houses were just finished. The trees out front were no bigger that this." He holds his hand a few feet from the floor. "Mud everywhere. Eileen hated it. The day we moved in, I promised her I'd make her happy. And I did. For a time, anyway. Then she found out she couldn't have children. I got on with things. I still had Eileen, after all. But it's different for some women. They get stuck in what should be instead of what is. She'd come back from visiting you and your boy and say, 'That's the natural order of things,' and have a little cry. I told her to stop going over if it upset her, but she said she couldn't help it."

"I'm sorry," I tell him. I try to picture Eileen in my head, but I can't. Her face eludes me. "I didn't know."

He places his hat in his lap. "When she got the cancer, she had to wear maternity clothes on account of her swollen stomach. A tumour instead of a baby. God has his jokes, I suppose."

The doorbell rings.

"I'm sorry," he says. "I shouldn't be talking like this. Not right before your party."

"There's no need to apologize. We can talk later. Excuse me for a moment."

Fern is wearing a red sequined top I've never seen before. Helen is wearing that straw hat again. Does she sleep with it on?

"I made the broccoli salad," Fern says. Her eyelids are blue, her lips a slash of bright red. Her breasts look like two red disco balls. Why is she all done up like this? She peers past my shoulder. "Is he here yet?"

"No," I say. "Just Mr. Sparrow. Where did you get that top?"

"I bought this in Michigan a few years ago. I've never worn it before. Someone told me gays love sequins."

Helen rolls her eyes. "You may want to put my potatoes in the oven until they warm up."

Fern slips past me. "I got the runs this morning, I'm so nervous."

"Dickie isn't coming?" I ask Helen.

Her response is a tight shake of her head.

"Hello, Mr. Sparrow," Fern calls out. "How goes it?"

"It goes fine," he says.

"He made a peach pie," I say.

"A peach pie!" Helen says playfully. "Aren't you a Renaissance man."

"No reason to make a fuss."

I run through the food. "We have meatballs and the vegetable tray. Fern's broccoli salad. Your potatoes. I also have buns and margarine. Am I forgetting anything?"

"Pie," Mr. Sparrow says, pointing at it.

"Is that what this is?" Fern leans over the counter. "I thought it was a round meat loaf."

A car horn honks.

"That must be Walter," I say, feeling my heartbeat quicken. I squeeze past the others. "Why don't the three of you go onto the deck? Helen, would you mind checking the chairs for bird poop?"

"She always gives me the fun jobs," Helen says.

I stop halfway to the door when I hear that familiar screech.

"... and *that's* the reason I don't like cars!"

I hurry over to the living room window and see Walter's white car out in front. From this distance, it looks as though there's a young girl sitting in the passenger seat with the window open. I almost manage to fool myself into believing it is, until that voice rips through the air again.

"I need to use the bathroom!"

Walter emerges from the driver's side, wearing a teal shirt and those black sunglasses. He pauses behind the car to rub his temples. "You're going to have to wait until we get inside, Mother Pender."

He walks around to open the passenger door. Taking each of her arms in his hands, he begins to tug.

"Watch it," Mrs. Pender says. "You're not deboning a chicken."

I should go out there to help but I'm rooted to the spot. I never thought I'd see Mrs. Pender vertical again, but there she is, upright on a pair of pretzel-thin legs. No wonder I thought she was a child. She's no bigger than an eight-year-old.

The floorboards creak behind me and I turn to see Fern approaching.

"I want to see Walter before he sees me," she whispers as she looks out over my shoulder. "That's him in the teal?"

"Yes."

"He looks like a little Liberace."

Walter takes a walker from the trunk and places it in front of Mrs. Pender.

"Careful, now," he says in a strained voice. He pulls a hand-kerchief from his back pocket and dabs his brow. "We've got a long driveway to go up and there are lots of cracks I need to step on."

"I'm going back out to the deck," Fern whispers, leaving me standing there. A few moments later, the doorbell rings. I take a deep breath and hold it in my lungs, afraid to let it go.

"I'm sorry, Joyce, but someone needs to use the bathroom," Walter says when I come to the door. He waves a finger over Mrs. Pender's head. "I hope that's all right."

"No problem at all."

Mrs. Pender's forehead is dotted with sweat and her bun is askew. She thumps past me into the house. "My god, it's a hundred degrees in here. Don't you have air conditioning?"

"I forgot to ask the nurses to put on a diaper before we left," Walter whispers hoarsely. "Do you mind helping her? I have my limits."

"I'll get Fern," I say. "She's good with these things. She had elderly parents."

The patio door slides open.

"Is everything all right?" Fern asks.

"Yes," I say, but there are too many people in my kitchen. "Fern, will you help Mrs. Pender to the washroom?"

"It's only number one," Mrs. Pender says. "No cause for alarm."

"Certainly." She clears her throat nervously as she extends her hand towards Walter. "I'm Fern, by the way."

"I'm Walter. Where did you get that top? It's screaming South Beach."

"Well, it was screaming fifty percent off when I saw it,"

Fern says, looking satisfied. She takes Mrs. Pender by the arm. "The bathroom is just down the hall."

"You look like a fireworks display," Mrs. Pender says.

I tell Walter to go out back and join the others. "Helen, my sister, is in the straw hat and you've already met Mr. Sparrow."

I stand for a moment, my palms pushing down on the laminate counter. I shouldn't have agreed to this. I'm in no frame of mind for hosting parties. Especially for strangers.

"That's the smallest bathroom I've ever seen," Mrs. Pender announces when she comes back into the kitchen. There's a bright smear of pink across her lips. Surely not mine, I hope. "You have to step outside to turn yourself around. Is that Hal Sparrow out there? I haven't seen him for years. Help me with this door, will you?"

I step over and slide it open for her. "Watch your step."

I pour glasses of wine and set them on a tray. Fern says she'll take it outside to pass around. I open the screen door for her and I hear Helen say something about cancer and then all eyes turn to me. My face grows hot.

"The meatballs should be done soon," I say. I head back inside.

I yank the cutlery drawer open to find my big serving spoon. Was she talking about John? I don't like anyone mentioning him while I'm not there. They have no right. The drawer slides all the way out, sending a clatter of silverware to my linoleum floor. I stare down at a tangle of fork tines and serrated edges.

"Oh," I hear myself say. Only that's not what I say. Instead, it's more a sound—a slow leak.

"What's the matter with John?" Helen asked when I told her we were heading to Toronto that night. I knew enough not to mention the details. I didn't trust her not to say anything.

"Fatigue, mainly."

"*Fatigue?*"

I winced hearing my word echoed back at me. "It's complicated."

"I see."

"You know John. He's always been a private person. He doesn't want me to say anything to anyone. It's not serious. There's nothing to worry about."

"Is there anything I can do?"

"Can you water my plants? I'm not sure how long we'll be gone. Likely a week. No longer."

I believed that. Charlie and I would stay with John for a few days after his release from the hospital to get him back on his feet. I planned to make large batches of dinners to freeze. And if John needed more time, I'd send Charlie home and stay on in Toronto until my son got better. I didn't care if it was a week or a month. I'd be there for him.

But I wasn't prepared for what I saw at the hospital. I looked down at the person lying beneath the white sheet. I couldn't understand what I was seeing. A mistake had been made. He was so emaciated. His cheeks were pockets, his brow a hard ledge. This wasn't the same person I'd seen less than three weeks ago. I'd just spoken with him, for god's sake.

I felt something close in around me as I stood beside my son's bed—a cellar's chill settling into my bones. I looked down at John's face, trying to find the son I'd known beneath the jutting bones and patches of beard. He was sleeping, his mouth open, a circle of darkness. An oxygen tube was attached under his nose and an IV drip was hooked to his arm. Maybe the liquid inside the bag was magic. It would make my son healthy again.

Charlie looked from John to me. "How can this be the flu?" he asked quietly.

I said nothing.

We sat by John's bedside, hypnotized by the slow rise and fall of his chest. Charlie's fingers fidgeted in his lap. He was a man whose hands knew what to do with wood and tools and pipes and chains, but never with the skin of another. I considered breaking my promise to John and telling Charlie the disease I believed our son had, but I was certain he'd be incapable of handling it. He didn't need confirmation of John's homosexuality or his disease. What Charlie needed was hope, and I wasn't about to take that away from him.

I suggested that he get a coffee. "It'll do you some good. When you come back, I'll go for a walk."

He nodded dumbly, a large child following instructions. I waited until he was out of the room. Then I leaned over my son.

"John, it's Mom. Can you hear me? Squeeze my hand if you can."

No response.

"John, you've got to pull through. You need to get well if you want to go to Mexico. I'll wear that bikini. I'll even get drunk and make a fool of myself and give you story after story to tell your friends when you get back home. Just wake up. Wake up and I'll do anything you want."

"He's been like that since this morning."

I looked up to see a man standing at the foot of the bed. He was wearing a red jacket and a Blue Jays ball cap. For a second I thought it was Kyle, but no. I'd recognize Kyle. That pug nose was burned into my memory. This was someone different.

"I'm Marty," he said. "The one who called."

I straightened up. "Yes. Thank you."

His hair was black and long enough to touch the collar of his jacket. There was a gold chain around his neck with a cross pendant shining out from the backdrop of his black T-shirt. He had a bump on his forehead the size of a Brazil nut. He smelled of cigarette smoke.

"He's been in and out of consciousness since I brought him in. Fever's broken at least. He has an infection in his mouth, too. Thrush. I'm assuming you know about the diarrhea?"

I blinked. "Diarrhea?"

"It's been bad for about two weeks now. He hasn't been able to hold anything in. It's been hell. He's been through so much."

I crossed my arms. "Who are you?"

"I'm sorry?"

"What is your relationship to John?"

He let out a short, awkward laugh and rocked back on his heels. "What do you think our relationship is?"

When I didn't answer, his eyes met mine. "I take care of him."

I saw a sharp ripple of ribs under his T-shirt. He had it, too, I thought. I was staring at the face of the disease itself.

"I appreciate you bringing my son to the hospital. But I'm his mother and I'm here now. John doesn't need you. You'll have to leave. My husband will be coming back any second and I don't want you to be here. He's going through enough."

His eyes held mine. His politeness slipped to hard edge. "John wouldn't want this."

"It doesn't matter what John wants."

His mouth twisted into a strange grin. "He always refused to say anything to you. I told him he should. I said it was better having things out in the open. But John said he wasn't raised that way." He took a step backwards. "He said he didn't have that kind of mother."

John woke once, briefly. We watched his eyes open and I heard Charlie catch his breath.

"John," Charlie said.

I got out of my chair. "It's Mom. We're here. You're going to be okay."

His eyes landed on mine, but only for a moment. His lids fluttered like butterfly wings and closed again. Had he seen me? Had he heard me?

"Is he in pain?" I asked the nurse when she came around to change the IV bag.

"He's made sounds. Groans."

She looked down at him. "I don't believe so."

"But how do you know?" I asked.

"I don't," she said. "Not for certain. But if he appears agitated, let us know."

The doctor came by at one point to tell us that John was suffering from a form of pneumonia. He suspected there was fluid buildup in the lungs. Words I didn't have a chance of articulating came out of his mouth. He told us John also had anal herpes.

"I'm sorry?" I asked.

"It's not uncommon," the doctor said. "But that's the least of my concerns right now."

John was scheduled for X-rays in the morning. They'd be able to see the extent of the infection in his lungs.

"I don't understand any of this," I said. "I was talking to him last week. How did he get from there to here?"

"The disease moves quickly. It's difficult to get a handle on everything at this stage. There's a lot we don't know about AIDS."

My knees almost gave out. That word. It screamed in my head. I glanced at Charlie. His face flashed confusion.

The doctor looked at me. "I'm assuming you knew."

I kept my eyes down and gave my head a slow shake. Charlie made a sucking sound, a gulp for air.

The doctor told us we should go home and get some sleep. They'd call if anything changed. We did as he suggested, even though both of us knew there would be no sleep that night.

We drove in silence to John's apartment, neither one of us wanting to speak of what we'd heard, what we'd seen, what it meant. We passed all-night convenience stores and restaurants with Sorry, We're Closed signs in the windows and pornography shops with triple neon Xs casting pink shadows onto the sidewalks. No one was out, save for a few lost souls. We stopped at a red light and I watched a beggar extend his hand towards my window. What kind of mother did he have? I wondered.

I held my breath when we unlocked the door to John's apartment. Charlie and I both stood in the hallway for a moment, uncertain if we should go inside. I found the light switch and we set our bags down. The air smelled like soap. There was a bowl filled with watery milk in the sink. A newspaper lay scattered across the kitchen table. A pair of peaches sat on the counter.

"Charlie," I said, "we passed a twenty-four-hour drugstore on the way here. Could you go and get me some Aspirin? I have a bad headache. I'm sorry I didn't ask before."

"John probably has some."

"Not the kind I need. Please."

As soon as the door closed behind him, I hurried around the apartment. I found nothing in the kitchen or living room. The bedroom door was ajar. For a brief moment, I was afraid I'd turn on the light and find Marty. But there was nothing, aside from John's unmade bed and the plaid comforter we'd given him that past Christmas. On the dresser was a photo frame. I picked it up. Marty squinted back at me. There were trees in the background. Where had this been taken? How long had they known one another? I felt as disturbed as when I'd discovered those muscle magazines. I shoved the picture beneath some sweaters in John's bottom dresser drawer. I changed the bedsheets. Inside his night table, I found a half-empty tube of Vaseline. I wasn't sure what it was for, but I buried it in the kitchen garbage. Then I stood in the centre of the living room, Marty's words swirling above me like an angry starling.

He said he didn't have that kind of mother.

I was still sobbing when Charlie returned with the Aspirin. He stepped over and wrapped his arms around me. We said nothing to one another. In the distance, the subways rattled towards their destinations.

I could not sleep. I tossed and turned in that bed, certain the sheets would spit me out at any moment. I was not welcome in this space. Marty continued to squint at me from his hiding place in John's dresser. Shortly before three, I surrendered to the fact that there would be no black pockets of forgetfulness that night. I walked out into the hallway, my bare feet on the cool tiles, and went into the living room. I tried to watch television, but found nothing except for infomercials and ads for telephone dating lines with scantily clad women. I couldn't focus on anything. At that moment, my son lay in the hospital while I sat on his sofa. It didn't make sense. If anything, Charlie or I should've been the sick one. John should've been the one worrying about one of *us*. I called the hospital, and after being subjected to fifteen minutes of elevator music, was told that John was still sleeping. There had been no change.

"You're sure he's not in pain?" I asked.

"If he was in pain, he wouldn't be sleeping," the voice said. She sounded middle-aged. Strangers were taking care of my son.

I stepped out onto the balcony, eager for the cool air to soak through my nightgown, my skin, my bones. There were no subways at this hour. Only the occasional flash of headlights passing on the road beyond the tracks. I made a promise that as soon as John got well again, I'd sit him down and apologize for everything: my nagging, my doubts, my reluctance, my fears. I'd accept him as he was, not as who I wanted him to be. He could even bring the occasional friend home, no questions asked. (Although we'd have to keep quiet about it.) I'd pave the way for new beginnings. Above all, we'd become friends again, just like we'd been in the early days.

The next morning, while Charlie sat on the sofa and stared vacantly out the living room window, I searched the fridge, looking for something to make for breakfast. The contents were a mystery to me: clotted cream, anchovy paste, chutney. I ended up poaching a couple of eggs and toasted some rye bread I found in the freezer. I watched Charlie push a piece of egg white around his plate with a corner of toast.

"What was he like when you were here?" he asked in a voice that seemed caught in his throat.

"Sick," I said. "But nothing like this. He had a bit of a fever. His energy was down and he'd lost some weight. But if I believed for one second he'd turn as ill as this, I wouldn't have left."

He looked up at me. "He should have come home, Joyce."

"Yes. He should've."

The telephone rang as I was clearing off the table, startling me so much that I dropped a juice glass. It was the hospital. John's blood pressure had dropped. They suggested we get there as soon as possible. Charlie went downstairs to bring the car around. I tried to wipe up the orange juice from the floor, thinking that John wouldn't want to come home to a messy house.

By the time we reached the hospital, the sounds coming from John were shallow, coarse, as though his lungs were filling up with sand. A nurse told me his breathing had become laboured around 6 a.m. and that it had gotten progressively worse.

"What are you going to do?" I pleaded.

"We've given him a shot of morphine," she said. "That's the best we can do at this stage."

At this stage. The floor gave way beneath me. My feet pedalled for traction.

She left. We settled quietly into the chairs on either side of the bed. Charlie placed his hand over John's. How much of our lives are lived too late?

"You couldn't ask for a nicer day," Walter announces as I set my big serving spoon into the bowl containing Fern's broccoli salad. "It's just perfect. Is this what they call Indian summer?"

We're sitting on the back deck balancing paper plates over our tightly closed legs. I found two TV tables. One went to Mrs. Pender, the other to Mr. Sparrow. I watch him bring a shaking fork towards his mouth, his meatball in peril of rolling away.

"That's not until the fall," Helen says. "Usually October. Before the first frost."

"What is Indian summer, anyway?" Walter asks.

"A late blooming," Fern says.

He laughs. "I could use some of that myself."

I join in but my laughter is alien. My meatballs have turned out dry, even though everyone says they taste perfectly fine. I should've added more eggs, but I wasn't paying attention. Helen's potatoes have turned out perfectly, of course. Fern's broccoli salad has too much mayonnaise for my liking. I pulled a hair from a floret and wiped it into my napkin. What a lacklustre memorial. Walter has to be disappointed in this turnout, these people, my dry meatballs. But he's managed to keep it hidden. He's been animated most of the time, telling stories about Miami. I'm sitting across from him, staring at the patch of skin revealed by his raised pant leg.

Why didn't you get it? I want to ask him. *How did you and Freddy escape the disease that claimed my son? What made your lives more important than his?*

I feel an impulse of anger towards him, his teal shirt, his white leg. I want to tell him what he can do with his Indian summer. My head swirls from the wine. It's been a long time since I've had a drink.

"That's one thing Fred said he missed," Walter says. "The seasons. I empathized to a point, but snowmen lose their appeal very quickly. Palm trees, on the other hand . . ."

"How long were you and Fred together?" Fern asks.

"That's none of our business," Helen says with a laugh.

"Thirty-three years," Walter says. "We were soulmates."

"Do I really need to listen to this?" Mrs. Pender asks.

"How did you meet?" Fern asks.

"My mother always wanted to go to Alaska so I took her on a cruise for her sixty-fifth birthday. Freddy was part of the entertainment on the ship. I stopped in my tracks the moment I saw him and was determined I'd get to know him before the cruise was over. Not so easy with Mother Darling attached to my hip. But thankfully, she tended to fall asleep after her post-dinner Drambuie. I snuck out one night and caught him performing in the ship's bar. He was a marvellous entertainer. I'm talking singing, dancing, acting—the whole enchilada. That night, he sang 'Moon River.' To this day, I can't listen to that song if it comes on the radio. There's no comparison. Anyway, I bought him a drink after his show and we talked under the stars. The rest, as they say, is history. We wanted to go on an Alaskan cruise when we found out he was sick. But it wasn't possible."

I look away as Walter slides the tip of a tissue under his bug glasses.

"He was a lovely man. I miss him in so many small ways."

"You're lucky to have found love," Fern says, surprising me.

"I was lucky to find Fred. Everything was underground in those days. So much secrecy and desperation."

"Soulmates." Mrs. Pender chuckles. "What a joke. The world is in sad shape and I can't leave it soon enough."

"I'm sure the world is devastated," Walter says.

"I'm getting more meatballs," Fern says, getting up from her chair with a grunt. "Does anyone want more?"

Mr. Sparrow raises his hand. "I could manage one or two."

Suddenly I feel overwhelmed. I want everyone gone. I want this to be over. They've all overstayed their welcome. My leg begins to throb and I reach down to massage my clotted veins.

"My son led a life of depravity." Mrs. Pender's face is a snarl.

"You shouldn't talk ill of the dead," Walter says, his voice rising. "Especially when they were wronged so much in life."

"He wronged himself!"

"I don't know how you have the audacity to say such terrible things about Fred," Walter says. "Especially in front of her." I look over to see him pointing at me. "*She* was the one who lost her son to cancer."

I feel everyone's eyes on me. Fern returns and is standing, dumbfounded, with a plate full of meatballs.

"Is that what she told you?" she asks Walter. She looks at me. "Is that what you said, Joyce?"

"I don't know what you're talking about." I get up from my chair. "I'll find a garbage bag for the plates."

"No point keeping secrets bottled up, Joyce," Helen says. "Not after all these years."

I point my fork at her. "Don't you dare talk to me about secrets. You know nothing about it. You've had everything you ever wanted and you're still not happy."

"Here we go again. Joyce and her tragic life. Always hard done by. Always the short end of the stick."

"Are you saying I'm responsible for the losses in my life?"

My sister rises out of her chair. "I'm saying you're a hypocrite when you accuse me of being unappreciative. At least I'm not a liar."

There's a flash of sparkling red. Fern's blouse between us. "That's enough."

"You didn't want anyone to know the truth about your son," Helen says.

Walter leans forward in his chair. "What are they talking about?" he asks Mr. Sparrow.

"My son . . ." I hear my own words trail to silence. I look at the faces surrounding me, searching for the one I want most but he's not here. "My son . . ."

"You're looking a little shaky, Joyce," Fern says. I feel her hand on my arm.

John died at 11:52 a.m. on Wednesday, July 25, 1984.

"My son didn't have cancer. He . . ."

There were no last words. No goodbyes.

And then I say it. "My son was a homosexual."

I feel myself fall.

* . . . .

No one can stop talking about the Queen.

"I still can't believe she's coming," Fern said the other night. She's beside herself. "Here, to our little city."

"Where does she go after Balsden?" I asked.

"Andover."

"Didn't she tour Canada a few years ago?"

"Yes, but this will be the longest royal tour ever. She's even going to the Northwest Territories, for crying out loud."

Fern feels the best place to watch the motorcade will be Century Park.

"They'll have bleachers set up. Mother and I are going down there with our flags and binoculars at the crack of dawn. Otherwise, we won't get a good seat. Thank god this isn't happening on a school day. I would have had to call in sick. Why don't you and John come with us?"

I tell her I'll think about it, but I really have no desire to be sandwiched between Fern and Mrs. Dover and their undying devotion to the monarchy. Helen said she hasn't decided if she's going. Mark and Marianne haven't shown much interest and Helen says Dickie could care less about the Queen.

"Just think of the crowds," Helen says with a shudder. "The newspaper said they're expecting ten thousand people. You'd think she was a movie star or something."

"Stop being a party-pooper. When was the last time something this big happened in Balsden?"

Every day for the past month, there's been a different article in the *Examiner*, giving updates about the Queen's visit. She won't be in the city for more than half a day, which has some people outraged over the cost of the festivities. But better a half-day than nothing at all, others have pointed out. The Queen is putting Balsden on the map.

Charlie finds it all ridiculous. "Why are they calling her the Queen of Canada when she doesn't even live here?" He says he's glad he has to work. But I overheard him the other night on the phone to his mother, making sure she knew the royal tour included a stop in Regina.

John can hardly contain his excitement, of course. He thinks he's friends with the Queen. In the fall, his kindergarten teacher, Miss Robinson, wrote a letter to the Queen on behalf of the class and included all the children's addresses. A few months later, John received a letter from Buckingham Palace. It wasn't from the Queen herself, but her lady-in-waiting, thanking him for the letter.

"What's a lady-in-waiting?" he asked.

"Someone who helps the Queen get dressed," I told him. "And plan out her day. Like a good friend."

"I could do that," he said.

I'd just put his Curly Q Sue doll in the spare room closet after a morning play. Charlie would never think to look there. "Boys can't be ladies-in-waiting. But you could be the Prince's butler."

I took a tea towel from the kitchen drawer, folded it in half and draped it across his wrist. "Now you say, 'Good day, sir. Would you care for some crumpets and tea?'"

When he repeated my words, he said "trumpets" instead of crumpets, which made me laugh.

Every day for the past two weeks, he's been asking, "Is the Queen here yet?" I've been asked what her castle looks like, why her husband is a prince and not a king, if she's bringing any dragons with her, if knights will walk beside her in the parade.

"Those kind of queens exist only in olden times," I told him. "This queen is modern and young. She's not that much older than your mommy."

Now I'm referred to as Queen Mommy.

"I think he's on to something," I said to Charlie.

The morning of the Queen's visit, before he slips out the bedroom, Charlie tells me to watch out for dragons. Within a few minutes, there's a knock on the door and John comes in, wearing his cowboy-print pyjamas. His hair sticks up in every direction. A soft explosion.

"Is it time yet?" he wants to know.

"Not yet," I say. I get out of bed, wrap my housecoat around me and take him into the kitchen to make a batch of pancakes. "The Queen is probably eating pancakes this morning, too."

His face lights up. "Do you think?"

"Absolutely," I say. "She has a big day ahead of her."

I help him ladle the batter into the frying pan and he lets me flip them, knowing that this is too complicated for his small hands. We stack the pancakes onto a plate and slide it into the oven while we wait for the others to cook. Outside, I hear the construction crews starting up. I thought they might have taken the day off, given the celebrations, but nothing, it seems, stands in the way of progress.

No matter, I think. Time has stopped in this moment, in my kitchen, for John and me. It's just us and the pancakes and the anticipation of something bigger than either of us can imagine building in the distance.

After we finish our pancakes, I have an idea. In a moment that seems both wrong and right, I take a paper napkin, some tape and a pair of scissors and make John a crown to wear on his head. I set it carefully on top of his dishevelled hair.

"There you are," I say.

"Here I am," he replies, and his smile is so instinctive, so natural, I ache.

■ ■ ■ ■

You'd think someone my age would be philosophical. I don't know if I'll live to see another year. Death is loitering in the hallway outside my room. Who knows when he'll decide to step through my door? I should've come to some sort of resolution by now. Some statement of fact. But I'm not philosophical. I'm not convinced that things happen for a reason. I suppose I could pull things out of the air, stitch together a quilt of lessons and give some semblance of order to those who have their whole lives in front of them. They need that much more than I do.

"There is a purpose behind everything," I'd say. "Ladybugs eat the aphids that destroy your garden and so forth."

I'd say something about idle hands. Maybe toss in a line about licking honey from a rose thorn. Whatever would suit the purpose and satisfy the need.

The truth is, I've lived through all my years and losses and I'm not any bit smarter or wiser than I was twenty years ago. Everything is still a ball of chaos. I seem to be able to do less

313

and less about it. But I'm fine with that. I've learned to let go. Of some things, in any case.

These are the thoughts that loop over and over in your head as you sit in your wheelchair with a blanket over your lap, looking at the pebbled roof of the convenience store across the street, knowing that there's an empty vase on the gravestone of your only child.

Ruth has been replaced. My new roommate is Claire. And, miracle of miracles, she can talk.

From what I make of her, she seems all right. She has short, practical hair and a thin, tall frame. She doesn't like wearing her dentures (only when she has visitors) so her mouth looks like one of those purses with a drawstring, all puckered and pinched at one end. There are photographs of her family on the wall and a small TV that broadcasts her Sunday-morning church service and a cactus on her windowsill that she says is forty-two years old. I don't think that can possibly be true, but why would she lie about a thing like that? She likes doing word puzzles and has the *Toronto Star* delivered on Saturdays. That's where she used to live. She came to Balsden because her daughter lived here. Then Claire's son-in-law lost his job and the family moved to Sudbury.

"You have to roll with the punches," she says.

Claire's husband died in the early '80s. She never remarried, although she dated someone for a while. They used to play cards with the neighbours. Then he died as well.

"I'm still open to anything," she says. "There are lots of eligible men around here."

"Most of them aren't worth much," I say. "I wouldn't get your hopes up."

"One less competitor for me." She shrugs and returns to her crossword.

I watch Claire as she goes about her crosswords or watering her cactus ("A dribble every three weeks. Never more. That's the secret") or poring over her newspaper. She seems so focused. Efficient. She's unlike anyone else I've shared a room with, and this makes me nervous because now I'm the weaker one. This time around, I have a feeling I'll be the one replaced.

The fire-headed nurse tells me it's Thursday. Timothy should be coming tomorrow night. I haven't seen him for two weeks. Part of me is frightened that he won't come back. What if I scared him away last time? I shouldn't have asked him to take me to the cemetery.

Claire looks up from her crossword.

"When is Trevor coming?" she asks, as if reading my mind.

"Tomorrow," I snap. "And it's Timothy, not Trevor."

I never should've mentioned Timothy to her, but it slipped out. She'll listen in. Perhaps she'll try to monopolize our conversation. Make small talk. She'll ruin everything. I'll tell Timothy to take me to the end of the hall. I won't share him.

"I wish I had a son to visit me." She licks the tip of her pencil.

"He's not my son."

"That's what you called him."

"I did not."

"Yes, you did. You said your son was coming for a visit."

My face goes warm. I *couldn't* have said that. My mind isn't gone. But why would Claire make this up? I fumble for the remote control and turn on the television. "He's not my son."

"Whatever you say, boss."

For lunch, we have meat loaf and peas that are more grey than green. For dessert, we're served a dish of apple crisp with a melting scoop of vanilla ice cream. It tastes like heaven. In the afternoon, they put on a movie in the recreation room. I don't usually go because it's hard for me to follow as most of today's actors say their lines too fast, as though they can't wait for the movie to finish so they can spend their millions. But today, I decide to go. I don't catch the name of the movie and I'm certain I won't enjoy it, but in the end, I do. It's a ghost story about a woman and her two children who believe they are being haunted. But really, they are the ones doing the haunting. They think they're alive, but they're dead. I think of Helen who fought her death until the very final seconds. I remember her thrashing in that hospital bed, as though her movements might provide a distraction. But death overpowered her in the end, as it always does. She didn't look peaceful so much as inconvenienced.

My telephone rings after dinner. It startles both Claire and me so much that she drops her crossword book and I drop the remote control.

"Joyce, it's Timothy. I won't be coming tomorrow night."

"Oh. I see."

"I caught a bug while I was away."

My stomach twists. A bug?

"I've been sick ever since."

"What's wrong?"

"Just a bad cold." He sneezes.

I'm overreacting. Gay men still get colds, I remind myself.

"My friend was just getting over one, so I suppose it was inevitable. This always happens when I go somewhere. I shouldn't leave home."

"Get plenty of rest," I say. "And drink ginger ale. That always seems to help me."

"Needless to say, I won't be coming in until this clears up."

"Of course not."

"I don't want to contaminate everyone."

"It's a bad time of year."

"When I'm feeling better, we'll go."

My fingers touch my lips. "Go?"

"To the cemetery. I've spoken to Hilda. We're all set."

He can't be saying what I think he is. I'd given up all hope.

"It's not necessary. I mean you don't have—"

"It'll be fine."

"No. It's too much trouble."

"Joyce, let me take you to your son."

I make a sound. Claire turns her head.

"All right."

"What kind of flowers should I bring?"

"Anything," I say, but I'm not sure he can hear me. "Anything at all."

CHAPTER TWELVE

WE SAT IN the hospital room, our son between us. John's mouth was open, a black hole. I pulled back the sheets and looked across his emaciated body, bones jutting from under his hospital pyjamas; the angle of his left foot; his lilac-tipped fingers. I knew this would be the last time I'd ever see him. I wanted to memorize every detail.

Charlie sat across from me, still holding John's hand. But by then, the holding had turned to soft strokes. A methodical brushing. Back and forth. Back and forth. The expression on his face was so full of hurt, I couldn't bear to look at him. A nurse came into the room and stopped when she saw us.

"I'll get a doctor," she said softly. "We need to officially pronounce him."

Then she left.

I tucked the blanket back over my son's chest. Charlie would not let go of his hand. I wanted to close John's mouth, but was afraid to lift the oxygen mask. So long as it stayed cupped to his face, there was a chance he'd start breathing again. But his mouth. Grotesque. A circle of pain.

Charlie looked up at me. Then he spoke. "When you went to visit him, did you know?"

"I didn't know anything, Charlie."

"But you saw him. You were there."

"He didn't tell me," I said, unable to take my eyes off John's face.

"That doesn't make sense." He slowly rose out of his chair.

"Charlie—"

"Did you keep it from me?"

"He said not to tell you. I was only doing what he asked. He didn't want you to know."

Charlie sank back down.

"He didn't want *anyone* to know," I said.

My husband began to moan and pressed his lips against John's cold hand.

I took my purse and left him sobbing. I walked down the hall, past the white walls and the rooms that housed their own tragedies, past the nurse and the doctor who were on their way to pronounce my child dead. I reached a pay phone. I opened my purse and found the coins I needed to make that first call. My hands shook and I almost dropped the coins, but I didn't. I picked up the receiver and heard its dull hum in my ear. I dialed Helen's number. She answered on the second ring.

"It's about John," I managed. "Cancer," I whispered before my scream escaped.

———

The evening of John's visitation, I stood in our bedroom and watched Charlie fumble with his tie knot over and over again. He said the fabric was too slick. It kept slipping through his fingers.

"Pay attention to what you're doing." I looked around the room. Our dresser. Our bed. The night table lamps I hated. Everything in its place. Unchanged. I remembered sitting at John's breakfast table, the dribble of milk caught in his beard. Had that only been a few weeks ago? Had all of that really happened?

We'd gone to pick out the cemetery plot a few days before. I don't think either of us thought in a million years we'd be doing something like that. Not at our ages and certainly not for our son. The director talked us through some of the options for a headstone. Did we want one with a rounded top or a square top? Did we want granite? How many people did we want to accommodate in this particular plot?

"Three," I said. I was already planning suicide. I wanted nothing more than to crawl into the ground next to John. Charlie said he wanted a wheat design engraved on the stone. I asked why on earth he wanted wheat and he looked at me blankly and said, "It's home to me."

I'd forgotten that. Perhaps not forgotten. *Not considered* is more accurate.

Helen and Dickie drove us to the funeral home. I couldn't comprehend that the grey casket at the far end of the room

321

held my son. It was . . . *obscene*. That's the only word. This wasn't the natural order. Children didn't die before parents.

Flowers encircled the closed casket. Big sprays of lilies and carnations and baby's breath. We said in the obituary we didn't want flowers. We told people to make donations to the Cancer Society instead. I don't even remember telling people what type of cancer it was. Maybe no one asked. I stood there, wanting to place my hand on the casket lid, but my arms were frozen at my sides. So long as I didn't touch it, I could convince myself that none of it was real. We went for two hours straight that night, shaking hands and hugging and accepting condolences. I reached behind me for posts and ledges that didn't exist, longing for some means of support. The entire night, I kept one eye on the door. Who would show up? What about the one from the hospital? Marty. If he came, people would notice him and put two and two together. The thought sickened me. My son was inside a coffin and still all I cared about was what other people thought.

I panicked when I saw John's friend Angela waiting in line. There was a man by her side and from where I stood, I couldn't get a clear look at his face. When they got closer, I saw it wasn't Marty.

"Mrs. Sparks, this is my husband, Tom," she said.

"I'm sorry for your loss," he said, taking my hand. His blue eyes comforted me. A good-looking young man. I remembered he was a lawyer. I suddenly felt light-headed. "Angela and I enjoyed John's company very much. He made us some unforgettable meals."

"John was always good in the kitchen," I said. "He didn't get that from me." I made a sound intended as laughter, but it came out too shrill, too deliberate. A few heads turned.

"Tom was the one who told John about the club," Angela said.

"That was very generous of you to get him the job," I said.

A look of confusion passed over his face. I watched Angela's grip on her purse tighten.

"John deserved that job," she said tersely. "Among other things."

"I'm so glad you were able to come." I knew my manner was off, that I was acting more like the hostess of a cocktail party, but I couldn't help it. It was easier to play this role than to deal with reality. I didn't know who I was. Without my child, was I even a mother anymore?

"Joyce."

I hear my name. A warm hand presses against my forehead.

"Joyce. Can you hear me?"

My eyes flicker open. Smudges of peach and grey and pink. A watercolour painting. Then the blurs come into focus. I make out the shape of my living room clock. The brass wall sconces on either side with their burgundy candles and virgin wicks. What's the point of having candles if I never light them? What good is any of this if it's all for show? My hollow, decorated world.

"Joyce," I hear again, and my sister's face hovers above me. Her jowls dangle. When did she get so old? "Are you all right?"

"I'm fine," I say, but my mouth is dry. The words get caught between my lips. I clear my throat. "What happened?"

"You scared the life out of me," Helen exclaims. "Please don't ever do that again."

"Do what?"

"Faint!" Her breath brushes my face. I smell broccoli. Ground beef. "Don't you remember?"

"You hit the ground like a ton of bricks," Fern's voice says from somewhere I can't see. "Scared the shit out of us, pardon my language. Can you feel your legs? Can you wiggle your fingers?"

"I'm perfectly fine," I say.

"We'll let the doctor decide that."

"I'm not going anywhere!" My voice is shrill. Cracked.

Fern's face appears next to my sister's, her sequins reflecting light onto the ceiling. "She wanted to call an ambulance. I told her to wait. We're taking you to the emergency. Walter will take Mrs. Pender back to the home."

"I *knew* this party wasn't a good idea," Helen says with a disapproving frown.

Fern nods. "Too much excitement."

"Please tell me she's all right." A different voice. Mr. Sparrow's.

Walter's face appears just over Fern's shoulder. "I feel just sick about this. Look at you, poor dear. You must feel like Dorothy waking up after her trip to Oz. Unfortunately, the Wicked Witch is still alive and eating meatballs on your back deck."

They gently help me to a sitting position, Fern and Walter taking my arms and Helen steadying my back with her hand.

Mr. Sparrow watches, concern etched in his face. I keep telling them I'm fine. I don't need all this fussing. Please. But truthfully, I feel as though I've just stepped out of a clothes dryer. I try to remember what happened before I fainted. We were out on the deck, having lunch. Mrs. Pender was there. Mr. Sparrow, too. Walter. Fern. There was an argument. Helen and me. I said something about John. But what? Then it comes back.

My stomach churns. I can't believe I admitted that, in front of all these people. I close my eyes and lie back down on the couch, wishing I could slip into unconsciousness again.

"We need to leave immediately," Helen says. "Fern, get Joyce's purse and a jacket for her."

"I don't need a jacket," I say. "It's boiling hot."

"Walter, you get Mrs. Pender ready. Hurry up, everyone."

"Have you ever seen a ninety-seven-year-old hurry?" Walter asks. "Look, let me drive you to the hospital. It's the least I can do. I feel terrible about everything. Fern, Mr. Sparrow, do you mind staying behind with Mrs. Pender? I'll come back for her as soon as I can. Promise."

"I suppose." Fern sounds a bit doubtful. "So long as Joyce doesn't mind."

"I doubt I'd be much good at the hospital anyway," Mr. Sparrow says.

"The only thing I mind is being forced to go there," I say. "For the last time, I'm fine. You're all acting like I've had a massive coronary. I fainted. It happens to people all the time."

An image comes of Mr. Sparrow lying on his bath mat, toothbrush in hand. I called the ambulance for him, in spite of his protestations. Now here I am, in the same circumstances. And I know I won't win.

Walter says he'll pull his car into the driveway. Fern goes to find my purse. Helen helps me sit up again.

"I don't want to go anywhere with that man," Helen says under her breath. "If it wasn't for him trying to shove his relationship with Freddy down our throats, you wouldn't be in this mess right now."

"I invited him," I say.

"Doesn't matter. He shouldn't have pressured you."

I refuse to go anywhere until I've at least fixed my hair and put some lipstick on. Helen follows me to the bathroom.

"How did I get from the deck to the couch?" I ask.

"Fern and Walter," she says. "It wasn't easy manoeuvring you around the kitchen table. A couple of glasses got broken. Mr. Sparrow wanted to stick a lemon wedge in your mouth. He said that's what they used to do in cadets when someone passed out. Needless to say, I managed to deter him." Her mouth stretches to a thin line. "I'm sorry about what I said. About John."

"Things got a little heated."

"You know that I'm here for you. Please tell me you do."

I nod as we pass the kitchen. I see the remains of our lunch on the table. Half-empty bowls, sauce-dampened paper plates, mangled meatballs. My simple cooking, my lack of finesse.

Lobster beak.

Hot tears spill down my cheeks.

———

The year after John's death, I was in the grocery store, setting things into my cart that I'd eat but wouldn't taste. I was unable to build up interest in anything. I couldn't tell if a blouse was nice or if a particular show was worth watching. I was frozen within myself, going through whatever motions were necessary to pass through the day. I'd become the Joyce Sparks "after." That was how we came to define our lives, Charlie and me. Things either happened before John's death or after. The world was cleaved in two.

I stood behind the back door screen that morning and watched Charlie take down the fence around our backyard. My husband, I'd come to learn (too late, always too late), never had the same issues with boundaries, with containment, that I had. He preferred open spaces. The sledgehammer became a blur. The air crackled with each swing. I'd pleaded with him to be careful.

"You're fifty-three," I reminded him.

But he didn't listen. He never listened to me anymore.

The back of his shirt was wet. His pants fell low on his hips. Every now and then he'd stop to wipe his brow before picking up the sledgehammer again.

"People grieve in peculiar ways," Helen said, as though she was some kind of expert. What did she know? Her children were still alive. "Men more so. This must be devastating for him. Especially when he never had a father of his own. Would he talk to a counsellor or a minister?"

"There's no way. How can you convince someone to talk about something when he doesn't think there's anything to talk about?"

"He needs a vacation," Helen had said. "Both of you do. Someplace tropical. Someplace *away*."

But there was no "away." No place where my son was alive.

I was almost through my grocery list when I saw her, standing by the seafood counter. It took me a moment to put a name to her face. Angela Dawber. I hadn't seen her since the visitation. My instinct was to turn around. But the possibility of talking to someone, *anyone*, who'd had a connection to John was too strong to resist. I needed reassurance from other people that my son was once in this world.

The corners of our carts touched. Red plastic bumped red plastic. I can only imagine what she must've seen. My unkempt hair. My grey face. No makeup. My sweater had a stain running down the front, a thin, dried-out river of a previous meal.

She was in town visiting her family. It was her father's birthday. Her husband was in the bakery section with their daughter. Emily, I was told, was four and wanted to help pick out a cake for her grandfather. Angela motioned with her head and her bangs swayed.

"I'm sorry I haven't called," she said. "You've been on my mind, Mrs. Sparks. How are you doing?"

"As well as can be expected," I said. It was my standard response.

"And Mr. Sparks?"

"He keeps himself busy."

Angela's eyes glistened. "I miss John a lot. I forget sometimes that he's gone. My head can't wrap around it."

She inhaled sharply, looked over at a tank of lobsters with
elastic-bound claws. "I don't know if you knew this or not,
but Marty passed away, too. This past spring. I went to the
funeral. His mother held the service in her garden. Marty
would've approved. He was a horticulturist."

"A horticulturist," I said.

"His family owns a nursery in Port Locke. Taylor's. They've
had it for years. Marty came from a long line of green thumbs."
She paused. "Sorry . . . I shouldn't assume you know about
Marty. I don't know what you—"

"They were together."

She paused again. "Yes."

"How long?"

"Maybe three years. They got along well. They'd go up
north and spend weekends with Marty's mother in Port
Locke. John would cook for everyone. Marty's father died a
while back. Heart attack, I think. But it was a big family. Two
sisters, if I'm not mistaken. And a brother. Good people."

My hands curled tightly around the handle of the shopping cart. A young girl with black pigtails came running up
and wrapped her arms around Angela's thighs. Angela smiled
self-consciously.

"This is Mrs. Sparks, Emily. Can you say hello?"

I bent down. "Hello, Emily. Nice to meet you."

But the little girl would have none of it. She stared at me
petulantly, her lips a thin, bloodless line.

———

I can never catch up, I think, watching the passing trees and houses as Walter and Helen take me to the hospital. Never could catch up to time. It evades me, slips through my fingers like cold, black oil.

Since my son's death, I'm early for everything. I'll leave the house a half-hour before I need to be someplace just ten minutes away. I can't even imagine the hours I've passed waiting in people's driveways or watching unenthusiastic store employees unlock automatic doors.

"Hurry up and wait," Charlie would say. "That's your motto."

I wish I were one of those people who sailed into doctor's offices just as the nurse was calling their name. Or someone who could pass an afternoon in conversation before glancing down at her wristwatch and announcing, "Would you *look* at the time?"

I often wonder what time must feel like for those people. Something that is always there, a guarantee, like air.

I don't need to go to the hospital. This excursion is pointless. I've said this until I'm blue in the face, but my protests fall on deaf ears. They don't understand. There's nothing about me that a doctor can fix. No pill for second chances. No prescription for fixing mistakes.

A year after Charlie died, I decided to do an inventory of the boxes in the basement. It wasn't something I'd been looking forward to. Many of them held evidence of a life that had long disappeared. Holiday decorations. Report cards. School photos of a cow-licked boy with a gap-toothed smile. But the contents of the boxes had to be sorted. I couldn't ignore them. I couldn't wish them away. And, I thought, it may not be that bad.

This was true for the first part. I opened boxes to reveal an old lace tablecloth that had belonged to my mother and a set of green-rimmed dishes with a jack-in-the-pulpit design and a set of Bobbsey Twins books from my childhood that I'd completely forgotten about. I set these boxes aside, took the old kitchen chair that sat next to the furnace and set it in front of the shelves. Making sure the chair was steady, I carefully stood up and, with my flashlight, discovered my old Christmas wreath and an orange and gold vinyl tablecloth that wasn't worth holding on to. In the far corner, I spotted what looked like a shoebox. I couldn't reach it on my own, so I stepped down from my chair and went to Charlie's workroom to see if I could find a yardstick. The workroom's smell reminded me of Charlie. Varsol and old rags and powdered cement. I'd have to deal with all these tools at some point as well. I found a yardstick and went back to my post and after a few unsuccessful whacks and grunts, I managed to slowly spin the box towards me. It was only when the box was in reach and out of the shadows that I saw the name written on the side in black Magic Marker.

JOHN

Small capitals. My husband's handwriting.

I stepped down from the chair, box in hand. I didn't want to open it, but knew I had to. I thought of how dark it was

inside the box, how dark it was inside my body, how everything functioned in complete absence of light: my stomach,
my kidney's, my heart. I sat down on the chair and set the box
on my lap. It wasn't a shoebox after all. It was from the refinery where Charlie had worked, the logo printed on the top.
I'd never seen this box before. I held my breath and lifted the
top. Newspaper. I parted the sheets, and then Charlie revealed
himself to me.

Years had passed, but the doll's eyes were still clear, her puckered lips still rosy pink. I reached in and gently pulled out Curly
Q Sue. So Charlie had found it. And when? I took the sheets of
newspaper from the box and searched for a date. August 25,
1998. Years after John died. Years before Charlie did.

When we found out that Charlie's tumour was malig-
nant, the doctor told us that treatment would buy us a few
months, but not much more. We were sitting in the sparse
hospital room he was sharing with an elderly man. I'd drawn
the curtain across for privacy, but I could still see the man's
shadow as he moved about his side of the room. Charlie had
said few words following his diagnosis. I didn't pressure him.
I knew enough by then not to push anyone down a path I
thought they should be following. We were watching TV
when Charlie said, "He was always good enough for me."

I didn't know what he meant at first. I was aware of the
man next to us shuffling in the room. Although I couldn't see
them, I knew the kind of slippers he was wearing. Black with
rounded toes, vinyl made to look like leather, soles polished
smooth. He was pulling open his night table drawer.

"I think you always knew that about me," Charlie said. "But I'm not sure it mattered to you, Joyce."

We'd been married all these years, but I couldn't remember the last time Charlie had actually spoken my name in a conversation. I placed a hand on his bedrail.

"What are you talking about?"

He shook his head. "You tried so hard. To keep everyone behind their battle lines when there was no battle to fight."

I heard something drop and watched as a tensor bandage rolled towards Charlie's bed.

"Did you ever stop to think that people deserve more credit than you give them? That your opinion wasn't the only one that mattered?"

The bandage unfurled, a flat, beige offering.

"I know you didn't think what you were doing was wrong. Not wrong for me. Not wrong for John. Your intentions were sincere. But that doesn't make it *not* wrong. Things never mattered as much to me."

This fatherless man. The sorrow I'd created but could never heal.

"He was my son, no matter what. I would've been happy with anything. Because it would've been *something*, Joyce."

Walter pulls up in front of the emergency entrance and steps over to the passenger side of the car.

"I don't think you can park here," I say as he helps me out of my seat.

Helen is beside me and takes my other arm. "Be careful," she says.

"For god's sake," I say, yanking my arms away. "I'm perfectly fine."

Walter leaves to park his car in the lot across the street. Once inside the waiting room, Helen and I go to the front desk. A nurse hands me a form to fill out and asks me to have a seat.

"I feel stupid being here," I say as Helen guides me over to a pair of orange vinyl seats in the far corner. People look up at us, sizing up our suffering compared to their own. I notice a young woman trying to control a toddler who keeps wiggling from her clutches.

"Arthur," she pleads. "Stop."

But Arthur doesn't. He refuses to be contained.

Helen sits down with an exasperated sigh and sets her purse in her lap. Her straw hat is looking a little worse for wear. "I don't care if you feel stupid," she says. "An ounce of prevention is worth of a pound of cure. That's what Mother always said. Besides, we're old, Joyce. We can't fall to the ground and simply pick ourselves up like we used to. We have to be cautious."

I ask her for a pen and she begins to dig through her purse.

"This party wasn't a good idea," she says. "I don't know why you were so hell-bent on it. You don't owe anyone anything."

She pulls out a nail file and frowns at it. "I know you don't want any part of that, either." She finds a pen and passes it to me.

I'm not sure how to respond, but she doesn't give me the chance.

"You were a good mother. No one thinks any less of you because . . . Anyway, you had a moment today. Emotions got the better of you. It happens. But I promise you we won't talk about this again. About John, I mean. We'll keep it under wraps."

Walter enters the waiting room, wearing his bug glasses. He attracts a few stares. Two young men nudge one another. He spots us and hurries over.

"I just paid two dollars to park," he says. *"For the entire day.* This city makes me feel like I've stepped through a time warp."

Helen excuses herself. "I need to find a pay phone. I should give my husband a call. He'll start to worry."

I watch my sister walk away.

"She's a little tightly wound," Walter says as he sits down next to me. "No offence."

"None taken."

I keep my eyes on the form.

"I've never liked hospitals," Walter sighs. "It's because of Nanna Kay. My grandmother. As a child, I was forced to visit her in the hospital every week."

"Mmm-hmm." I wish he'd be quiet. I'm having a hard enough time concentrating on writing.

"I'm afraid of getting old," he says. "Well, not that I'm not already old. But elderly. Incapacitated. Alone."

"It's something we all face."

"Not Fred," he says. "Not your son."

My pen comes to a stop. I glance sideways and see him turn his bug glasses over delicately in his hand, as if he were holding an ornate flower.

"I'm sorry about this afternoon, Joyce. It was too much for you."

"It's fine," I say. I try to fill out the address field, but the pen won't write.

"Was your son out to you?"

I don't know what to do with his question. "What do you mean?"

"Did he tell you he was gay?"

I clear my throat and glance nervously around. "He didn't talk much about his personal life. He was a private person."

Another lie. John wasn't private. *I* was the one who demanded privacy. No, not that. *Secrecy.*

"I see," Walter says. And I can tell by his tone, by the clip of his words, that he does. He can see through me as though I were made of glass. The same as my husband. The same as my son. I huddle over the form, trying to make myself as small as possible.

"It's different," he says. "Nowadays, I mean. People hardly bat an eyelash. Sometimes we guard these things so fiercely, only to find it doesn't matter all that much. At least, not as much as we thought it would." He pauses. Looks from the glasses in his hands to me. "Or is that what you're afraid of?"

CHAPTER THIRTEEN

I'M TAKING a trip tomorrow. I made a phone call this morning to confirm my destination and then I called the bus station and ordered my ticket. I haven't told anyone about this. I don't want anyone to know. This trip is mine.

I'm going to try to fix something I broke. It's a partial fantasy, I know, as most things are in life. Three-quarters wishing to one-quarter reality. But it's all I've got at this point. And I have to do something. I have to try to take something back.

The good thing is that I don't have to travel that far. Port Locke, where Marty's mother lives, is only three hours away. It will make for a long day, but I'll be back in my bed by nightfall. Safe.

Walter calls from the hotel early this morning and asks me how I'm feeling.

"Fine," I say. "I'm supposed to go through some more tests, but nothing serious. At least, the doctor seemed to think that."

"That's good," he says. "You can never be too sure. Do you plan to be home for the next hour or so? I'd like to see you before I head back to Miami."

Although I've softened to him somewhat since the party two days ago, I still have no need for goodbyes.

"It's out of your way," I say. "You'll have to drive all this way and then back out again. It makes no sense."

But he won't take no for an answer. "I have something for you, Joyce."

Good lord, I think. A plant? A bouquet of flowers? A rainbow kerchief? I don't want to see Walter. I've had enough of him and his offerings and his bug glasses and his knowledge about my son.

"I'll be there around ten," he says. "I'll drop by the Sunset first and say goodbye to you-know-who."

I have no choice but to run around and wash the dishes and sweep and vacuum and try to make my house presentable when it's the last thing I feel like doing. My mind is elsewhere, focused on conversations yet to happen. Dots that have yet to be joined.

Mrs. Taylor?

Yes?

My name is Joyce Sparks. My son's name was—

John. Of course.

I stand in the middle of my living room. The TV informs me I'm in store for another beautiful day. Across the street, I watch Mr. Sparrow slowly unravel the garden hose from its hook at the side of the house. He twists the tap and the hose stiffens as water rushes through it. He holds the silver spout in one hand, gives the hose a tug with the other and slowly drags it across his lawn to the bright red geraniums under his living room window. He presses the handle of the spout. A crystal shower arcs through the air. The geraniums sway in response.

We'll both be dead before we know it, I think.

Walter arrives shortly after ten, looking more than a little winded.

"Sorry I'm late," he says. "Mrs. Pender was sleeping when I got to the home."

He's wearing a new shirt. It's electric blue with yellow lightning bolts. Does everyone dress like this in Miami? When he takes off his sunglasses, I see that his eyes are puffy.

"Don't ask," he says with a wave of his hand. "The last thing I want to do is give the old crow that kind of validation."

I invite him in. "I can put on some coffee if you like. I've got cookies."

"No thanks. I don't have time."

"Are you sure?" I ask.

"My dear, I've already been too much of a nuisance in your life," he says, reaching into his back pocket. He pulls out an envelope. "I thought you might like having these." He passes it to me. "Just a couple of pictures of Fred. One when he was young and the other one taken a few years ago, before he got sick. We were in Vegas, which explains all the drunk Midwesterners in the background. But it's a good picture. You can see him as he was."

There's a scalloped edge sticking out of the envelope and I pull out a black-and-white photograph. "Thank you," I say. When I look at it, my heart contracts. It's Fred in his white suit, the one he was wearing when he led the band that day, so many years ago. I was a young girl then. I still remember what Fred meant to me that day. The dreams I held close.

I leave the other photo inside.

"There's a story behind this white suit," I say to Walter. "Do you know it?"

He shakes his head.

"Let me tell you."

Fern calls later.

"Do you want to try out that new restaurant on Langley tonight? I heard it's cheap and the portions are a fair size. The desserts are good, too. I haven't had a decent slice of pie in I don't know how long."

"I don't have much of an appetite," I say.

"You will by supper. It'll do you good to get out of the house."

She asks me how I'm feeling and I'm not sure what to say. I could say "fine." It'd be easier. But even if I wanted to tell the truth, I don't know how. This is my problem. I'm buried inside myself.

"I'm surviving," I say. It's as close to the truth as I can get.

"It's certainly been an interesting couple of days."

"Yes."

There's a pause and I close my eyes and wait. I know she's struggling, too. We're a lot alike, Fern and I. Too much of our lives goes unspoken. The same could be said for my sister. This is what's kept us together all these years, huddled with our silences, talking *around* the things that mattered most, rather than talking *about* them. But we used to talk. I remember those days, those conversations. When did they stop? When did we start living only on the surface?

"Maybe we can go for dinner tomorrow night," Fern says. "Would that be better?"

"I can't tomorrow night." I'll be on my way back from Port Locke. But she can't know this.

"You were lucky," she says abruptly. "To have had a family. I know that, given everything, it might not seem that way to you. But you had something. And you still have it, even if it seems like sometimes you don't. I don't know if I'm making any sense."

"I'll call you about dinner," I say.

I dreamed about John in the years after his death. Sometimes the dreams took place at his apartment in Toronto. Other times, at our house in Balsden. I dreamed of running after him. I dreamed of knocking on his door to no answer, even though I was certain he was there, on the other side. I dreamed of the shape of his back, his silence, his attention focused on everything else but me. Sometimes John was a boy. Other times he was a man. I never dreamed of him as I most wanted to see him: as he'd be now if he were alive. My mind couldn't picture his face in the present. My imagination didn't have that capacity. Perhaps it was for the best.

For years, I had a recurring dream. I was standing on our street, but not in front of our house. Things were off balance, a mixing of details, the way dreams always are. John came up behind me. He was sixteen or so, a backwards baseball hat on his head, wearing an oversized jean jacket. (I don't know why. He never wore baseball hats, let alone backwards ones, and I don't remember him owning a jean jacket.) He wanted something from me. Change for the bus. I looked down the street and saw a bus turning the corner. A flash of light. I pushed my hand deep into my pocket and pulled out whatever coins I had and passed them to him. He took them and the bus pulled up. John stepped inside and I watched him take a seat next to someone.

Charlie.

John put his head on his father's shoulder and closed his eyes. Charlie placed his hand on my son's head. Then the doors shut. I watched as the bus disappeared in the distance like a popped bubble.

I haven't dreamed of John lately. This has bothered me, because as painful as the dreams are, at least I get the chance to see him again. Sometimes, I tell myself that the absence of dreams means his soul is at peace. But I also know it's not John's soul that's in question.

There's a knock on the door shortly after dinner. It's Mr. Sparrow, holding an ice cream pail full of greenish-red tomatoes.

"I didn't get as many this year," he says with an apologetic shrug. "Just set them on your windowsill for a few days. They should ripen up."

I have no idea what I'm going to do with this many tomatoes, but I take them. "Thank you."

I invite him in, but he declines. He has to get back home. He needs to start clearing out his closets.

"I have to get organized." He turns slightly when he says this and I feel a tug of concern.

"Oh? For what?"

"After our talk the other day," he says, "about you moving, I got to thinking. Things are becoming too much to handle. Even this blasted garden. I never eat half the stuff. I don't know why I grow it in the first place. I suppose to keep myself busy, but I'm not sure that's a good enough reason anymore."

"Of course it's good enough," I say, stepping out onto the porch.

"What I mean to say is that people should have a purpose in life," he says. "And if your purpose is something you've invented for the sake of having one, well, that seems to me to be even worse than having no purpose at all."

"Mr. Sparrow, what is it you're getting at?"

He surveys the black iron rails surrounding my porch. "I called my nephew the other day. Gerald. I told him to put me on the waiting list for some seniors' homes in the area."

"There's no need for that. I'm not moving anytime soon. It was just talk—"

He holds his hand up. "It's got nothing to do with your plans, Joyce. I need to start being practical. My fall shook me up pretty bad. What if you weren't home? What if you hadn't come over?"

"But I *was* home. I *did* come over."

"But what about the next time? I don't want anyone worrying about me. I don't want to be anyone's burden."

"But you're not a burden," I say, my voice rising. "Mr. Sparrow, you're part of this neighbourhood. You're the reason I've stayed in this house for as long as I have. We take care of each other. That doesn't have to change."

He slowly shakes his head. "It does, Joyce, whether we want it to or not. And better we're the ones making that change than have life do it for us. We keep a little piece of our dignity that way. We've been lucky to have had one another. Just think of all the years we've been here." He turns around and begins to make his way down the front steps. "It's time for some new blood on this street. Young folks. People with energy and dreams to spare. Kids. Remember the sound of kids?"

He's halfway down my driveway now, the evening closing in around him.

"Mr. Sparrow!" I want to call after him. "Who will make sure my blinds are up?"

This morning, I wake up early (although I didn't sleep well throughout the night) and, after breakfast and the morning news (a fire in the west end, an increase in property taxes, a chance of showers later this afternoon), I get dressed, put on my makeup and slip out the back door. I'm catching the 8:30 bus. I know I could drive, but I don't want to press my luck.

The bus to Andover is half empty. I buy a magazine to read while I wait in the Andover terminal to board the bus to

Port Locke, but I can't concentrate. The words slide past me.
I keep thinking about her. Marty's mother. I try to picture
what she looks like. The clothes she wears. If she resembles
her son.

*They'd go up north and spend weekends with Marty's mother in
Port Locke.*

That's what Angela told me that day in the grocery store.
To think of this stranger, this unknown woman, doing the
exact thing that I couldn't: opening her doors, no questions
asked, and taking my son in. A true mother. My fist curls and
thumps against the side of my leg. This has to work.

The bus to Port Locke is even emptier than the bus from
Balsden. There are six of us, a hodgepodge of strangers, making
this two-hour trip north on a Tuesday morning in September.
The sun slides shyly between the clouds, coming out every now
and then to spread its shadows. I stare out the window at
the blurred evergreens and church signs with what I assume
are messages of hope, the letters too small for my eyes to read.

Marty's mother can't be much younger than me. But she'll
be spry. Eager. A woman who has spent her life in open land-
scapes. A visor on her head and gardening gloves on her
hands. She'll be holding a pair of pruning shears. There'll be
a faint smudge of dirt on her forehead. She'll feel the tap of
my finger on her shoulder. Turn around. Smile politely.

Mrs. Taylor?

Yes?

We stop in a town called Milner. It's nothing more than an
intersection. I watch the bus driver squat and remove a pair

of boxes from the luggage compartment before heading into a convenience store that apparently doubles as the post office. The bus door is left open. I eye the blue velour seatbacks and the few domes of hair and consider getting up. Putting on my coat. Stepping down onto ground I haven't touched before. Someplace new. Unknown. I can leave everything behind. No one will know about my son. My life. The grief I wear like a pair of sandbag earrings.

I can begin everything again. And get it right this time.

The bus driver steps back onto the bus. Closes the door.

"Port Locke," he announces, "the next and final stop."

The bus deposits me in the middle of downtown. I go to the bathroom at the terminal and check my makeup in the mirror. There's a yellow and red plastic container next to the sink for depositing hypodermic needles. I blink at it. Has life really come to this?

I wander along what I assume is the main street. There are bookstores and a couple of women's clothing stores with vacant-looking mannequins staring out from the display windows. I pass a bingo hall and a flock of teenagers huddled under a cloud of cigarette smoke in front of a Tim Hortons. I spot a bakery across the street.

"I'm looking for Taylor's Nurseries," I tell the woman behind the counter.

"That's out on Highway 4," she says.

"Too far to walk?"

She nods. "But only ten minutes or so by car."

"I'll have to take a cab."

She says she'll call to order one and I thank her. While I wait, I decide I should buy something in appreciation. The display case holds neat rows of sugared doughnuts, cookies and pastries. There's a chocolate cake dotted with ground nuts and tight spirals of icing. I notice a Chelsea loaf on the counter.

I tell her I'll take a loaf. "I haven't had a Chelsea loaf in ages," I say.

"Just made these," she says, snapping open a white plastic bag.

I'll give Marty's mother the loaf. The cab arrives and I get in. The driver's radio crackles. I hold the loaf, feeling the warmth seep through the plastic bag and spread across my thighs.

Mrs. Taylor?

The nursery is bigger than I expect. A white sign announces that mums are on special. The doors silently slide open and I step through a miniature green forest. Around me are bird baths and shiny wheelbarrows and shelves of painted pots. A voice above me requests that *Joel come to the service desk, Joel to the service desk, please.* I pass a woman in a red smock with the word "Taylor's" stitched in gold embroidery above her breast. She looks at me and my breath catches. No. Too young.

I walk by the service desk and see another woman standing behind the counter. She's plump with blond hair scooped high on her head like icing. Older. But still not old enough. At the opposite end of the nursery, I see a sort of teahouse, a small café tucked into a corner, with wrought-iron tables and chairs and surrounded by a white picket fence. Silk vines coil up some of the fence posts. What a nice idea, I think, making my way towards this oasis. With all this greenery, you could almost convince yourself you were in a perfect park setting. A sign announces that the lunch specials of the day are crab quiche and shepherd's pie. The prices seem a little steep to me, but no matter. They're running a business, after all. As I'm standing there, a young girl whisks by me with a pair of coffee mugs in her hand. She stops.

"Are you here to eat?" she asks.

I nod, realizing I haven't had anything since breakfast, and she tells me to take any seat I like.

"I'll be with you in a moment."

It's peaceful in here. Calm. I hear the sound of water running softly. An invisible brook. Lights twinkle from shoulder-height artificial trees. I set the bag containing my Chelsea loaf on the chair next to me. The girl comes back and hands me a menu. I'm told there is no chicken soup today.

"It's not very good anyway," she says. "The noodles are always mushy."

I order the crab quiche and a cup of coffee. If this is a family-run business, she could be Marty's niece. Her eyebrows are thick. Straight lines of disapproval. She's tired of her job, I can tell. Just as she's about to walk away, I say, "Excuse me."

She turns around.

"Is Mrs. Taylor here today?"

"You mean Jean?"

"I don't know her first name. She had a son. Marty."

"That's Jean," the girl says. "The owner. She died last spring."

All my hopes escape like a released balloon. What did I expect to accomplish? I look down at the table. "Did you know Jean? I didn't," I say.

"She was a nice lady." The girl says she'll be back in a minute.

From this vantage point, I can see the comings and goings of the nursery. The employees and the customers. The skids of packaged dirt within brightly coloured plastic bags. The hanging ferns and the racks of mums. Nature contained.

Always a good business this time of year.

She's sitting next to me. Blue kerchief. Silver eyebrows. Tanned skin. The same mouth as Marty.

Going on fifty years now I've run this place. Hard to believe. Marty would've taken it over. Had things turned out differently.

I know.

Shame. They always leave us behind, don't they? Men.

I thought things would go a different way, Jean. I had an idea in my head at the start of everything.

We all do.

I couldn't get the idea to fit.

Nothing ever goes according to plan.

I've been thinking that you can only ever deal with something with whatever means you have at that particular moment. I suppose one advantage in getting older is that you do have a better frame of reference. But you're also left with the memories of all those moments when you didn't know any better. Lately, I've wondered if I *did* know better, only I chose not to see it. I closed my eyes and barrelled through.

And it was only when I reached a clearing that I had the gall to turn around and see the mess I'd left behind.

What's done is done, Joyce.

He asked me not to tell my husband. We stood in the entrance of his apartment and I was leaving to catch the train and John specifically asked me not to tell Charlie. If I had known for one second, if I knew how quickly things would turn . . .

Best to let that all go now.

The girl had come back to the table, startling me. She sets the quiche and my coffee in front of me. I won't be able to eat any of it. I look at the chair next to me. Empty, except for the bag of Chelsea loaf.

"Is there anything else you need?" the girl asks.

"No," I say.

Nothing.

- - - -

Claire is sitting by the window, her magnifying glass and crossword puzzle book in her lap. She wants to know where I'm going.

"What's happening? I've never seen you in a dress before. Are you moving out?"

"Dare to dream," I say and excuse myself to the bathroom. I want to apply a little lipstick before Timothy gets here. He called me the other night to say he was feeling better.

"I can take you to the cemetery Sunday afternoon. It's supposed to be a nice day. I'll come by after lunch."

"You're sure about this?" I asked.

"I'm sure," he said. "You?"

"Yes."

The past couple of days, I've been practising standing, holding on to something for support, trying to build up the strength in my legs.

My fingers can't grasp the tube of lipstick properly and it keeps falling into the sink with a clatter, leaving red gashes on the white ceramic. I'm about to give up when the fire-headed nurse knocks on the door and offers to help me.

"I don't need any help," I say.

Her hands go to her hips and she looks at me sympathetically. "You're sure?"

Why do I refuse people at every step? "Maybe a little."

"I hear you've got a day trip in the works," she says, slowly running the lipstick along my lips.

"Don't make me look whorish," I say.

"I wish I had a young man coming to take me away. What's your secret?"

"Luck." How strange to think in those terms. I've never considered myself a lucky person. And yet it's the only word that springs to mind.

Timothy arrives just after one and wheels me down to the elevator. Mae MacKenzie does a double take when we pass her, but I keep my eyes straight ahead. I don't want any questions. Once the elevator doors close, I feel my body sink into my chair, and I watch the lit circles slowly move from 4 to 3 to 2 to G.

"I asked one of the orderlies to meet us out front," Timothy says as he wheels me out into the foyer. "I feel better having some help at the start."

"Of course," I say.

The day is beautiful. Early fall with a souvenir of summer. Tiny yellow leaves are piled along the gutter and wedged between the sidewalk gaps. They look like fingernails, the artificial kind.

The orderly is waiting for us next to Timothy's car. I recognize him. An Italian fellow. Bald. He's wearing a gold chain around his neck, thick as rope. He shows Timothy how to lift me up and lower me into the passenger seat. Then he takes my ankles and gently pivots me around so that I'm facing the windshield. I hear them discussing my wheelchair and feel the thump of the trunk closing. The inside of Timothy's car is very clean. I smell peppermint and something else. I inhale deeply, trying to place it.

Flowers.

He wants to know what John was like. "That is, if you don't mind talking about him."

"I don't mind," I say. "I haven't talked about him enough. I'm never sure what to say. Or how much to say. I always assume people will react negatively. But it's different now . . . with you."

We stop at a red light. My back is hurting me, but I ignore it. Instead, I focus on the houses and cars we pass. Life carries on. I feel the energy of a younger world. There are sales, groceries to buy, buses to catch. There are teenage boys, getting ready for their first band trips.

"John was kind. And thoughtful. When he was young, he gave me a necklace for my birthday. It was all sparkle and shine. Fit for a movie star. I suppose all boys go through that stage. Idolizing their mothers."

"Sometimes it's more a matter of seeing Mom how she should be," Timothy says.

My old heart throbs at these words.

The light turns green. "He was angry, too. It wasn't something I saw every day, but it was always there. When he was born, I thought he'd fix everything in my life. But that's not the way it worked out. How unfair to expect that of him."

I look at Timothy. "Do you think I could've made my son happy? If I'd accepted him, I mean?"

His shoulders rise. "I don't know, Joyce. There could have been other things he was angry about. It doesn't always have to do with being gay."

He's right. There were more things to my son than his homosexuality. So why did I always stop at that?

My breath catches when we turn into Lakeside Cemetery. I'm not sure I remember the way. It's been so long. I tell Timothy to turn left. Then make a right. "Just a little farther. See that oak tree? Pull over next to it. Here. Right here."

He gets out of the car and tells me to wait while he looks for the stone. I squeeze my hands together. My back burns. The passenger door opens.

"I found it," Timothy says. "The ground doesn't look too bumpy. We should be fine with your chair."

He undoes my seat belt and slowly gets me into position. His hands slip under my arms and it feels wonderful to be this close to a man so young. It's almost like we're dancing.

"Easy now. We're in no rush." He guides me to my chair and wipes his brow when I'm finally positioned. "It's just over here."

He starts to push me, but then I remember the flowers and Timothy turns back to the car to get them. I can see the stone from here. I feel something between desire and dread. Timothy sets a bouquet in my lap. Tiger lilies. A dozen of them. Licks of bright orange.

"They're beautiful," I say. There's no sense, no point, in trying to hold back my tears. He wheels me over the gravel and then the quieting grass.

Even after all these years, I'm shocked by the names etched in granite. The letters and numbers, so matter-of-fact, so impersonal.

Charles William Sparks

Jonathan Charles Sparks

"My two men. What I wouldn't give for five minutes with each of you." It takes me a moment to realize I've said the words out loud.

The vase atop the stone is empty, as I knew it would be.

"My husband wanted the wheat border," I say. "He was from the Prairies." I feel Timothy's hand on my shoulder and close my eyes. "I remember the first time it rained after John died. I couldn't stand the thought of him being out here, alone, in the ground. So I came and sat over his grave with an umbrella. But I was too late to protect him, you see. Always too late."

"You loved him, Joyce. He knew that."

"I loved him on my terms. Never on his." I clear my throat. "Timothy. I want you to meet my son. His name was John Charles Sparks. He died when he was thirty-one . . ."

A breeze passes me and I inhale, holding it in my lungs.

"From AIDS."

I've never said it before. Strange how such a small word can carry so much weight.

"There are some important things you need to know about John. He used to sing in the church choir. He also played the baritone for his high school band. He ran away once and left my world at a standstill. He graduated from college and became a chef at a private club for wealthy people." I pause here, uncertain if I can go on. But somehow I do. I *have* to. "He was in love with someone when he died. A man named Marty, although I never got to know him, something I regret to this day. The most important thing you should know about my son, though, was that he was loved. Desperately. By both his father and me. I hope you understand that, in spite of the mess I made."

I reach my hand up and place it over John's.

"I know," he says.

Air like gauze. Fog. My feet slide between the smooth sheets. I'm halfway between the sleeping world and the waking one. My favourite place to be. I've learned how to control my dreams in this state. I can conjure up all kinds of worlds and all seems possible. Nothing is out of reach. Right now, I'm thinking of a table in a small dining room. The tablecloth is blue-and-white check with a fringe border like eyelashes. I imagine beads dangling from the fringe. Crystals that shine in the morning light. From where I sit, I can see trees, older than me. A breeze exposes the pale green underbellies of their leaves. The sky is ocean blue. It's going to be a hot one today. But not yet. There are bowls arranged on the table, spoons, white napkins, small juice glasses. Everything neatly laid out. All in its order.

My son sits across from me, his face suspended in the transition from boy to man. I put him in his favourite green jacket, knowing it won't fit. But no matter. This is my creation. I can do what I want. There's someone behind us, in the kitchen. I hear the sound of water swallowing things up, the soft echoes of dishes hitting the bottom of the sink. Charlie, of course. Always there. Around the corner.

There are so many things I want to say to John. But I don't know where to start.

I reach across the table, wipe a drop of milk from his beard. "Come home," I say.

I thought I'd be dead by now. If someone had told me when I was seventy that I'd last as long as I have, I would've laughed. Then screamed. All these lonely years on my own. People wish for a long life, but they don't consider the casualties along the way. Now, it's only me and this black purse and a bucket of memories. Things could be worse, I tell myself. I could be out of my head, knee-deep in dementia. And yet, I'm not convinced that would be worse. It might actually be a blessing of sorts.

The trees out front have changed colour. From where I lie in bed, I can see the leaves fly past, waving in the wind like little hands. Sometimes, I wave back. I'm told it's Thanksgiving weekend.

"Gobble-gobble," the Filipina nurse says when she comes to get me out of bed. She's later than usual. I've been awake for an hour, waiting for Timothy. He's going home for the holiday but said he'd drop by.

"I have something for you," he'd said.

I have no idea what it could be.

Claire is still sleeping. She doesn't usually get up before eight.

"Have you seen a turkey running around here?" the Filipina nurse asks as she raises my bed. I feel like Dracula emerging from his coffin. "It escaped from the kitchen. It's not under your bed, is it?"

She winks. Someone is feeling playful today.

"I see a lot of turkeys around here, my dear," I say. "But none with feathers."

She laughs and there's a glimpse of authenticity between us. It's rare, but it does happen every now and then. She gets me sitting up and then wheels in the large contraption that will carry me to the washroom. Arms through straps. The whir of the motor.

"When was your last bowel movement, Mrs. Sparks?"

"I don't remember."

"Do you think you can go this morning?"

"Your guess is as good as mine."

I sit on the toilet while the nurse wakes Claire and gets her ready for the day. I hear them exchanging words but can't make out the conversation. I know that the nurses like Claire more than me. She's friendly. Doesn't hold her situation against them. It's not their fault. They're only doing the best they can.

"I can't imagine we're much fun to be around," Claire has said. "It's hardly like we're guests at a party."

The nurse's head pops into the washroom. "Anything yet?"

I shake my head. I can't poop on demand. Everything is rush, rush, rush. "You need to give me something. A laxative."

"I'll give you some more time," she says and pulls the door closed.

Everyone is downtown. I expected crowds, but this is overwhelming. Almost frightening. I didn't think there were this many people in Balsden. Perhaps we should've gone to Century Park as Fern suggested. No matter. The bus has dropped John and me off in front of the library. I grab his wrist and begin twisting my way through the crowds along Parker Street. We pass a man selling photographs of the Queen. John asks if we can have one, but I tell him no. His heels dig into the sidewalk.

"But I want one."

"John, if we don't get a spot now, we'll miss seeing the Queen. Now what's more important to you—a photograph of the Queen or the real thing?"

This puts things into perspective for him and we carry on. Eventually, we find ourselves in front of city hall. This seems to be as good a place as any and there's a small gap on the curb. I take the blanket from my bag and cover the curb. Then I sit down and pull John onto my lap. The sun is directly overhead and I slip a hat on him, even though he doesn't like to wear it. He's holding the letter he received from Buckingham Palace. I know it's going to be a tattered mess by the end of the day, but he was intent on bringing it. He says he'll wave it like a flag when the Queen goes by. He also wanted to bring the crown I made for him this morning, but I drew the line. While he was in the bathroom, I threw it into the garbage before piling the leftover pancakes onto it. If he asks me for it, I'll plead ignorance. If he's upset, I'll make him another one. He's so unpredictable. He'll forget about some things as though they never existed and other things, he'll hold on to for dear life. I can't pretend to figure him out.

"Which way will she be coming?"

"From the right," I say, pointing. "Keep your eye on the right. They'll be turning onto Parker Street."

"Is that the street we're on now?"

"Yes. It's the street all the parades go down."

The day of the big game, Fern and I went downtown. You never saw such a big to-do, but that's the way it was. Our football team had made it to the finals. Balsden has always been a sports town. What our parade lacked in razzle-dazzle it made up for in spirit. The streets were lined with people. It seemed like all of Balsden was there. And do you know who was leading this parade of parades? I'll give you one guess.

She's forgotten about me, the Filipina nurse. I've been on the toilet for twenty minutes at least.

"Nurse!" I holler and feel something snap inside of me, a violin string breaking.

"Claire."

But the name comes out more as a gasp. I close my eyes and see red rapids, surging. No escape. My hands fumble for the pull cord.

"Nurse."

He turned down that street, all dressed in white, leading the parade. And he had that peculiar hat, perched on his head just so. He was bursting with pride that day. You could see it in his smile, his posture. And when he flung that baton in the air, he caught it every single time.

Bleating in the distance. Sheep. Always those sheep. They never stop. My face is pressed against something flat and cool. It may be the floor. I hear the door slide open.

"Joyce!" He kneels beside me.

"You're just in time, John."

"It's all right. Everything will be okay."

So this is how it goes, I think.

I squeeze his hand and see something bright. A fireball turning the corner.

There's chaos around us. Children running, peering down the street towards the point where the Queen will appear. Some people have flags and wave them. The older ones sit in lawn chairs. One man has a radio. I can make out the squeaking sounds and static.

I wish Charlie were here. Sometimes, he misses out on too much.

A dull roar spreads itself along the line of people until it reaches us and moves on. A ripple of electricity. John runs out into the middle of the street before I can grab him. His neck strains to the left and right.

"John!" I call. "Get back here!"

But he doesn't.

"John!"

Then he rushes back to me, wrapping his arms around my neck. I can smell the detergent on his striped shirt, maple syrup on his cheek. He turns around and I hold him tight against me. I feel the rapid rise and fall of his chest under my hands. I crane my neck and see a flash at the end of the street.

"Here it comes," I say and lift my son up.

ACKNOWLEDGEMENTS

Thank you to Nita Pronovost and the team at Doubleday Canada, Dean Cooke, Ann Ireland, Shaun McCarthy, Patricia Visser and, as always, my partner, Serge, and family.

© Paula Wilson

A NOTE ABOUT THE AUTHOR

BRIAN FRANCIS' first novel, *Fruit*, was a 2009 Canada Reads finalist. It was also named one of NOW Magazine's Top 10 Books of the Year, picked as a Barnes and Noble "Discover Great New Writers" selection and was an Extended Book Sense Pick. Francis is a recipient of the Writers' Union of Canada's Emerging Author Award. He lives in Toronto.

A NOTE ABOUT THE TYPE

The text of *Natural Order* is set in Adobe Jenson (aka "antique" Jenson), a modern face which captures the essence of Nicolas Jenson's roman and Ludovico degli Arrighi's italic typeface designs. The combined strength and beauty of these two icons of Renaissance type result in an elegant typeface suited to a broad spectrum of applications.

The chapter headings are set in Neutraface Display.

Book design by CS RICHARDSON